Beauty and the Blade

BOOK ONE

THE TALENTED FAIRY TALES

S.C. GRAYSON

Editing: Lisa Green

Cover Design: Mibl Art

Interior Illustrations: Lulybot

To Amanda. You gave me my first fairy tales. Now it's time to give you one of your own.

Chapter One

As Contessa prepared for her wedding, there were no tittering bridesmaids to remark on the fashion of her gown or to gossip about what eligible bachelors they might dance with at the celebration. There was only her maid, Ada, solemnly buttoning up her gown. Despite the decadent lace dripping off the wide sleeves of her dress, Contessa couldn't escape the feeling that she was a knight donning armor for battle as Ada tightened her corset.

Ada drew Contessa from her imaginings as she began pinning the veil to the crown of her head, the ivory of the lace only a few shades lighter than her silvery blonde hair. It was the same veil her mother had worn on her wedding day, and Contessa couldn't help but feel comforted by the thought of her. After all, if it weren't for her, Contessa wouldn't be getting married today at all. Ada lowered the blusher over her face like a knight's visor before combat. She was ready.

Contessa emerged from her room to find her father waiting on the landing. As soon as she stepped out the door, his gaze darted over her form, taking in every detail as if he were cataloguing evidence for a police report.

"Yes, you'll do nicely. Every bit the beautiful bride that rabid dog bargained for." Her father's tone was clipped and business-like, as usual, even in his approval of her. After all, this wedding was the first step in a plan that was as much his as hers.

Her father turned on his heel and marched towards the front door. Once Contessa picked up her hem and maneuvered her skirts down the stairs as well, they made their way to the carriage that waited for them on the cobblestoned street.

The ride to the church was blessedly short. Only the harsh clop of hooves on the cobbles and the clatter of wheels broke the silence in the carriage. Contessa pushed back the curtain in the window to peer out into the gray city streets of London. People paused to watch the carriage pass, knowing it belonged to the chief of the Royal Police from the crest on the side. The closest bystanders smiled and waved at Contessa as they wove their way from the upper city towards the spires of the palace and the church at the top of the hill. As Contessa looked longer, though, she noticed people peering from darkened doorways and curtained windows, their faces shadowed with fear.

It seemed that the respect commanded by Chief Cook was laced with a healthy dose of apprehension. The number of Cursed—or Talented as they had once been called—he had sent to the gallows in the Inquiries kept the city safe, even as it frightened many. And the fear burdening the people of London was only made heavier by the growing rumors of the King's illness.

Only when the carriage jerked to a halt in front of the church did Contessa's father speak.

"This is the last moment we have to talk openly. From here on, you must appear to be the perfect and demure wife. You cannot expose your true motivation in marrying Mr. Woodrow to anybody, or you risk your safety."

Contessa nodded, already having heard this information a dozen times but unwilling to interrupt her father to tell him so.

"We're lucky to have this opportunity to get you so close to Mr. Woodrow. We can't afford to squander it. It's incredibly fortunate that he took a liking to the way you looked and was rash enough to want to marry you despite you being my daughter." Her father's hard gray eyes softened fractionally as he continued. "It's no wonder, though, with you looking so much like your mother. She always was so beautiful. I'm glad you take after her. Remember, we're doing this for her, Connie."

At his words, steel snaked its way into Contessa's spine. The use of her mother's nickname for her brought back memories of smile lines and gentle lullabies—brighter times, before her father had become consumed with his work in the Inquiries. No matter what lay ahead, she could be strong if she remembered her mother's laughter, her light.

"We're doing this for her," Contessa echoed.

Her father smiled tightly. "She would be so proud of you."

Together, they stepped out of the coach and made their way into the church. Organ music swelled within as they pushed open the double doors to the Sanctuary. At the end of the aisle, she could just make out the horrifically scarred face of her groom, but it wasn't his disfigurement that imbued icy hatred into Contessa's veins.

Waiting for her at the end of the aisle was the man who had murdered her mother.

♟♜♞♟♟♟

For a wedding with so much riding on it, the ceremony was unremarkable. Contessa kept her eyes fixed on the golden buttons of her groom's waistcoat as the priest's words washed over her like the droning of mosquitos. She almost snorted when she found the gilded buttons were emblazoned with a rearing lion. Her groom mocked the authorities desperate to arrest him by paying homage to the name people called him in fearful whispers on the street.

It was said that, when he was young, he'd challenged the former leader of the Lion gang to a fight. The man had pinned Nathanial down and tried to claw his eye out, but Nathanial had bitten his finger clean off. It was the fight that left him with the name everybody in London called him in hushed tones: the Beast.

The priest reached the end of his lengthy homily and moved on to the vows. Contessa was pleased her voice didn't waver when she said, "I do," although it did come out stony. Her father stiffened infinitesimally.

To Contessa's surprise, her groom's vow came out equally cold. She had expected enthusiasm from the man who had suggested the marriage to begin with. After all, he'd approached her father to ask for her hand after only laying eyes on her once—without even speaking to her. Surely, he was pleased to wed such a lovely bride if he had been willing to have the Chief of the Royal Police for a father-in-law just to have her. Maybe Contessa's bitterness had put him off.

Contessa didn't have any more time to ponder Mr. Woodrow's motivations as the ceremony moved to the exchanging of rings. She succeeded in not flinching as he took her left hand in his to slide a simple gold band onto her finger. Mr. Woodrow withdrew his touch quickly, but not before she spotted a myriad of scars crisscrossing his knuckles. She'd spent so much time concerned with his disfigured face, she hadn't considered the possibility that he was similarly marked elsewhere.

With the rings exchanged, the only part of the ceremony left was the moment Contessa had been dreading the most. The guests applauded, but the sound rang hollow in the vastness of the sanctuary, echoing sparsely among the rafters.

Mr. Woodrow lifted the veil from Contessa's face, and she found she could no longer get away with fixing her gaze on his buttons. She steeled herself and lifted her eyes to see the face of her husband up close for the first time.

Contessa understood why people called him the Beast. His legendary scar overtook most of his face, a gnarled rope of tissue running from the left side of his chin to the right side of his forehead and into the edges of his shaggy auburn hair. It pulled up the right side of his lips to create a permanent snarl and bisected his right eye so it squinted until its hardened hazel was barely visible.

Contessa was so taken off guard by the expression in his good eye that she'd forgotten why she was looking at his face so closely until he leaned in. As much as Contessa had known the kiss was coming, the feeling that washed over her at the sensation of his mouth on hers caught her by surprise. She was used to her anger for her mother's murderer freezing the blood in her veins. Now she felt unbearably hot, fire taking the place of jagged ice at the base of her spine. Perhaps her rage demanded action instead of steely resolve as she stood so close to the object of her hatred.

The roughness of his scar scraped her lips, and the warmth of his breath brushed her face. Then it was over as quickly as it began, the kiss leaving only a simmering warmth in its wake. Contessa felt rooted to the spot until the Beast took her hand to lead her down the aisle to the celebrations and the night beyond.

♟♟♜♟♟

The wedding meal wasn't as dreary as it could have been, given the general solemnity of the rest of the day. White roses bedecked the ballroom, and flickering candlelight lent a surreal look to the room. Lilacs peaked through the windows, blooming on the bushes in the adjacent park. Contessa had to admit it was a lovely venue, if not as grand as the palace ballroom would have been. Her father made no secret of his resentment for not being able to host the celebration in one of the London palace's smaller ballrooms, as he would have before he lost his position as the King's personal bodyguard. However, Contessa preferred the less ostentatious location.

Contessa endeavored to enjoy a piece of cake, but she was constantly aware of the man at her side, the same way she would be aware of a sharp pebble that had worked its way into her boot.

The Beast sat up perfectly straight, hands fisted on the table. Contessa found herself staring at the untouched piece of cake in front of him. His lack of celebratory mood perplexed her. Perhaps the realities of having the chief of the Royal Police as a father-in-law were setting in. There were a lot of officers in the room after all.

The Beast's uneaten dessert was cleared, and his chair scraped harshly against the wooden floor as he stood. A scarred hand appeared in her line of vision and Contessa realized she was going to have to take it to participate in their first dance. She took her time folding her napkin before placing her hand in his much larger one. Rough calluses rubbed against her palm as he led her onto the dance floor.

The orchestra began to play a waltz, and the Beast placed his other hand on her waist. The warmth of his skin seeping through her dress was at odds with the shiver that ran up her spine. Contessa managed not to recoil from his touch and placed her own hand on his shoulder. Once again, she found herself inspecting the buttons of the Beast's waistcoat, noticing how they strained across his powerful chest when he lifted his arms.

As they began to move to the music, something became clear: both Contessa and the Beast were horrendous dancers. Contessa had never spent the time mastering dance beyond the basics, avoiding balls to convince her father she wasn't as girlish and silly as her peers. If Contessa had hoped the Beast was skilled enough at leading to disguise her incompetence, she was in for a disappointment. Within the first few bars, he had stepped on her toes twice, which was quite a feat considering the width of her skirts. Although Contessa hadn't given it much thought before, it occurred to her that being the secret ruler of the most feared gang in London didn't leave one with time for dancing.

The only good thing to be said for the waltz was that it was blessedly short. Contessa found herself whisked into the arms of her father for a stiff, but thankfully, more elegant dance. It wasn't long before she found herself tossed around between distant relatives and high-ranking members of the Royal Police. They all wished her well until she found herself in a set of arms she felt more comfortable in than the rest.

"Joey," Contessa sighed, relaxing for the first time in hours, "Thank goodness."

He succeeded in turning her around the floor without stepping on her toes. He was used to her poor dance skills and had adjusted after many gavottes that left him limping. "I'm glad I finally stole you away. It was much harder than it should have been for your father's protege to get a turn. I must say, I had hoped attending the wedding of a friend who might as well be my sister would be emotional in the joyous way, instead of anxiety inducing."

Contessa tried to scowl at his indiscretion but found she was too glad to see a friendly face to commit to the expression.

"It's very kind of you to wish me well," Contessa responded politely as they passed a distant relative from the country who was staring at them.

"Wish you good luck is more like it," Joseph responded, seemingly oblivious to the danger Contessa would be in if their plot was discovered. "Hopefully, you can find the evidence we need and be a sympathetic young widow within a month."

Contessa squirmed at the casual mention of a man's death, even if he was a murderer. "You make this sound as easy as a walk in the park."

"It will be easy for you," Joseph encouraged. "Nobody expects girls as pretty as you to be capable of treachery. You look too angelic to be plotting. That's what I thought before you beat me at chess ten times in a row."

Contessa furrowed her brow. "Historically, aren't the beautiful women the dangerous ones? Using their feminine wiles to bring down powerful men?"

"You read too much," Joseph scolded with no real disapproval. After all, he was the one that lent her novels to supplement the vast tomes of history and politics kept in her father's library.

Contessa opened her mouth to retort that she hadn't had as much time to read as she would have liked recently, but Joseph jumped in before she could speak. He leaned in close to whisper in her ear, "Please come home soon. I don't want defeating an enemy to come at the cost of losing a friend."

Contessa swallowed. Having to stay away from Joseph meant

losing the only confidante she had. As her father's protégé, though, Contessa doubted the Beast would take too kindly to him.

"Just think, seeing me less means losing at chess less often." Contessa tried for levity, but it fell flat.

The music ended, forcing them to step apart. Contessa tried to draw strength from the encouraging smile Joseph gave her, but it was ruined by the telltale creases between his brows as he sketched a polite bow. *Be careful,* he mouthed before turning to weave his way back through the guests. His dark head retreated, leaving Contessa to feel alone in the crowded ballroom.

She was jolted out of her reverie by a tug on the full sleeve of her gown. She startled to find her new husband at her elbow. His gaze followed where hers had been, and her heart froze at the thought that he may have overheard their conversation. It resumed beating when she saw his expression was not angry but merely pensive. His disfigurement made it hard to be sure, though.

"The festivities are winding down. You should distribute your flowers to your friends before we leave."

This was the first time she'd heard his voice besides when he'd said, "I do," and she'd been too busy inspecting his buttons at that moment to pay attention. It wasn't what she anticipated. She'd thought somebody of his appearance and reputation would have a coarse, grating voice, evocative of the monster she knew him to be. Instead, he had a smooth tenor, sounding much younger than she had expected. She didn't know how old he was. Before this moment, she hadn't even thought to ask.

Finding the Beast still staring at her, she looked down at the bouquet in his outstretched hand.

"Oh, well," she hedged. "I don't have any bridesmaids to give flowers to. I have some cousins here, but I don't know any of them well."

The Beast's face twisted into an expression she couldn't identify on his unorthodox features, but it smoothed itself out again just as fast.

"Good. I never did like the tradition anyways."

He took her elbow to guide her through the crowds of well-wishers to the exit. Contessa's attention narrowed to the point where his fingers touched her arm, an electrifying feeling making her freeze before she remembered she was supposed to be walking. As she allowed herself to be led through the grand room, the cake she had eaten turned to lead in her stomach. She'd been so distracted by surviving the festivities that she'd managed to keep her mind off what came after the celebration. Now, though, the heat of her husband's hand seeping through the sleeve of her dress was an inescapable reminder that she would no longer be able to keep him at arm's length. By the time she stepped up into the Beast's carriage, Contessa was beginning to think her wedding cake might make a reappearance based on the churning in her gut.

The coach she arranged her skirts in was a good degree smaller than her father's carriage, although the benches and curtains were luxurious in their upholstery. Contessa found her voluminous dress dominated the confined space. She wasn't even sure the Beast would fit. He stepped up into the coach after her and managed to wedge himself onto the bench across from her. In the enclosed space, his frame looked wider and more hulking, and Contessa found herself shrinking back against her seat. In the darkness of the evening, the shadows cast by the ridges of his scar were even more pronounced on his face.

Contessa clenched her jaw and looked the Beast full in the face. If this plan was going to work, he was going to have to believe her a willing participant in their marriage. The only nerves she could show were those expected of any young woman on her wedding night.

To Contessa's surprise, the Beast looked away first, cramming his considerable bulk into the far corner of the coach so his coattails didn't so much as brush the ruffles of her dress. As the carriage lurched into motion, he pulled back the curtain on the window to peer out into the night. Contessa settled for staring at her hands where they rested in her lap, rearranging them into a more relaxed position when she found them gripping her skirts with white knuckles. Only the clatter of wheels broke the silence. It seemed as though she was not going to have a conversation with the man before she shared his bed. His physical presence seemed to make the space grow warmer, causing sweat to prickle the skin at the nape of Contessa's neck.

She tried to convince herself it was a blessing he didn't expect her to speak, for it would be difficult to hide her disdain. It should be a consolation that she didn't have to converse with the criminal who had murdered her mother. Still, she found it impossible to stay silent.

"It was a lovely party."

The Beast's head snapped around, and he fixed her with an incomprehensible look. "Do you generally enjoy parties?"

"No," she admitted, caught off guard by his question.

There was a long pause while he considered her answer. Contessa resisted the urge to return to the study of her fingernails.

"Neither do I," he said flatly, before turning back to watch the passing street.

Contessa followed his gaze to find the manicured green of the park had given way to the elegant rows of houses in the wealthier districts of London. She knew the Beast's home was in the upper city, although not as close to the palace as her father's. The Royal Police were very familiar with his residence, given that her father had men watching it night and day. Despite his efforts, the Royal Police had been unable to find evidence confirming Nathanial Woodrow's identity as the leader of the notorious street gang, the Lions. Still, the entire city whispered he was the Beast, cutthroat gang leader and ruthless murderer. The only reason nobody could prosecute him was that nobody who saw him left the scene alive. Instead, he left a trail of corpses with three slashes cut across their face—the calling card of the Lions.

The carriage trundled to a stop. Contessa was surprised to find herself looking at a house featuring a cheery blue front door and a row of neatly trimmed hydrangea bushes out front. She chided herself for her disbelief. The Beast wouldn't keep the heads of his enemies on pikes or have a dozen thugs armed with crowbars waiting outside his front door. That was why he hadn't been caught. His facade was so immaculate that nobody could pin down any proof of his crimes. Contessa was walking into the lion's den to find the evidence everybody else had failed to get.

She just hadn't expected the lion's den to have a front door the color of a clear sky.

Contessa followed the Beast out of the carriage and trailed him up to the front door. Before he could even reach for the knob, the door sprang open to reveal a woman in a neat gray dress and white cap. She looked to be a few years younger than Contessa and was currently bouncing on her toes, trying to look over the Beast's shoulder.

"Welcome home, sir," the woman offered. She stepped aside to let him in, although her gaze remained fixed on Contessa behind him.

The Beast ignored her behavior, stepping inside and immediately shrugging off his coat. Contessa followed after him.

"Take her to the rose room and see to it she is prepared for bed," was the Beast's only greeting before he stomped off into the house, tossing his coat over the back of a chaise lounge as he passed.

The maid didn't seem concerned by her employer's behavior, her attention already on Contessa. She appeared to be quivering in excitement, her curls bouncing where they spilled from her cap and onto her round face.

"Oh, aren't you lovely! No wonder Mr. Woodrow was in such a rush to marry you," she exclaimed, looking Contessa up and down. "Oh, and you still have your flowers! Let me take those so we can get you a vase of water. They'll be a nice touch to add to your room. Liven the place up a little bit."

Contessa numbly handed her bouquet off to the girl, surprised by her bubbly demeanor. Meanwhile, the maid was practically skipping up the stairs, keeping up an impressive stream of chatter as she went, commenting on everything from the fashion of Contessa's dress to the weather. She acted oblivious to the fact she was working for a monster who was currently prowling through the downstairs, waiting to devour Contessa.

As Contessa followed the maid, she took the opportunity to examine her new personal prison. While the outside of the home had been welcoming, the inside of the house was sparse. All the furniture was good quality, but none of it drew the eye. A few generic landscapes decorated the vast walls, but there were no signs of the homeowner's tastes or preferences. It lent the place a sense that it was simply inhabited and not really lived in.

As they reached the top of the stairs, the women turned to the left down a darkened hallway until the maid pushed open a door.

"This will be you room, Mrs. Woodrow."

Contessa startled at the use of her new name but schooled her features quickly.

"Thank you, Miss..."

"Pinsberry," the maid supplied, "but I'd prefer it if you would call me Julia."

Contessa stepped into the room and wrinkled her nose. The

entirety of the room was wallpapered in a print of small red roses. The blotches of crimson on a cream background made Contessa think of drops of blood. She shivered.

Julia didn't notice Contessa's displeasure, herding her towards an intricately carved dressing table. Contessa kept herself from looking towards the bed against the other wall, richly hung with thematic crimson drapes.

"We call this room the rose room. Mr. Woodrow suggested this one for you himself."

Contessa exhaled sharply through her nose as Julia began to unpin her hair. Of course, a man who married a woman he had never spoken to would put her in a room that resembled an overgrown garden. It was odd he hadn't brought her to his own room. Although considering the Beast didn't know her at all, maybe he desired to keep his space to himself and keep her elsewhere for his amusement. Contessa took a few moments to even her breathing at the thought.

Julia's ability to chatter endlessly extended through Contessa's nighttime preparations. As she brushed her hair and changed into her nightclothes, Contessa listened, hoping she might start uncovering hints about the Beast and where she might find evidence of his crimes. Contessa was left disappointed, although she found the maid's energy to be infectious. She'd never spent significant time around women her age, and she welcomed the distraction of Julia's company in her current predicament. While the wedding had been nothing more than an act, it was refreshing to hear Julia gush over every detail of her flowers and her dress.

Once Contessa was perched on the edge of the bed, Julia left with a quick curtsy and a friendly, "Goodnight, Mrs. Woodrow."

As the door clicked shut behind Julia, a heavy silence descended in the room. Contessa strained to hear movement in the hallway, but there was no noise except Julia's receding footsteps. Her earlier tension had returned tenfold now that she was alone, and her fingers gripped the fine fabric of her nightdress until her knuckles blanched. She tried to distract herself from the thundering of her heart by counting the gaudy red flowers on the wallpaper. She couldn't keep herself from listening for heavy footsteps in the hall, though, as she waited to be devoured by the Beast.

Chapter Two

Contessa woke to sunlight streaming through windows covered by scarlet drapes, turning everything in the room an unearthly shade of red. Shivers shook her body as she found herself curled in a tight ball on her side, hugging her knees. She was still lying on top of the coverlet, never having climbed under it the night before.

As her consciousness returned to her, she pushed herself up and looked around in confusion. It took Contessa a moment to register her surroundings, realizing she was not in the bedroom she'd slept in since she was a small girl.

Awareness chased the last vestiges of sleep from her mind, and Contessa jolted to her feet. She couldn't remember the Beast coming to her bedroom last night. She looked down at herself, trying to discern what had happened. She found her nightdress undisturbed, and her hair still neatly plaited over one shoulder, just as Julia had left it. Whipping her head around to double check, she found that she was indeed alone in the bedroom.

Contessa furrowed her brows in confusion before icy terror shot through her veins. Her true intentions must have been found out. That's why the Beast hadn't come to her the night before; he was furious with her deception. Soon, Contessa would find her throat slit at his hands, just as her mother's had been.

She took a step forward, preparing to search the room for something to defend herself with. Something sharp would be best, but a heavy candlestick might do the trick. Contessa wouldn't go down without adding another scar to the Beast's horrific face.

The door to the bedroom sprang open before she could take more than two steps. Contessa's hands flew up in preparation to defend herself, but she let them fall to her sides when it was not the Beast but Julia who traipsed through the door. Her wide smile just peeked over the fluffy magenta bundle in her arms.

"Good morning, Mrs. Woodrow," Julia greeted, giving no sign that anything was amiss. "You're up early! I thought you would want a bit of a lie-in after yesterday's excitement, but apparently not. I thought I heard you get up, and I realized I hadn't shown you how to ring the bell to summon me. I apologize if you've been waiting long."

"Not at all," Contessa responded, keeping her distance for fear this was all some elaborate plot to catch her off guard.

Julia simply approached her and shook out the bundle in her arms. It revealed itself to be a gown, which the maid laid across the covers of the bed. Contessa grimaced as the magenta clashed violently with the red coverlet.

"Mr. Woodrow ordered a set of dresses for you as a wedding present, but this is the only one that's arrived so far," Julia explained as she set to work getting Contessa out of her nightdress. "He has no sense of fashion, so he told the dressmaker to outfit you in whatever the most popular styles are. The color is so lovely. It'll be gorgeous with that pale hair of yours."

By the time Contessa was laced into the fuchsia monstrosity, she was forced to disagree with her maid. While the general shape of the dress was flattering, that was the only positive feature Contessa could find. The ribbons and bows and ruffles made Contessa think of last night's wedding cake. She prayed the rest of the dresses would show a touch more restraint.

Contessa schooled the distaste from her face as Julia wove a matching ribbon through her hair. The maid seemed to be enjoying styling Contessa so much, she didn't have the heart to ruin her fun.

"Oh my, you're so lovely," Julia tittered. "I've never gotten to dress a lady as beautiful and stylish as you. Not that I've dressed many ladies at all before. I mostly just learned how to style hair by practicing on all my friends."

"You're quite good at it," Contessa praised her honestly, twisting her head to get a better look at the maid's handiwork. While the color of the ribbon wasn't Contessa's favorite, she had to admit the way her hair was piled on top of her head made her neck appear impossibly long. A few choice ringlets framed Contessa's heart-shaped face, accentuating her gray eyes, the only physical feature she'd inherited from her father.

"Oh, thank you." Julia bounced on her toes. "I've always wanted to be a lady's maid. I was so worried I wouldn't be any good at it."

"How did you come to be working as my lady's maid then?"

"Oh well, I was working for a friend of Mr. Woodrow's." Julia twisted her apron between her fingers. "When it became clear that Mr. Woodrow would need a maid for you, his friend mentioned my interest. Put in a good word for me, as it were."

"So, you were a maid for a friend of Mr. Woodrow's?"

"Something like that," Julia responded, looking down at her feet.

Contessa's eyes narrowed as she scrutinized her maid in the mirror. The woman's nervousness betrayed that there was more to the story than a simple reference. Perhaps there was a link to her employer's illicit activities. Still, it seemed cruel to interrogate the maid when her involvement was likely minimal and possibly involuntary. Contessa would use Julia as a last resort for collecting evidence.

"That was very kind of your former employer," Contessa settled on as a response.

Julia nodded and changed the subject. "Well now that you're all dressed, I'm sure that you're absolutely famished. Let me show you down to the dining room for some breakfast, Mrs. Woodrow."

Contessa let the subject drop and followed the girl downstairs into the living areas of the house. As Julia directed Contessa into the dining room, she glanced around for the Beast, but he was nowhere to be found. Instead, a sandy-haired man about her own age entered the room and pulled out a chair.

"Good morning, Mrs. Woodrow," he said, indicating she should take a seat.

Contessa slid into the proffered chair. "Thank you, and who might you be?"

"Mr. Topps at your service, but you may call me Gregor," the man offered, picking up the teapot.

Contessa was surprised that both servants preferred to be called by their first name, but she supposed that when you murdered people for a living, you didn't have to stand on ceremony with your household staff.

"Will Mr. Woodrow be joining us?" Contessa ventured.

"Oh no, he left early this morning," Gregor commented, as if this wasn't out of the ordinary as he served her breakfast.

"I see."

Once her plate was filled, Gregor stepped back and asked, "Will that be all, Mrs. Woodrow?"

Contessa dismissed both him and Julia but didn't start eating.

Her stomach tangled into knots, and she didn't feel putting food in it would help the situation. Why had the Beast gone to all the trouble to marry her, then not joined her in bed the night before? Now he was completely absent. If he was regretting his decision, it was going to make her mission to discover the truth of his crimes more difficult. If he wouldn't even speak to her, gaining his trust was out of the question.

Maybe it had nothing to do with her at all. Maybe some matter of business had come up. Surely that was it. She would be able to winnow his secrets out of him as soon as he handled whatever matter had stolen his attention.

Contessa began picking at the food in front of her. If she were to make any good of this situation, it wouldn't do to have her fainting in the middle of the day. She didn't know who the cook was, but the meal was excellent. Even the bacon was perfectly chewy, just how she liked it. Before she knew it, Contessa had cleared her plate.

Neither Gregor nor Julia reappeared to clear the table, so she made her way out of the dining room. There was still no sign of anybody else. It wouldn't hurt to have a look around, especially if the Beast wasn't there. Perhaps she could find some piece of evidence and bring the man to justice without even speaking to him.

Contessa set off through the living room, poking at cushions and pulling open drawers. It wasn't as if she expected a bloody murder weapon to tumble out from a hidden compartment, but Contessa still found them shockingly empty. The drawers were devoid of any personal effects, not even a matchbook to be found lying about.

She moved through the drawing room and the parlor with similar findings. In fact, the cushions on the sofas and chairs were so smooth, it looked as if they had never been sat on. The only significant thing Contessa was able to discern was that whoever decorated the house was fond of flowers. In every room she passed, she spotted multiple vases of fresh flowers, all blooming so beautifully that it must have cost a fortune. It seemed odd in a house that barely appeared inhabited otherwise.

When Contessa reached the hallway in the back of the house, she was greeted by a dark wooden door. She hadn't found an office yet, and of all the rooms she might investigate, it seemed an office was the most likely to contain useful evidence. Maybe some records of his underhanded business dealings or letters from accomplices. After all, the Beast had accumulated wealth so rapidly that it set off the initial rumors of his criminal activity. Gossip claimed that nobody could be that fortunate with investments without having meddled. Still, no one managed to find anything incriminating. He had never even been seen entering a gambling hall, which, while legal, tended to be crawling with gangsters with unnaturally good luck.

Contessa strode towards the closed door, hoping to finally confirm the years of rumors. Her heart sank when she found it locked. Of course it was locked. The Beast didn't trust her enough to leave her alone with all his potential evidence, and he was right not to.

Somebody cleared their throat behind her. She whirled around so quickly she nearly tripped on her ridiculous skirts and toppled over. After correcting her balance, she looked up to find Gregor staring at her and wearing a bemused expression.

"May I help you find something, Mrs. Woodrow?" he asked, his tone polite but still managing to convey that he didn't approve of her walking around trying random doors.

"I just thought I'd explore my new home a bit. Get to know the place a bit better." Contessa stepped away from the locked door.

"Well, is there anything I can get you to entertain you for the afternoon?" Gregor offered, once again implying there were more suitable activities for her than poking around in his employer's belongings.

"I do like to read."

"I could show you to the library," Gregor suggested, although he looked amused for reasons Contessa couldn't puzzle out.

When he led her through a door at the top of the stairs, the reason for Gregor's earlier amusement became clear. While the room obviously was a library, for the walls were lined with bookshelves and there were several comfortable looking chairs scattered about, it was not filled with books. Instead, the shelves lay barren. Contessa got the impression that if she were to run her fingers across them, they would come away caked with dust.

She caught Gregor's eye and he smiled sheepishly, his honey brown eyes sympathetic.

"Mr. Woodrow hasn't gotten around to stocking the library. He's a busy man," Gregor offered.

Contessa took the opportunity to pry. "It would seem so. What business did he have that was urgent enough to call him away the day after his wedding?"

"I wouldn't know." Gregor pointedly avoided Contessa's narrowed gaze. "But I'm sure he wouldn't mind if you took the liberty of acquiring some books."

"That would be nice," Contessa lied. She didn't intend to be around long enough to build him a worthy collection. "Do you have a newspaper I could read in the meantime?"

Reading the paper was a practical habit her father had instilled in her as soon as she could read. Contessa didn't intend to let it go by the wayside because of her current predicament.

Gregor fetched her the paper and suggested she might like to read it in the garden. Contessa agreed, hoping the sight of the open sky might make her feel less like an exotic bird in a cage.

As Contessa stepped out of the back door and into the hazy city sunshine, she found the gardens might as well have been in a different world than the interior of the house. Where the inside had seemed completely devoid of life, here it overflowed. Plants bloomed everywhere. Full hedges lined a brick path to a trickling fountain in the middle of the courtyard, and flowering vines adorned the wrought iron fence surrounding the small lawn. Rose bushes of every variety filled the beds, and there were even some flowers which Contessa had never seen outside of a greenhouse.

It struck Contessa how different this was from the garden outside her own home. Where that garden had been neatly trimmed until the hedges took on unnatural shapes, this garden was bordering on overgrown in a way that made it seem anything but neglected. It was a perfect sanctuary from the austerity of the house.

Contessa settled herself on the edge of the fountain, fanning her skirts around her to sit more comfortably. She turned to the newspaper and opened it on her lap, frowning immediately.

The headline announced a set of public executions that would take place within the week. The Inquiries had uncovered three more Cursed wreaking havoc in the streets. Apparently, one of the offenders was capable of conversing with birds and was using it to spy on and blackmail officials for the Scorpions, another one of the street gangs. Contessa felt a mixed bolt of concern and pride upon reading that Joseph had been responsible for his arrest. Another Cursed could summon bright lights that could blind an opponent in combat, and a third was accused of using her ability to murder her husband.

Contessa shifted in her seat, dreading another set of executions. She hated magic as much as anybody else, but she never enjoyed watching the hangings. The fearful eyes and twitching legs of the sentenced always made Contessa want to look away. She never did, though. She could hear her father's voice in her head telling her the hangings were a show of strength—that they made London safer. They ensured there would never be another assassination attempt like the one that killed King Royce, the current King's father. It hadn't been the first time the Talented, as they had been referred to then, had threatened the monarchy, either, with a group supposedly responsible for the end of the Stuart line with the murder of Queen Anne. The resulting chaos had nearly torn England apart before the Royce family managed to reunite the country under the crown once more.

As Contessa flipped through the rest of the paper, her sympathy for the accused lessened further. The Scorpions had burned down a house in the middle city, the owner and his wife locked inside as the flames burned an unnatural shade of blue. Two nights ago, a family had been found dead in their home, turned to stone by another one of the Cursed.

This was why the Inquiries had to continue. The gangs were full to bursting with Talented who used their powers for fear and destruction. Her father was right—they must be stopped and brought to justice.

Chief Cook made it his life's work to stop the Cursed's reign of terror, working tirelessly since the assassination of King Royce. He had been King Royce's bodyguard, standing watch outside his bedroom as one of the Cursed used their power of invisibility and slit the King's throat in the night. It had lost her father his reputation, his status, his job, forcing him to be demoted into the Royal Police. In his new position, he led the Inquiries with unmatched fervor, to root out and destroy the Cursed—to make sure nobody else had all their hard work destroyed by a perversion of nature.

When one particular gang had come knocking for revenge, and Contessa's mother had paid the price, Chief Cook had thrown himself into his work with even more vigor. That was why Contessa had attended every execution in the last five years, and why she was sitting here in the home of the most notorious gang leader of them all.

By the time Contessa finished the newspaper, the sun in the sky was no longer sufficient to thaw the ice in her veins. The descriptions of the atrocities committed by the gangs had renewed her purpose. She would stop this monster, and she would avenge her mother.

Still, she would have to keep her wits about her if she was to succeed. Contessa took a few fortifying breaths and looked around the garden to calm her pounding heart. It still seemed so odd that the Beast would have a sanctuary this lovely, especially when the rest of his home was so bleak.

That night, Contessa mentioned her observations about the garden to Julia.

"The garden is all Gregor," Julia responded, brushing Contessa's hair until it fell in pale ripples past her shoulder blades. "Mr. Woodrow doesn't spend much time thinking about the house, but he's given run on the landscaping to Gregor. He loves all things gardening. I do wish somebody would liven up the inside of the house, though. Maybe you could help."

Contessa met the maid's eyes in the mirror over her shoulder and softened at her optimism. "I doubt Mr. Woodrow would appreciate me interfering in his home. He seems like a...volatile man."

"I don't think he'd even notice much if you spruced the place up. He spends most of his time either out of the house or locked up in his office in the back."

Contessa stayed quiet, hoping Julia might give her a hint of how to gain entry to the office, but she was disappointed.

"I'm sure you know best, though, Mrs. Woodrow, being so sharp and classy," Julia said, tying off the plait she'd woven Contessa's hair into for bed.

As Contessa perched herself on the edge of the bed once more, Julia curtsied and left the room with a cheerful goodnight. Though the Beast had been called away the evening before, Contessa was convinced he would pay her bed a visit sooner rather than later. Why else would he marry her and dress her up like a ridiculous paper doll if not to take advantage of her appearance? Again, Contessa listened for footsteps in the hall until her eyes drifted closed of their own accord.

Chapter Three

The next three days in the Beast's house passed similarly to the first. Contessa woke and was dressed by Julia. Each morning her dress was more horrendous than the last, but Contessa found herself thankful none of them were the same magenta as the first. Still, the third dress was a canary yellow that did nothing positive for her complexion and only served to make her look mildly jaundiced.

It turned out not to matter how sallow Contessa's clothes made her look because she saw nobody but Julia and Gregor. She was beginning to think she'd dreamed up the Beast's existence entirely as she sat out in the back garden and read the paper. She was reassured of her purpose in the den of her enemy, though, when she read about a series of raids at the harbor by the Lions. Gang members had burned three ships and left several police officers dead in the harbor with three slashes cut across their faces. Contessa let out a sigh of relief when she skimmed the names of the dead and found none that she recognized.

What was odd about the raids was that the police couldn't identify what the target of the attack had been. The gang had crept in and caused a large amount of chaos, then left just as quickly without having stolen anything. It was peculiar, but then again, that was the way with the Cursed. They used their power to cause pain and spread fear, while decent folk were just trying to live their lives.

The raid on the docks must have been why her new husband had been absent. It seemed violence and death were more important to him than getting to know his new bride. Contessa couldn't say she was surprised. Although, she wasn't sure if she was relieved he had been missing or disappointed she hadn't been able to make more progress on her mission.

Every day she went through her same routine of searching the house for clues, and every day, she came up just as empty-handed as the last. She tried the dark wooden door at the back of the house, and each day she was less surprised to find it locked. It felt like the door stood between more than her and an office. It stood as a barrier between her and her way home. It stood between her and revenge.

At night, Contessa sat up for as long as she could, spine rigid and ears pricked for footsteps outside her door. Dread kept her alert late into the night, and each morning, she woke up both relieved and concerned that she would never get her chance to earn her target's trust.

On the fourth day, the routine changed jarringly. Contessa walked into the dining room and nearly crashed face-first into the table. Sitting in the seat opposite hers was the Beast himself, tearing into a piece of buttered toast as if it had personally offended him. His deformity pulled at his mouth in such a way that made him chew with his mouth partially open, and he sprayed crumbs across his plate as he ate.

Contessa looked on in horror for the briefest moment before she remembered her role and composed herself.

"Good morning," she greeted him in what she hoped was a polite but not forcibly cheery tone.

The Beast jumped as if he too hadn't been expecting a companion, and his hand sprang to his belt. Finding no weapon there, it came back to rest on the table in a fist as he responded with a "Good morning" of his own. He turned back to his toast without even making eye contact.

Contessa must have displeased him at the wedding if he couldn't even look at her. Perhaps he had been intoxicated when he had asked her father for her hand in marriage. But then it wouldn't make sense that he had gone through with it. He certainly didn't seem the type of man to have a strict sense of honor. No, his displeasure must stem from something Contessa herself had done. Maybe she wasn't as beautiful as he had first thought, or perhaps she hadn't been guarded enough with her hostility towards him.

Now Contessa did her best to school her expression into the vacant but pleased look so many men seemed to favor. She also made a note to try to acquire clothing in more flattering shades. Her father would hate Contessa fussing over her appearance, and it twisted something in her gut to make herself try to appear vapid and suggestible. She reminded herself it was all a means to an end.

Still, as she served herself porridge, her efforts seemed to be in vain. The Beast continued to keep his eyes firmly fixed on his plate. With an internal sigh, she dug in and hoped the conversation would improve.

"You don't take any honey or milk on your porridge?"

Contessa jumped for the second time that morning and glanced up. Her husband still wasn't looking at her face, but his eyes were firmly fixed on her spoon. She supposed it was an improvement.

"I've always eaten it plain. I never really considered trying it any other way," Contessa replied.

The Beast made a noncommittal noise and turned his face back to his plate, although his mangled brow was now wrinkled like he was trying to solve a complicated puzzle. Contessa concluded he had earned his nickname not only from his appearance, but from his unappealing manners.

He didn't speak again until Contessa laid down her spoon across her empty bowl. Then he motioned to Gregor, who Contessa hadn't noticed was stationed somewhere off her shoulder, and asked him to bring around the carriage.

"Where are we going, Mr. Woodrow?" Contessa asked once Gregor had left, pleased her voice continued to sound friendly.

"The executions."

"The executions?" Contessa failed to hide the distaste from her voice. She'd hoped she wouldn't have to attend considering she wasn't currently under her father's roof, but she was mistaken.

"Yes. You would have read about them in the papers." The Beast's tone made it clear that there was no doubt in his mind she'd been reading the news. Even if he hadn't been home, he wasn't ignorant of Contessa's activities.

Of course, a murderer would want to watch his competitors' demise. Contessa wasn't sure why her attendance was expected, but she decided not to ask. After all, this was her first opportunity to observe the man since their wedding.

Contessa simply nodded and braced herself for the day.

♟♙♜♙♟♙

If Contessa hadn't been to any executions before, she would have thought she would stand out in the crowd wearing a garish shade of purple at such a somber occasion. However, as usual, the crowd was clad in all manner of bright colors, and even her hat bedecked with feathers didn't seem out of the ordinary for the occasion.

The crowd bristled excitedly, and loud chatter filled the square surrounding the gallows. Contessa avoided looking at the stark wooden platform in the center of the courtyard, looming over the crowd in judgement.

Public executions had gone out of fashion, having been seen as barbaric. But after the last king was assassinated by a Cursed, there had been public outcry. The masses demanded to see justice done, and her father had been at the head of the charge. So, the gallows had been constructed and the Inquiries began.

Contessa scanned the crowd in favor of looking at the wooden platform. A lump formed in her throat as she saw children among those gathered in the square. Her father had brought her to her first execution at the age of seventeen, just after her mother had died, but there were some in the crowd much younger than that.

The Beast stood next to Contessa. He was so still she might have mistaken him for a statue if not for the slight stretch of his waistcoat when he breathed. His presence next to her only served to worsen the churning in her gut.

Trying to ignore her husband's tension, she returned to scanning the crowd. She managed to spot her father standing with the rest of the Royal Police at the front of the square. His salt and pepper hair was parted so meticulously that Contessa was sure his manservant must have used a ruler, and his moustache was polished so it shone in the thin sunlight. He was every inch the Chief dutifully protecting his citizens from the threat of the Talented.

Standing next to her father was Joseph, and Contessa allowed herself to be comforted by the sight of a friendly face. He was currently laughing at something the officer to his right had said, his crooked smile reminding her of sunny days and playing pranks on each other.

Contessa was ripped from her contemplation by the jeering of the crowd as three figures were marched onto the platform. Contessa stayed silent and forced herself to look each of the convicted in the face. While the front of the crowd where Contessa usually stood with her father heckled and mocked the accused, she noticed that more people in the back where she stood now stayed quiet.

The first two figures who stepped onto the gallows were the image of the Cursed everybody had in their minds: burly men wearing fierce scowls and looking like the stuff of children's nightmares. Contessa squinted to see the tattoo on one of their forearms, indicating his membership in the Scorpions.

The third gave Contessa pause. The woman couldn't have been any older than Contessa herself, a slight thing who stumbled up the wooden steps to the gallows. Her trembling was visible even from this distance, and red rimmed the woman's swollen eyes.

As the charges against each of the sentenced were read, the Beast reached up and removed his top hat. Contessa peeked at him out of the corner of her eye, but the Beast's eyes remained fixed on the sentenced. A muscle twitched near his jaw under his warped skin.

Contessa returned her attention to the platform as the executioner stepped forward to fasten the rope around the necks of the sentenced. The woman was still shaking, but she didn't speak or beg. She kept her eyes straight ahead and lifted her chin as the noose was slipped over her head.

Contessa dug her nails into her palms and gritted her teeth as she waited for the executioner to pull the lever that would bring three lives to a sudden end. There was a ringing in her ears that made it difficult to hear the noises of the crowd, but she'd long since trained herself not to look away.

After a moment that seemed to last forever, the executioner pulled the lever, and the three victims dropped to their deaths. The necks of the two gang members snapped immediately with cracks that Contessa could hear over the ringing in her ears. The woman's weight was insufficient to break her neck, and she dangled, jerking sickeningly as the life was choked out of her.

The moment went on for an eternity before Joseph stepped forward, wrapped his arms around the woman's legs, and jerked down decisively. Joseph had confided in Contessa that he hated watching the lighter criminals strangle to death nearly as much as she did. At the sound of the woman's neck snapping, the Beast jerked. His reaction was enough to distract Contessa from the horror of the moment. She wouldn't have expected somebody with so much blood on their hands to flinch at one more death. Still, as she peeked at the face of her husband, she found it was white as a sheet. Even the usually reddened tissue of his scar had turned pale.

Feeling as if she shouldn't be watching his distress for some reason, Contessa looked forward once more to find her father looking directly at her. He began weaving his way through the milling crowd towards her, the sea of people parting to let his distinguished figure through.

"Excuse me for a moment, Mr. Woodrow," Contessa asked, hoping it wouldn't raise too much suspicion for her to have a few words with her father.

The Beast grunted and stayed rooted to the spot, which Contessa took as assent, and she set off through the crowd to meet her father.

As soon as father and daughter reached each other, Chief Cook grabbed Contessa's wrist to pull her close, murmuring in her ear, "Have you made any progress?"

Contessa shook her head infinitesimally, eyes darting about to ensure they weren't being observed. The crowd seemed entirely preoccupied, chatting excitedly about the gruesome executions.

"I've tried, but he doesn't even speak with me. It makes it difficult to gain his trust."

Chief Cook's moustache ruffled as he blew out a disappointed breath. "Surely, I've trained you to be resourceful enough to try other methods. What about looking through his belongings?"

"He keeps everything in his office, which is always locked. I can hardly convince him he doesn't need to if we never converse," Contessa's eyes continued to dart around the crowd as she spoke as quietly as possible.

Chief Cook shook the wrist he was holding, rattling her bones. "Then pick the lock, girl. Those pins in your hair can do more than make you look fashionable, you know."

He was right, but Contessa had hoped to avoid something so risky. Picking locks was time consuming, and the chances she would be caught in the act seemed high. Still, Contessa had all the training of a police detective. Her father had made sure she was prepared for exactly this eventuality. She wouldn't let him down.

"Alright, I'll do it as soon as possible," she promised, and Chief Cook's eyes softened.

"Good. You're doing me so proud, Connie. I'm glad to see you safe and whole." His hand slid from her wrist to her hand, where he gave it a tight squeeze.

Contessa's usual steely resolve returned at his words. After several disheartening days in her new home, her father's encouragement was just what her soul needed. If he believed in her, then she would complete her mission and come back home with her mother avenged.

The moment was broken when Chief Cook pulled his hand from her own, "The devil is looking for you right now, and he's motioning for his carriage. Get back to him before he gets suspicious."

"I won't let you down," Contessa promised before turning and picking her way back through the crowd. Sure enough, her husband stood at the edge of the square where Gregor had just pulled the carriage up. His eyes scanned the crowd for her and caught hers just as she separated herself from the edge of the masses.

Once again, Contessa was surprised by the contrast of their warm hazel to his ravaged features. The intensity of his gaze almost made her trip over her hem, but she matched his stare with the piercing glare she'd learned from her father. He blinked and turned back to the carriage. He climbed in before she reached him, leaving Gregor to help her into the coach.

Once they were settled inside, the coach jerked into motion, bouncing and jostling over the cobbles.

"How was your father?" the Beast asked, fixing her in his gaze once more like a predator sighting his prey.

Ice slid into Contessa's gut, but she didn't back down.

"He is in excellent health. Thank you for asking."

The Beast exhaled sharply through his nose in what might have passed for a sign of amusement.

"I'm sure he is. Today must have been a proud day for the Royal Police." As much as Contessa had been having difficulty reading him, the disdain in his tone was clear.

"Of course, as it is a proud day for us all when murderous gangsters are brought to justice." Her tone was insipidly sweet, like sugar hiding the bitterness of poison.

Contessa had been sure her statement would have stoked his rage, but instead, the Beast blinked as if perplexed and then turned to the window. Silence fell, and Contessa felt unbalanced, despite having landed a verbal blow against the Beast.

She didn't have time to dwell on the hollow victory as the Beast interrupted.

"Stop!" He shouted, banging his fist against the roof. "Stop the carriage, Gregor!"

The sudden halt caused Contessa to nearly tumble off the bench, but she caught herself. Her hands landed on the seat where the Beast had been sitting half a second before, but he had already thrown himself out the door. Contessa took a second to follow him, yanking on her dress as it caught on the steps. By the time her feet hit the ground, the Beast was already darting around the corner of a house into an alley. Contessa ran after him, feet slipping on the cobbles and internally cursing the dainty slippers that came with the dress. She didn't even know why she was chasing the Beast, but there was a buzzing in her head clouding her reason. He had sounded so urgent.

Contessa rounded the corner just in time to see the Beast grabbing a man by the front of his tattered shirt, dragging him away from a lady huddled against the wall and clutching a parasol like a weapon. As the Beast backed the man up, he stuck out a leg behind the thug, making him lose his footing. As the thug slipped, the Beast used the hand twisted in his shirt to bodily lift him and throw him down. His back hit the ground with a painful thud. The noise finally chased the buzzing from Contessa's mind, and she darted over to the woman.

"Are you alright?" Contessa asked, arriving at her elbow.

"I think so," she said shakily. "He was after my purse, but you arrived so fast, I hadn't even screamed..."

Contessa followed the woman's gaze to where the Beast kneeled next to the thug, still wheezing for breath after his violent introduction to the ground. The Beast leaned in and whispered something to the man. Contessa couldn't hear what it was, but the effect was immediate. The man blanched and struggled to his feet, stumbling and tripping out of the alley before he had fully stood.

"Thank you, sir!" said the woman at Contessa's elbow.

The Beast stood, brushing off his coat and turning around.

The woman drew breath as if to continue, but the words turned into a choked noise in her throat when she saw his face.

"I—I must be going," the woman stammered, before beating a hasty retreat out of the alley. She walked close to the wall, trying to keep as much distance between her and the Beast as possible, before nearly running around the corner.

The Beast didn't acknowledge her reaction, taking a moment to straighten his cuffs. Contessa stood quietly, watching a rapid transformation of the man in front of her from feral Beast back into the man she'd stood next to at the execution. Picking up his hat from where it had fallen on the ground, he dusted it off before jerking his chin to indicate they should head back to the carriage.

Gregor didn't comment on their short stop, clucking the horse back into motion. Contessa herself couldn't help replaying the moment the Beast had picked up the thug and bodily thrown him to the ground. Remembering the way his muscles had flexed in his back and imagining the strength it would take, Contessa shivered. Her face and chest felt hot at the thought. It must be the fear of knowing she was living with an enemy this dangerous. She'd known it before, but the actual demonstration of the Beast's power caused a much more visceral reaction.

What she didn't understand was why he'd stopped the attacker at all. Perhaps he'd recognized the member from a rival gang and didn't want them stealing the Lion's quarry. How he had even known about the attack was another issue. Perhaps there had been a commotion and Contessa had been too lost in thought to hear it. Contessa shook herself. Whatever the Beast's motivation for stopping that offense, her job here was to find evidence of his own crimes.

Chapter Four

Contessa sat up longer than usual that night, convinced her husband would finally visit her bed. After all, she'd finally seen him today for the first time since their wedding. She knew he was no longer otherwise occupied. Still, the clock ticked on in the silence, and she remained alone in her chambers.

What she'd begun to suspect now became clear in her mind; the Beast didn't intend to bed her at all. Perhaps he had married her simply to torment her father. Not only could the police not pin him down for his crimes, but he could steal away first the Chief's wife and then his daughter.

Contessa slid off the bed and began pacing. While the days were still warm, the night was cool, and the wooden floor chilled her bare feet. Contessa welcomed the cold as it kept her alert and helped her think.

Her hopes of gaining her husband's trust had been thoroughly dashed. It seemed the only choice left to her was force—far from Contessa's preferred method, but she was capable enough.

Making up her mind, she strode to her dressing table and pulled out several hair pins. Then she donned her dressing gown and slipped out her bedroom door, silent as a shadow.

She tiptoed down the hall, listening at every turn for signs of life. This wasn't a task she wanted to undertake if the Beast was awake in any of these rooms, but her ears met only silence.

She crept down the stairs, alert for any signs of life on the lower level. If the house seemed devoid of life during the day, it was positively macabre in the still of the night. The ticking of a grandfather clock echoed loudly through the living space. Long shadows distorted the room until even Contessa, in all her practicality, could have been convinced the place was haunted.

Finally, she arrived at the locked door in the back of the house. Its dark wood loomed larger than life in the shadows of the night, and Contessa chided herself for letting her dramatic sensibilities get the best of her.

Sinking to her knees, she pulled the hairpins out of her pocket and got to work. It was slow going, and Contessa kept pausing to listen for the click of tumblers and signs of life in the house. After long, tense minutes, the last tumbler finally fell, and the door swung open on blessedly silent hinges.

Groping about, Contessa managed to locate a lamp and matches on a sideboard near the door. She memorized their position in her mind so she could replace them before moving to light them. After a few seconds of struggle, she managed to cast a dim light in the office.

She made her way to the center of the room where a desk dominated most of the large room. As she lifted the lantern higher to get a better view, she gasped as the light caught on a gleaming piece of metal. Lying in the center of the desk was a knife, flat enough to slip into a boot but long enough to easily deliver a killing blow.

The sight made the blood run cold in Contessa's veins, but she continued to scan the desk. As much as Contessa's heart hammered at the sight of the knife, simply owning a weapon was not enough proof to warrant an arrest. Still, a dark voice in the back of Contessa's mind wondered if that very blade had slit her mother's throat.

The rest of the desk was unremarkable, sporting only a few fountain pens and a handsome malachite paperweight. Just as Contessa was reaching to open one of the top drawers, she heard a sound almost like a growl behind her.

She whirled around, her stomach dropping sickeningly, to find the Beast standing with his hand braced against the doorframe, effectively blocking her way out. Her mouth opened but no sound came out. She'd been found, and now she would meet the same end as her mother. She would fail her father, and she would never get to see Joseph again.

"I suppose this is what I get for not giving you a proper tour of your new home."

Contessa opened and closed her mouth a few times. She was unsure what she'd expected the Beast to say, but it hadn't been that.

"I'm a curious person," she eventually settled on as a response.

Contessa could hear his exhale, but she couldn't make out any change in his expression in the dim light.

"Let's have a drink," the Beast said before turning and stalking out of the office.

Contessa blinked at his broad back a few times then followed him. She supposed she could have grabbed the knife from the desk next to her and charged at him, but she knew it would be futile. The Beast wouldn't turn his back on her if she posed any sort of threat to him.

He led them to the living room where he set about lighting more lamps while Contessa stood in the middle of the room awkwardly hugging her dressing robe around herself. Now that she was slightly less concerned with her impending death, she was far more aware of her state of undress. Goose bumps crawled up her spine as the Beast glanced at her.

Once the lanterns were lit, the Beast turned to the sideboard where there was a single decanter filled with amber liquid. He poured two glasses and turned back to her.

"Here," he handed Contessa a glass before throwing himself down in the nearest armchair.

She continued to stand there, dumbly staring at the glass in her hand.

"Drink. I'm not trying to poison you," he said, taking a sip from his own glass in demonstration. "Unless you don't like whiskey, in which case I'm afraid I don't have anything to offer you."

"Whiskey is fine," Contessa responded, perching herself on the edge of a nearby settee and taking a delicate sip. She raised her eyebrows as she found it was the same brand Joseph had pilfered from his father's cupboard on several occasions to drink with her in secret. It wasn't an expensive brand, surprisingly modest for somebody as wealthy as the Beast. Despite the odd situation, she found the familiar warmth calmed her.

"So," the Beast bit out the word as if he were having great difficulty formulating exactly what to say. "I think it's time we stop beating around the fact we don't have a traditional marriage."

"That's an interesting way of describing our situation," Contessa said, her formerly sweet demeanor nowhere to be found. Considering he had caught her breaking into his office, it seemed all pretense of earning his trust was thoroughly destroyed.

"And how would you rather I phrase our situation?"

"How about being honest about the fact I've been sold off to a Beast?" Contessa's frustration at her continued failure was getting the better of her, and her voice was bitingly cold.

The Beast's twisted eyebrow shot up in surprise at her use of his notorious nickname. "An ungrateful spitfire like you is no walk in the park," he shot back.

Contessa floundered for a response. It was bold of him to assume she should be grateful he had deigned to marry her. The only thing he had done for her was dress her in hideous clothing and relieve her of her mother.

The Beast took the opportunity of her silence to continue. "I can't give back the opportunities you've lost. But considering we are stuck with each other; what do you say we endeavor to not make each other's lives a living hell? I've tried to stay out of your way, but today I couldn't help but notice some signs of...hostility from you."

Contessa suppressed a derisive snort. She would love to make his life a living hell, but it was more important for her to bring him to justice.

"I'd love to put our hostility to rest." She silently added that she would like their hostility to end with him on trial for murder.

"Then we're in agreement," he said before taking a long sip of his whiskey.

Contessa took the opportunity to observe the man. He was still fully dressed despite the late hour, but he seemed exhausted. Where he had always sat rigidly in her presence, now he was slouched in his chair in a way that almost looked defeated. There was a purpling circle as dark as a bruise under his good eye and his unruly auburn hair was even more wild than usual.

"Are your rooms to your liking?" he asked suddenly.

She stuck with the theme of honesty for the evening as she answered, "Not particularly. I've always hated roses."

The Beast tilted his head. "I would have thought red roses were your favorite based on the frequency with which your suitors had them delivered to your house."

Contessa was unsurprised that he had been having her house watched, just as her father was watching his. His reconnaissance must have been thorough to notice the flowers from her few admirers before her father shoed them away.

"That's because men always assume women want red roses, considering they are the flower of Aphrodite. Everybody thinks women want to be associated with the Goddess of love and beauty."

"And what Goddess would you rather be compared to?" he asked.

Contessa swirled the amber liquid in her glass as she weighed her answer. "Nemesis, the Goddess of retribution."

The Beast's eyes appeared to be a glittering gold in the light of the oil lamps as he raised his drink in a toast. "To revenge."

"To revenge," Contessa echoed, lifting hers in return.

The Beast drained his remaining whiskey in a single swallow and Contessa watched his Adam's apple bob in the dim light. Then he set his glass down on the floor and pushed to his feet. He began to stalk out of the room, but he paused in the doorway. The lighting was such that Contessa could only make out his silhouette, his powerful shoulders taking up the entire doorframe. Contessa's skin tingled.

"I would recommend you don't go through my things anymore. I assure you that you will end up in far more trouble that you bargained for." Despite the implications of his statement, the Beast's tone remained conversational. He slipped down the hall without waiting for any response from Contessa.

Contessa stayed in her seat nursing her whiskey long after he had disappeared. When she did eventually make her way up to the rose room, she didn't sit up and wait, but slipped under the covers and went straight to sleep.

♟♟♜♟♟

Despite her escapades the night before, Contessa woke as soon as the sun began peeking in the window. Her body was too regimented to sleep in much past dawn unless she was deathly ill.

Today, Julia dressed her in a sky-blue dress edged with delicate white lace. The sleeves were far too voluminous for Contessa's usual taste, but the color was an improvement.

Julia tittered and gossiped as usual while braiding Contessa's hair in a crown around her head. It seemed she was unaware of Contessa's transgressions the night before—or if she was, then she was a far better liar than Contessa ever would have guessed. Something about the girl gave Contessa the impression she would struggle to be anything but completely genuine.

Contessa picked at her cuticles as she sat at her dressing table, a habit her father had broken her of years ago. Now she picked until a bubble of blood formed on her thumb as she pulled at a hangnail.

Working her way out of her current predicament would be a complicated game of chess. She'd wasted her opportunity to search the Beast's office. Now that he knew she could pick the lock, he would set more protections on his documents. The plan of using her womanly wiles on him had apparently never been an option at all, which was a revelation as perplexing as it was relieving. Admitting defeat was not an option Contessa was willing to consider. She couldn't contemplate her father's disappointment should she fail to collect incriminating information. Not to mention she was officially married. She wouldn't be free until her husband was hanged for his crimes. The thought made Contessa shudder after yesterday's executions.

She was left with no time to examine her predicament further. As she entered the dining room, she found a figure already occupying her usual seat. Her immediate reaction was to think she'd seen more of her husband in the past day than in the first five days of their marriage put together. She then realized the back of the head she was staring at was covered in black curls instead of the Beast's auburn mane.

Gregor was currently pouring the man tea as he told some raucous tale, gesticulating widely. The story was apparently so engaging that Gregor didn't notice the teacup overflowing until steaming water spilled over his hands.

Gregor yelped and nearly dropped the teapot, and Contessa moved to grab it from him. The mysterious man beat her to it. He snatched the pot from Gregor and grabbed a napkin to tend to his scalded hands before Contessa had even taken a step forward.

"Are you alright, Gregor?" Contessa asked, taking a napkin from another place setting to mop at the spreading spill.

Gregor nodded, his round face turning beet red as the man dried his hands with the napkin.

"Really, I'm fine," Gregor stammered. "Just let me grab another cloth to clean the spill and boil you some more water."

He snatched up the teapot and beat a hasty retreat, looking mortified by a simple spill.

"He's an odd duck, that one," said the man, and Contessa recognized a slight lilt to his words that placed him as being from the northern part of the continent.

He turned away from the door Gregor had exited to face Contessa where she was still working to contain the spill with a thin napkin. He immediately let out a low whistle upon seeing her.

"And you are a pretty little bird. Nate failed to mention how lovely his wife was when he told me he was getting married."

Contessa gave up on managing the spill and turned her full attention to her surprise breakfast companion. Taking in his appearance, she finally had an image in her head for what an author meant when they described a character as a handsome rogue. His curls were messy in a way that appeared to be perpetually windswept, and his eyes held a twinkle as he fixed Contessa with a crooked smile.

"Mister Kristoff Mainsworth at your service," he introduced himself, offering an outstretched hand to Contessa in greeting. Several rings sparkled on each finger.

As Contessa reached out to shake his hand, she caught a glimpse of tattooed ink encircling Kristoff's wrist beneath his cuff. The rounded *r*'s in his accent lent his speech a distinctly friendly air, and Contessa couldn't help the smile tugging at her mouth as she introduced herself in return.

"Contessa C—er, Woodrow. May I ask what brings you to our home this morning?"

Kristoff slid back into his chair and resumed buttering his toast, which had escaped the flood of hot water.

"Oh, I'm a business associate of Nate's. I stopped by this morning to give him some help with his affairs." Kristoff brandished the butter knife with an unconcerned air as he spoke. "I always like to stay for breakfast after our meetings. Gives me more opportunities to torment poor Gregor."

It took Contessa a moment to comprehend that Kristoff was referring to the Beast when he called him Nate. Still, she perked up immediately upon hearing he was a business associate.

Looking more closely at his appearance, she could see scars across his knuckles and could just spot the gleaming handle of a revolver poking out from his belt. She knew what type of business associate her husband might have. While she'd recently hit a dead end in her investigation, she saw another avenue as she looked at Kristoff's open smile.

"I see. And what kind of work do you do for Mr. Woodrow?" she asked with wide, innocent eyes as she reached to serve herself some porridge.

"This and that." Kristoff looked at her with narrowed eyes as he took a bite of toast.

"Well, you must be instrumental if you're here this early. You're the first guest I've seen in the week I've been here," Contessa flattered.

"Mrs. Woodrow, Nate may not have mentioned that you had the face of an angel, but he did say you were sharp as a whip." Kristoff waggled his piece of toast at her. "You will be getting no information out of me."

Contessa managed to look taken aback even as she internally cursed. "I'm sure I don't know what you mean, I was just curious as to the nature of your work."

"Oh, you know exactly what I mean, but if we are all going to play the idiot here, I'll humor you. I just deal with day-to-day aspects of Nate's business so he can focus on the big picture of his work." Kristoff finished off his toast and spoke with his mouth full. "And that is all the details you'll be getting out of me, so don't go pressing for more."

"I suppose it makes sense," Contessa quipped back. "Mr. Woodrow is too high and mighty now to really get his hands dirty, but you look far too concerned with your appearance to be the hired muscle. You're stuck being the middle management."

Kristoff choked on his last swallow of toast and had to cough enthusiastically before responding with a chuckle. "No wonder Nate has been keeping so busy recently. He certainly has his hands full here."

If Contessa wasn't going to get information on the Beast's gang involvement from Kristoff, then perhaps she could at least unravel the mystery of why the man had married her at all.

"You can't possibly mean his hands have been full with me. We've scarcely spoken since our wedding day."

A crease formed between Kristoff's arched brows as he responded, "Well, that's too bad. He may have finally met his match in you."

Contessa suppressed a frown of her own at the comment. "Yes, well, if he didn't want to have anything to do with me, then why go to the trouble of marrying me?"

"For the same reason that you agreed to it." Kristoff fixed her with a knowing look, and Contessa stiffened in her seat.

She'd thought she was the one trying to get behind enemy lines, but it might be the other way around. Still, he was doing a rather unsatisfactory job of gaining information on her father. Contessa opened her mouth to quip about how the Beast would have no such satisfaction from her, but at that moment, Gregor returned with a fresh teapot and Kristoff became thoroughly distracted.

"Ahh, Gregor, you've returned," he said, gesturing broadly. "You must let me take a closer look at those talented hands of yours. Can't have that green thumb impeded by any nasty burns."

Gregor regained his earlier flush, and Contessa smiled into her porridge.

♟♙♖♙♞♙

Kristoff left shortly after breakfast, and he spent the rest of the meal too busy flirting relentlessly with Gregor for Contessa to weasel any other hints from him. Contessa would have felt bad for Gregor if she hadn't thought he was enjoying the attention.

Once she was alone again, Contessa was briefly at a loss for what to do. She eventually settled for her usual routine of finding the newspaper and heading out into the garden to read.

She was settled in her spot on the rim of the fountain, the paper spread across her lap in the sunshine, when a shadow fell across the page. She looked up from the article she was reading about how a physician from the Southern Continent had arrived to treat the king's illness, to see the face of the Beast looming over her. She resisted the urge to immediately jump to her feet. Instead, she asked politely, "Is there something I can help you with, Mr. Woodrow?"

"I was looking for the newspaper. Gregor said you had it."

"Well, he was right. I'm reading it right now," she said, looking back down at the article, not in a particularly accommodating mood. If she wasn't going to weasel information out of him, she saw no purpose in being nice to a murderer.

The shadow didn't move from over Contessa. The Beast's hands clenched and unclenched at the edge of her vision. Good. Let him feel a fraction of the frustration this marriage had caused her.

"Standing over me isn't going to make me read any faster," she commented without looking up.

There were a few seconds of stillness until the Beast moved away. Instead of heading down the path back to the house, however, he simply moved to the side and sat down on the edge of the fountain a few feet from Contessa.

Contessa flipped the page, but her eyes scanned over the same sentence several times.

"So, this is what you do all day?" the Beast finally broke the silence.

Dropping the pretense of reading, Contessa looked up to find him staring at her with his head tilted to the side. Contessa was still unsure of her ability to read his expressions. His scar made him seem constantly hostile. Or maybe that really was his expression, and the scar just enhanced the effect.

Remembering his question, she answered, "Well, it's not as though you've given me many options to entertain myself with around here."

This creases between his brows deepened.

"What do ladies like you do to entertain yourselves?"

Contessa considered his question, finding it an odd thing to ask. "I personally read a lot of books."

The Beast exhaled sharply through his nose, clearly spotting her predicament there. "Aren't there other things you like to do to pass the time?"

"Don't you dare suggest I embroider cushions. Not every young lady enjoys straining her eyes over a needle and thread."

The Beast huffed again in what could have passed for a laugh had his face managed more than a slight grimace. "No, you don't strike me as the type to embroider. You have to enjoy something besides reading, though."

"I do. I play a lot of chess, and I like a good walk in the park." Contessa thought wistfully of spending Joseph's afternoons off in the parlor laughing over a chess board and the rolling pathways of the Grand Park. She'd been cooped up in this sterile house for too long.

"I have a chess board," the Beast offered.

"That's rather unhelpful if I don't have anybody to play against. I learned long ago that I can't stay objective enough to play against myself," Contessa pointed out.

The Beast fixed her with a thoughtful stare. "I can play."

"Then perhaps we should see who the better strategist is."

The silence between them stretched. He broke the it first.

"Why haven't you gone for a walk in the park if you enjoy them?"

Contessa opened her mouth to answer but paused. She'd thought the answer was obvious. Realizing her mouth was hanging open like a fish, she shut it with an audible snap.

"I married you; I didn't kidnap you," said the Beast, having the nerve to sound disgruntled by her assumption that her mother's murderer might have hostile intentions.

"That was rather unclear when you married me and then refused to speak to me," Contessa retorted and then winced. She wasn't sure why she made it sound like she wished he would speak to her. Maybe a week in a foreign house barely seeing anybody but Julia and Gregor had begun to affect her head.

The Beast considered her for a moment. She waited for him to snap and say something in his defense. Instead, he said, "If you ask Gregor, he'll bring around the carriage to take you to the park."

Contessa just nodded in thanks. After a moment, the Beast stood, straightening his cuffs before heading back down the garden path.

"Wait," Contessa said before she could stop herself. "You can have this now." She held out the paper for him to take.

He stared at the offering in her outstretched hand for long enough that Contessa almost pulled it back. Then he took it with an inclination of his head before turning back to the house.

Contessa watched his receding form, feeling as though every conversation with him confused her more than the last.

Chapter Five

ontessa was surprised to find that she would have company for dinner as well. Gregor was just placing a bowl of pea soup in front of Contessa when the Beast stalked into the dining room and threw himself down into the chair across the table. He grunted something that may have been a greeting as he did.

Gregor, for his part, didn't seem perturbed, and moved to fetch another place setting. Contessa peeked through her lashes as she blew on her soup to cool it. She didn't speak. The Beast didn't object to the silence and set about ladling a large amount of soup into his bowl as soon as Gregor set it in front of him.

As they ate, the silence was only broken by the slurping the Beast made as he spooned soup into his crooked mouth. Contessa was used to quiet meals, her father not being particularly loquacious. This silence, however, made her sit up so straight she felt as if she might float off her chair.

As the meal ended, Gregor brought the Beast a glass of whiskey.

Contessa prepared to excuse herself from the table and the silence that put her on edge. Before she could stand up, the Beast spoke.

"I thought we could play that round of chess this evening."

He sounded almost uncertain, as if the fact he was asking her surprised him as well.

Against her better judgement, Contessa nodded in assent. If she couldn't beat this man at his own game to bring him to justice, then she certainly would enjoy beating him at chess.

He pushed from his seat and moved around her to lead the way out of the dining room. As he brushed by her, he passed close enough she could smell the whiskey that clung to his breath. The hair on the back of Contessa's neck stood up and she took a step back.

The Beast led the way to the parlor where there was indeed a Chess board on a low table. She thought she would have noticed it during her earlier investigations, but perhaps the Beast usually kept it in his office. He perched himself on stool near the table, and Contessa arranged her skirts around her on the end of a chaise lounge opposite him. As the Beast leaned forward to ensure the tiles were properly arranged on the board, Contessa couldn't help but think that his large form looked a little ridiculous crowded onto the small wooden stool, his powerful build making it seem like furniture for children. Perhaps he could have taken her seat, but Contessa wasn't one to argue with him if he was determined to be uncomfortable.

Once the board was set up, the Beast jerked his head towards her, indicating she should make a move since she was sitting closest to the white pieces. Contessa picked a simple first move, hoping for him to underestimate her. He responded as she hoped he would, and the game was afoot.

They played in silence, but Contessa took pleasure in the sharp exhales of surprise she was able to elicit from the Beast with her strategy. She almost smirked when he ran a wide hand through his hair in frustration, but she schooled her face to neutrality.

Contessa found herself enjoying the match despite herself. It reminded her of evenings spent playing chess with her father. He had taught her to play at a very young age and always encouraged her to sharpen her strategic mind. She could still remember her mother scolding her father when he won repetitively, but he insisted she wouldn't learn otherwise.

Now she could best her father nearly half the time, and her current adversary wasn't nearly as skilled. The Beast hadn't even finished half his whiskey by the time she had him on the ropes.

"Oh dear, it looks like I've backed you into a corner here," Contessa commented in feigned surprise as she executed her final strategy.

The Beast looked up at her with one brow lifted.

"I wonder how that happened," he mused in a tone that made it clear he wasn't shocked in the slightest.

Contessa was loath to admit she was disappointed he didn't rage at his defeat. She'd hoped making him angry would make her feel less frustrated at her current predicament. Instead, he took a long sip of whiskey and calmly accepted his fate.

"You play very well," he commented, clearing the board.

"My father taught me."

Any sense of a truce that had fallen between the two immediately vanished as the Beast's eyes snapped up to hers, flashing gold in the dimming lamplight.

"Of course, your father would train his daughter to be a sharp one."

"It's fortunate for me that he did."

A beat of silence passed before Contessa pushed to her feet saying politely, "I'm afraid I must be going to bed now. Thank you for the match, though. It was certainly enlightening."

Contessa turned to go in a rustle of skirts, but not before she caught the hard glint in her opponent's eyes. She swept from the room feeling smug. By the time she got to her rooms, her victorious glow had faded. A game of chess had been a temporary outlet from her frustration, but it still didn't get her any closer to justice.

♟♜♖♙♜♙

The Beast seemed to have developed a vested interest in besting Contessa at chess. For the next two nights, after dinner, he would materialize with a glass of whiskey in hand and challenge her to a match. Contessa accepted each time, telling herself it was a chance to get to know her adversary better. Indeed, Contessa began to be able to read the signs of his frustration as he played—the way he gnawed at his bottom lip and the heavy exhales through his nose when Contessa thwarted him.

They played mostly in silence, broken by only short bits of conversation. Contessa debated trying to talk more, thinking perhaps she could get him to let some important piece of information slip. The silence, though, seemed to be an integral part of a small truce they had created, and Contessa was inexplicably hesitant to violate it.

One of their brief conversations occurred when Contessa had managed to knock over her teacup with the oversized puff of her sleeve. She cursed in a way that would make her father scowl, and the Beast's eyes shot up from the board at her expletives.

Contessa tried to mop the spreading stain from her skirts with her handkerchief, but it was no use.

"Well, this one wasn't my color to begin with," she mused, tucking the soiled handkerchief away.

The Beast scowled at her periwinkle skirts. "The dressmaker assured me this color is what all the ladies are wearing."

Contessa was taken aback that the Beast had conversed with a dressmaker. She couldn't picture him entering a dress shop at all.

"Be that as it may, pastels make me feel like a porcelain doll."

"What colors do you prefer?"

Contessa found it odd that they were talking about something as mundane as favorite colors, but she supposed stranger things must have happened.

"Gray," she responded honestly. "And blue."

The Beast considered her with a tilted head. "The same color as your eyes," he commented thoughtfully.

If the conversation had been unusual before, it felt downright bizarre now. The Beast seemed to feel similarly and quickly turned his attention back to the game board. Contessa found herself distracted by his implementation of a new strategy and pushed the comment to the back of her mind for further consideration.

Two days later, she was dressed in an elegant day dress made of gunmetal gray silk, and she was forced to consider whether the color choice was a coincidence.

Contessa resolved to ask the Beast about the dress that evening over their nightly game of chess. However, he didn't appear as she finished dinner to challenge her to a match. Presumably, he was delayed, so Contessa moved herself to the parlor to set up the board herself.

By the time the board was set, he still hadn't materialized. Contessa had nothing better to do than sit and wait. Settling back on the chaise lounge, she considered her strategy for the coming game. With the Beast's increasing prowess, she would have to employ more sophisticated tactics. As she contemplated, the candles burned lower and lower. Eventually, they burned out, but Contessa didn't notice, for she had dozed off.

♟♜♔♟♖♟

Contessa was woken by the sound of a child crying out. It took her a moment to place the noise, for it wasn't something she was accustomed to hearing. As soon as she recognized it, though, she jerked awake, sitting bolt upright amongst her rumpled skirts.

The noise of the crying child was the loudest, but it was accompanied by the pounding of footsteps and panicked words in a distinctive northern brogue. Just as Contessa recognized the voice, Kristoff rounded the corner into the parlor, and she located the source of the wailing. Bundled in the man's arms was a child, no older than seven or eight, based on his size. The child was wearing the grubby clothes of an urchin, but the shoulders were darkened by blood dripping from his scalp. He was howling and clutching to Kristoff's shirt sleeves, marking the crisp white fabric with crimson handprints.

Contessa leapt to her feet. Kristoff looked slightly taken aback to find her in the parlor, but the expression didn't last long. He strode over to the chaise Contessa had been dozing on and gently laid his cargo down.

Even as he arranged the screaming child carefully on the cushions, he barked at Contessa, "Find Gregor. Out back, in the garden."

Without another thought, Contessa hiked up her skirts and dashed from the room. As she flew around the corner into the back of the house, she saw something that made her heart skip a beat.

The door to the office was flung wide open.

Contessa skidded to a halt in front of the open doorway. The desk lay beyond the threshold, a few papers scattered across its surface. She made to step inside, see what clues the papers might hold.

Her foot hovered in the air before she could enter the forbidden room. In her mind flashed the image of the young boy in the living room, dark blood dripping down his face.

Cursing internally, Contessa whirled in place and sprinted towards the back door to the garden. Bursting out into the night air, she spotted Gregor kneeling in a bed of hydrangeas.

"Gregor," Contessa shouted, heaving for breath in her too tight corset after her brief sprint. "It's Kristoff, there's a child in the parlor, he's bleeding."

Gregor, looking concerned but less surprised than Contessa might have thought, shot to his feet before she could get Kristoff's name out. He brushed his muddy hands off on his work apron as he rushed towards the house.

"Apply pressure to the wound, I'll be right there with my kit," he instructed, pushing through the back door.

Contessa ran back to the parlor, pointedly avoiding looking at the temptation of the open office door. When she arrived back in the parlor, she found Kristoff already trying to staunch the bleeding with his bare hands. The child was still whimpering and squirming, but he had stopped screaming. Sliding to her knees next to him, Contessa could see the blood was coming from a long, jagged graze across the boy's forehead and into his hairline. Gathering up a handful of her skirts, Contessa pressed the gray silk against the wound, the fabric instantly turning dark and heavy.

Kristoff glanced over at her with a grateful expression, wiping his reddened hands on his pants. Just then, Gregor pushed into the room, carrying a leather case. Kristoff sprang to his feet to give up his space next to the boy. Contessa pulled her hands away so Gregor could inspect the injury.

He hissed between his teeth at the ripped skin.

"Bullet graze?" he asked as he began pulling supplies out of his leather case.

"Broken cable," came Kristoff's voice from over her shoulder. "One of the machines was hit by a stray bullet in the escape, and the broken wire caught him across the face."

Contessa looked at the child in front of her again as he spoke, taking in the gnarled hands of a laborer in a textile factory.

Gregor nodded in understanding as he pulled out a bottle and began pouring the contents on some rags. A harsh chemical smell filled Contessa's nose.

"I'll need to clean this and then stitch it up. Somebody will have to hold him steady."

At Gregor's words, the child began to wail anew, flailing his arms and batting at Gregor and Contessa where they knelt. Contessa slid onto the chaise, pulling the child's head into her lap as she did so and stroking his hair gently away from his wound.

She shot a pointed look at Gregor as she began to speak, indicating he should work quickly.

"You've been so brave," Contessa cooed. "What's your name, brave one?"

"P-Paul." The boy's lower lip trembled as Gregor approached him with an antiseptic-soaked rag. He flinched as the cloth touched his wound, but Contessa placed her hands on either side of his face and held him firmly in place.

"Well, Paul, I'm Contessa Woodrow, and I'm so sorry we had to meet under such painful circumstances. You are in good hands now though, and Gregor is going to fix you up perfectly." As she finished, Contessa shot Gregor a look that made it clear he needed to deliver on her promises. He nodded once and set back to cleaning the wound.

"You're Mr. Woodrow's wife," the child said, his eyes becoming round, and he seemed to relax into her lap just a touch.

"Yes," Contessa said, eyeing the needle and thread Gregor was pulling out of his kit and tightening her grip, "and I'm going to help you. Your parents must be worried sick about you."

As Contessa spoke, Kristoff begin to shake his head, but it was too late.

"I-I don't have any parents," Paul stammered. "It's just me and my little sister, Olivia."

The boy's eyes widened even further as if he had just remembered something important. He began to squirm in Contessa's lap as he yelled, "Olivia! Where is she? We were running and then..."

Contessa tried holding the boy still and stroking his hair, but he remained distraught until a familiar voice sounded near the door.

"She's safe with the others, and a tough little thing too."

Contessa's looked up to find the Beast standing in the doorway looking disheveled. His overcoat had a long rip on the sleeve, and his hair was even messier than usual, but he seemed uninjured. His gaze was trained on the little boy in Contessa's lap, and his eyes were softer than Contessa had ever seen them. Maybe it was just the dim lighting.

The boy calmed his squirming, but Contessa knew the worst was yet to come, so she returned her attention to him.

"I'm sure your sister would be very impressed with how courageous you're being. Do you think you could be brave for just a little bit longer?" Contessa encouraged the boy.

The boy nodded, and Gregor began to approach him with the needle. Contessa held his head firmly in her hands but let her thumb stroke through his hair in reassurance. She heard a rustle next to her and glanced up to find the Beast had also settled on his knees beside the chaise. He took one of the boy's small hands in both of his large ones, and despite the difference in size, in that moment, Contessa couldn't help but notice the similarities in their scarred fingers.

Her attention was drawn back to the boy when he screeched in pain as Gregor began to make his first stitch. He attempted to jerk away, but between Contessa and the Beast, they managed to hold him steady. Contessa cooed out soothing nonsense as best she could between gritted teeth. The cut was not as severe as it had initially appeared once the blood had been cleared away, but it still looked painful. To everybody's relief, the boy had fallen unconscious by the time Gregor was making his third stitch.

The room was silent as Gregor worked, and Contessa remained still with the boy's head cradled in her lap while he finished. The Beast didn't move, either, Paul's hand still clasped in his. Contessa snuck glances at him out of the corner of her eye and could see the muscles in his jaw clenched under his uneven skin. His eyes didn't waver from the boy's face the entire time.

When Gregor had tied off the last stitch, the entire room breathed a collective sigh of relief. Gregor mopped away the blood with a clean rag to reveal a neat line of sutures marching across Paul's forehead and into his hairline.

"The cut was pretty jagged. It will leave a scar. It should heal quickly, though," Gregor commented as he packed up his kit.

"With luck, it will just make him look dashing when he's older," Kristoff commented.

Contessa couldn't help the way her eyes flicked over the Beast's own scar, hard won in the fight for the leadership of the Lions. Thankfully, Paul's wouldn't be nearly as severe.

The whole room seemed to shake itself from its reverie as the Beast spoke.

"We need to get him out of here, Kristoff. Take him out the back and bring him to the rendezvous point with the rest of them. Rhosyn will make sure he's taken care of from there."

Kristoff stepped forward and lifted Paul out of Contessa's lap as if he weighed nothing more than a house cat. He arranged the boy so his head didn't loll. Then Kristoff made to leave the room, but before he did, he leaned towards Gregor and whispered something Contessa couldn't hear. Then they both left, leaving her alone in the now deafening silence with the Beast.

Contessa stared down at her lap, the silk now completely darkened with blood.

She contemplated her stained dress as she waited for the Beast to break the silence, but he remained quiet. He stared at his own bloody and scarred hands as if they might hold the secrets of the universe.

Contessa was so full of questions that, eventually, one burst forth.

"What happened to Paul's parents?"

Perhaps it wasn't the most urgent question, but she couldn't banish the pain she'd felt when Paul had said it was only him and his sister. Losing one parent had nearly ruined her. Losing both wasn't something Contessa wanted to consider.

The Beast looked up from his hands, tilting his head as he responded. "The same thing that happened to the parents of all the factory children."

When Contessa showed no signs of comprehension, he elaborated.

"They were hanged in the Inquiries."

The air rushed from Contessa's lungs of its own accord until she felt hollowed out. Her vision narrowed at the edges and wavered until the sight of the living room was that of a different one, five years earlier. The blood on her hands was no longer Paul's, but her mother's.

She could still feel her mother's head cradled in her arms as she screamed for her father. She'd found her on the ground. The blood that poured out of her mother's ruined throat seeped into her flaxen hair, which had tumbled out of its elaborate rolls as if yanked by violent hands. More blood trickled out of three scratches raked across her mother's cheek. Contessa would never forget the look in her mother's eyes as the light faded out of them. It was one of pure rage. Rage that Contessa had absorbed into herself until her life had been consumed by the need for revenge against her mother's murderer as well as all the rest of the Cursed in the city.

Now, Contessa found herself drawn out of her terrible vision by the warm hand of the murderer himself. It rested softly on her shoulder, and Contessa realized he hadn't touched her at all since the dance on their wedding day.

When her husband's hazel eyes met hers, Contessa was surprised to find they didn't fill her with the rage she normally felt when she thought of her mother's murder. Instead, she just felt incredibly sad. She had lost a single parent to the Cursed, but how many orphans had the Inquiries left? Those children had been forced to endure watching their parents dying in public executions, in front of a crowd who was glad for their death. Perhaps those orphans were just as full of anger as Contessa, ready for vengeance that would make more orphans.

It left Contessa feeling cold to her soul. The Beast removed his hand from her shoulder as quickly as he had placed it there.

"I feel awful for them," Contessa murmured.

"You weren't the one who murdered their parents."

That wasn't exactly true. She might not have pulled the lever that sent them plummeting to their death, but her father was the one sending them to their executions. She'd stood in the crowd as they died, just as full of fear as the rest of the spectators.

"What happens to the orphans?"

Contessa needed to know. As uncomfortable as the executions had often made her feel, she hadn't stopped to consider the dangerous gangsters being hanged might have children of their own.

"Most of them start working in factories, trying to make enough money to eat. They eventually fall into enough debt that they aren't much better than slaves, worked to the bone, punished for falling behind." The Beast's eyes were pointed towards Contessa, but she got the impression he was far away as he spoke.

"And where do you and Kristoff fit into all of this?"

"We try to give the children...another option in life," he answered.

Contessa's heart sunk. It was out of the frying pan and into the fire for these children. Rescued from the harsh factory life only to be thrown into a life of crime in the gangs, likely ending with their own hanging. She didn't know why she'd hoped for something better from the Beast.

She found her eyes drawn to his scarred hands still resting on the lounge and covered in Paul's blood. Part of her itched to reach out and touch them, to wipe them clean and soothe the scars. Not all the marks could be from knife fights, and she pictured the small boy's hand clutched tightly in his own.

While the textile factories offered harsh working conditions, the street gangs couldn't be much better.

Contessa's head whirled. She needed to take a step back, regroup, and develop a new plan of attack. She pushed to her feet and attempted to smooth her now ruined skirts.

"I think I need to retire for the evening," she offered, desperate for a chance to think on her own.

The Beast just nodded and remained kneeling on the floor. It was odd to have her mother's murderer in such a vulnerable position before her. It was something she'd envisioned many times, usually with him begging for her forgiveness. Now that she was here, though, it felt vastly different than she had imagined.

Banishing the thought from her mind, Contessa turned to leave the room. Just as she was about to step into the hallway, she heard a voice behind her.

"Thank you for your help tonight, Contessa."

She glanced over her shoulder.

"It was no trouble at all, Mr. Woodrow."

She made her way upstairs to her rose infested bedroom, thoughts of everything that Mr. Woodrow had told her swirling in her now troubled mind.

Chapter Six

The next morning at breakfast, Contessa was greeted by a neat, white envelope waiting for her at her usual seat. Her heart sped up in her chest as she recognized the green wax seal emblazoned with a set of scales that belonged to her father. If he was taking the risk to write to her in Mr. Woodrow's house, it must be of utmost importance.

Contessa endeavored to eat her porridge at a normal pace, not wanting to appear too anxious. She tucked the letter into her dress to read once she made her way out into the privacy of the garden. She preferred not to read it here, where Gregor might enter and see something untoward over her shoulder.

By the time Contessa had arranged herself on the fountain in the back courtyard, she had to keep herself from ripping into the letter like a child opening a present. She broke the wax seal with quick fingers, letting her eyes rove the page and take in her father's aggressively neat and angular handwriting.

She'd known her father wouldn't put any explicit information about her mission in the letter. Her brow furrowed as she read. She'd been prepared to decipher a hidden message artfully concealed in seemingly mundane news. Instead, the page held nothing more than a short note telling her the weather tomorrow was supposed to be ideal for a stroll in the park.

Contessa's brow smoothed once again. Her father was suggesting she go to the park so she could converse with him in person. It wouldn't be seen as unusual for Contessa to go for a stroll with her father, although they would still have to be careful not to be overheard.

♟♞♜♛♝♛

The sun managed to warm Contessa's face, even through the parasol she carried. She would just as soon have gone without the lacey accessory, but Julia had been so pleased it matched her hat that Contessa had been persuaded to take it with her. Now she was glad of the shade it offered as she squinted, searching the shrub-lined paths of the park for her father. She ambled along as casually as she could for a minute before spotting his angular silhouette standing alone, contemplating a nearby fountain with his hands clasped behind his back. As Contessa stepped up beside him, he glanced at her out of the corner of his eyes.

"What on earth are you wearing?" he asked.

Contessa glanced down at her dress and grimaced. It was exactly the type of frivolous ensemble her father would look down his nose at.

"Mr. Woodrow bought this dress for me," she answered, smoothing the skirts as best she could, wishing she could make them take up less space in the tight alcove.

"Perfectly predictable. That Beast would like to show off the money he stole through blood by having ostentatious taste," her father scoffed.

Contessa considered the sparse house with the blue door and thought maybe the ostentatious taste was that of the dressmaker and not Mr. Woodrow's. She kept that observation to herself as her father continued.

"What progress have you made? I assume I have received no evidence because you have been unable to communicate with me, so I took the liberty of making you an opportunity."

Clasping her hands in front of her, Contessa responded, "I have been working to find evidence, but progress is slow. He is not as trusting as his proposal may have initially led us to believe."

Chief Cook sniffed. "He is a violent man ruled by his baser urges. Surely, after sharing his bed for two weeks, you must have gotten some small piece of information out of him."

"He is more cunning than you give him credit for," Contessa retorted, for some reason feeling loathe to speak to her father about the fact she hadn't been warming Mr. Woodrow's bed.

"Are you defending the man?"

Contessa's spine went rigid. "I'm simply stating why I have had to be more cautious in my approach."

Chief Cook sighed, the action ruffling his moustache. "Well, I am glad you're being careful. I do want my daughter home in one piece at the end of this."

Contessa relaxed her hands where they had fisted in the folds of her dress. Her father was simply pressing her because he was anxious to get her home. Being back in her own element did sound appealing. The world within the walls of Mr. Woodrow's house had begun to turn her head.

"Father," Contessa began, needing to find some clarity in the confusion, "what happens when those hung in the Inquiries have children?"

Chief Cook's gaze darted over to his daughter. "What an odd question. I would think most of them go to work in the factories. The factory owners will look after them and pay them an honest living until they are old enough to learn another trade."

Contessa nodded, staying silent as her brain integrated her father's response.

"Why do you ask? Has this got something to do with Mr. Woodrow?"

Contessa opened her mouth to tell him what had brought on her question, but the breath caught in her chest. She remembered Paul's scared face and scarred hands and couldn't bring herself to admit the whole story. If she told her father about Paul, he might be found and punished for running away from the factory.

Instead, Contessa told a half truth.

"I think Mr. Woodrow might use the children of the Cursed as a recruiting ground for his gang." Contessa mentally patted herself on the back for her carefully crafted response. Now her father could work to prevent children from being forced into the gangs, but Paul and his sister wouldn't be hunted down and made an example of.

Chief Cook smoothed his moustache in thought.

"Interesting. It makes sense I suppose. It explains why the Lions seem to always have endless numbers. I'll see what I can do about these children, make sure they don't get pulled into a life of crime."

The tension in Contessa's chest ebbed a bit. Her father might be harsh, but everything he did was to serve the Kingdom. If he was going to protect the children from the hardships of lives on the streets, then they would be safe.

"Thank you for that information. You have done well after all," her Father praised, reaching out to squeeze her hand briefly.

Contessa squeezed back. "I must go before Mr. Woodrow's man misses me."

"Then go and keep using that sharp wit of yours. It will get you home in no time."

Contessa did as she was bid, glancing over her shoulder at her father one last time before stepping around a topiary and back onto the main path. Here she blended in with others enjoying the nice weather. She spotted couples strolling arm in arm, and her heart squeezed. She looked away and began walking around the loop, back towards where Gregor waited for her, but a hand reached out and yanked her into a gap in the hedges.

"Joey!" Contessa scolded when she saw who had grabbed her, adrenaline fizzling in her veins.

"Chief Cook said you were safe, but I had to know for myself." Joseph held her by the shoulders, scrutinizing her from head to toe.

"I'm fine," she reassured, happy to see him—happy to have a friend as her world grew more complicated.

"Then what's happened?" Joseph pressed. "What's taking you so long?"

Contessa sighed. "Things are more complicated than I thought. Mr. Woodrow...he's not exactly who I thought he was."

"He's not the Beast?" Joseph's eyebrows shot up.

"He is," Contessa hedged, "but he's not what I was expecting beneath the façade."

Joseph's grip on her shoulders tightened. "Are you defending him? Saying he's not a monster?"

"No," Contessa shook her head, "but there's more to the story than his crimes."

Joseph released her shoulders as if they had burned him, taking a step back.

"He's broken the law, committed *murder*. Nobody is above the law, no matter their infraction and no matter their reasons."

For a moment, Contessa saw her father's fervor in Joseph's eyes, and she stammered.

"It's not that..." Contessa trailed off, trying to communicate to Joseph how nothing was turning out how she expected.

"Remember who's side you're on." Joseph's voice was cool. "The Royal Police are trying to keep London safe. Don't let the Beast change you."

Joseph turned on his heel and ducked back onto the path, leaving Contessa feeling lost. Maybe he was right, and everything was as black and white as he said it was. Still, she couldn't rid herself of the feeling of Paul's blood on her hands.

Chapter Seven

At dinner that night, Contessa found the table set not with two place settings but three. Already seated at one of them was Kristoff. He sat slouched jauntily to one side, his feet propped up on the chair beside him and absently twirling a silver fork in one hand. Upon Contessa's entrance to the dining room, though, he leapt to his feet.

"Ah, the lovely and ever poised Mrs. Woodrow," he said, taking one of her hands in both of his and bowing over it in truly dramatic fashion. "What a pleasure it is to be joining you for the evening meal."

Contessa felt a smile tugging at the corners of her lips despite herself. The man could charm a teakettle.

Just then, Mr. Woodrow stalked into the room. His eyes darted quickly over the scene in front of him before saying, "Stop terrorizing her, Kristoff."

Contessa was surprised to find he didn't bark the phrase like a command, but his voice was light as if he were used to Kristoff's antics and they had ceased to bother him long ago.

Kristoff did as he was bid and resumed his seat, but not before throwing Contessa an exaggerated wink.

Contessa and Mr. Woodrow also moved to their places, and Gregor stepped in to begin serving the meal. Kristoff's eyes roved quickly over Gregor, and Kristoff opened his mouth to say something. Seeing the wicked glint in Kristoff's eye, Contessa determined it would be in the best interest of Gregor's poor nerves to interrupt him.

"To what do we owe the pleasure of your company, Kristoff?"

Kristoff turned his attention away from Gregor and to Contessa.

"You mean besides the fact that eating dinner with Nate night after night must get incredibly boring, and I thought it time to save you from that torturous monotony? I had some business to attend to that ran late, and I wasn't going to be able to make it to my own home in time for supper, so I decided to stay."

"Working this late on a Sunday? You must be uncommonly dedicated," Contessa commented as she accepted a bowl of onion soup from Gregor.

"On the contrary, if I had my way, I wouldn't be keeping these long hours. It's Nate over here and his utter disbelief in leisure that keeps my nose to the grindstone. Maybe if he learned to lighten up a touch then I would not suffer so," Kristoff said, clutching his chest in mock drama.

Mr. Woodrow glared at him over his spoon, but Contessa sensed no real malice in his gaze. For her part, she'd never imagined that anybody would dare tease the most notorious mass murderer in the city, yet here Kristoff was. She'd never considered the possibility that Mr. Woodrow might have friends.

They made an odd set, Mr. Woodrow's constant tension and

surliness clashing with the twinkle in Kristoff's eyes suggesting he saw most things as a joke. Still, something about the way they mirrored each other signaled to Contessa that they had shared a life-long friendship—something Contessa herself had never experienced.

"Why, Nate, when was the last time you did something purely for your enjoyment?" Kristoff prodded.

Mr. Woodrow paused in the middle of a slurp of soup and furrowed his brow.

"I've played chess with Mrs. Woodrow most nights," he defended, sounding offended by Kristoff's asserting that he didn't know how to have fun.

"You only do that because I forced you to admit you have nothing else amusing to do in this house," Contessa argued. While their nightly games had certainly been preferable to boredom, she'd gotten the impression they were engaging in them as a test of wits rather than a form of entertainment.

"I have been enjoying our nightly games." Mr. Woodrow tilted his head, sounding honestly wounded.

Contessa struggled to formulate a response. The best she came up with was a soft "Oh."

Kristoff sipped his own soup, pointedly staring over the spoon at Mr. Woodrow. Mr. Woodrow in turn shot him an indecipherable look, but Contessa was saved from her puzzlement by the return of Gregor with the next course.

The rest of the meal passed without incident, Kristoff and Contessa chatting idly about articles she'd read in the newspaper. They spent a while discussing whether they thought the King would survive the fever he was suffering from and another few minutes examining the merits of each of his sons as successors.

They stayed pointedly away from any news that involved gang violence or police activity. While Contessa still knew her role in this house was to gather evidence of gang activity, she found she genuinely enjoyed Kristoff's company. There would be other opportunities to ferret out incriminating details, so for now, she allowed herself to enjoy some of the first real conversation she'd had in weeks.

To her surprise, Mr. Woodrow also offered his opinion from time to time. He seemed much more at ease in the presence of his friend. Contessa reminded herself that he was a young man, not much older than herself, and not just the figure of legend he had built himself up to be on the streets of London. The realization made Contessa shift uncomfortably in her seat.

When the plates had been cleared from the table, Gregor came in and delivered Mr. Woodrow his customary glass of whiskey. He turned to offer one to Kristoff as well, but Kristoff waved him away.

"Today has been a long day. I think I should be getting home. You two enjoy yourselves, though." He looked pointedly at Mr. Woodrow who shot him an inscrutable look over the top of his glass.

Kristoff turned to Contessa, giving her a small bow as he said his good-byes.

"Maybe I'll work late and stay for dinner more often, just for the pleasure of your company."

"I might enjoy that," conceded Contessa, inclining her head to him.

With that, Kristoff took his top hat from Gregor and swept from the room. Contessa could have sworn he gave the manservant a wink as he left.

The room grew noticeably quieter with the lack of Kristoff's presence, but some of the levity he brought remained, hovering in the air.

"Would you like to continue with another game of chess tonight?" Mr. Woodrow broke the silence. "I would hate to think you were only feigning interest in our matches out of a sense of duty."

"Well, I am your wife," Contessa shot back, but her tone lacked its usual venom.

Mr. Woodrow exhaled in amusement but gave her a look that said he knew perfectly well what she'd meant.

"I would actually enjoy a game of chess tonight," Contessa admitted.

Mr. Woodrow nodded and made to lead the way from the dining room. As he rounded the table towards the door, he reached out and snagged the decanter of whiskey and another cut crystal glass from the table.

When they arrived in the parlor with the chess set, Mr. Woodrow poured a few fingers of whiskey into the glass and handed it to Contessa.

She took the offering but tilted her head curiously.

"Most people could use a drink after having dinner with Kristoff," he offered by way of explanation.

Contessa let out a small giggle as she took the glass, then froze immediately. It was an odd feeling to giggle like a gossiping flirt, and she realized she hadn't laughed in weeks. The noise felt foreign in her throat, and she stole a glance at Mr. Woodrow.

His expression surprised her more than her own laughter. While Contessa often had trouble interpreting the expressions on his scarred face, the look he wore now was unmistakably a smile. It was a small thing, just curving up the corner of his mouth and crinkling his good eye, but something about it made the way his scar warped his face appear less grotesque.

Contessa quickly looked away and began arranging the tiles on the circular board.

They began as usual, in silence, but the whiskey Contessa sipped against her better judgement must have turned her head. Soon, she looked down at the board and found Mr. Woodrow had decimated her strategy. She tried quickly to salvage her pieces' formation, but it looked to be a lost cause.

"You've improved immensely," she commented, trying not to sound petulant as he took one of her knights.

"I have Kristoff to thank, actually."

"Kristoff?" Contessa asked as she managed to move a rook to safety, if only temporarily.

"Yes, I told him of our games. He suggested I try implementing a different strategy. Something a little less aggressive that involves my pieces working together more," he explained, quickly circumventing her escape strategy.

Contessa knew they were no longer just speaking of chess, but she wasn't sure what Mr. Woodrow was suggesting.

"It seems to be working for you," she hedged, "but doesn't that force some of the pieces to compromise their strengths?"

"Maybe it is worth compromising for the greater good."

"It depends what kind of game you are playing," Contessa countered, feeling as if she was losing her footing in the conversation and the chess match.

"And what kind of game are you playing, Mrs. Woodrow?"

Contessa looked up from the board to find Mr. Woodrow looking at her, not with hostility, but with genuine curiosity, as if she were a puzzle with a missing piece. She chewed the inside of her cheek for a moment before answering.

"Justice."

"Then we play the same game," he responded, his voice soft.

She shook her head. "It doesn't count if we play for the opposite team."

"There is only one team when it comes to justice," Mr. Woodrow said, making a final move to corner her king and win the match.

Contessa turned her attention back to the board in front of her, taking in her scattered tiles. It felt like an accurate reflection of her brain right now. Her mind was filled with scattered images flicking through her consciousness. Her father staring up at the gallows with fervor on his face. Joseph, insisting that there was no gray area. Her mother's eyes, angry and empty. The bloodstain left on the skirt of the gray dress.

"If there is only one side, then why is so much blood spilt?" Contessa wondered aloud.

"Seeking justice can be a dangerous profession," Mr. Woodrow's fingers brushed over his scar for the briefest of moments. Still, it was enough to make Contessa wonder if the tales about how he had gotten it were true. It was possible he had earned it in a street fight, but gossip and rumors had been known to be untrue.

Contessa stayed silent as she considered his words, and Mr. Woodrow sighed.

"I know you're smart, Mrs. Woodrow," he paused to throw back the last of the whiskey in his glass. "Just use that impressive intellect of yours to think on what I've said."

With that, Mr. Woodrow pressed to his feet and inclined his head to her before leaving the room. Contessa stayed frozen on the stool she occupied in front of the chess board. She looked at the chair Mr. Woodrow had just vacated. It was in the same place the chaise lounge had previously occupied, but the new wingback armchair was noticeably free of stains.

Perhaps that was why the furniture in the house was so impersonal, so it could be burned and replaced if it suddenly became evidence in a crime. Contessa thought it much more likely that the furniture was generic because nobody had spent time in the living area of the house before she'd moved in. Maybe Contessa should consider trying to liven the place up a little bit if she was going to be inhabiting it much longer.

Contessa shook herself at the thought. She was not here to become a society housewife. She was here to... Well, truthfully, she wasn't sure what she was doing anymore. She couldn't endorse the activities of murdering thugs, but she was forced to reconcile with the fact that their breaking children out of forced labor in the factories might be doing some good. Not to mention that she liked Kristoff far too well to believe him to be capable of the degree of the violence that was always attributed to the Lions.

Pressing to her feet, Contessa resolved not to think of these confusing issues until she'd slept the last traces of whiskey out of her system. She would need her full wits about her to devise a plan reconciling all her interests.

Contessa considered heading upstairs and climbing directly into her bed but dismissed the idea. Her head was still spinning and, for some reason, she kept picturing the way Mr. Woodrow's face had looked when he smiled. It wouldn't do to have him appearing in her dreams. She would go for a quick turn about the garden to clear her head before going to sleep.

Contessa headed to the back of the house and out into the garden. She passed the entrance to the office that had taunted her, and lamplight flickered through the crack beneath the door. It seemed that Mr. Woodrow had returned to his work after their game. She paused for a moment as she passed the office but then continued out the door to the back garden.

She took a breath of the still night air, and instantly, her twirling mind began to slow. The night was quiet, the only sound to be heard the clop of horse hooves from the street in the distance and the trickling of the fountain.

The cool of the night was refreshing in comparison to the warm weather they had been having and it made Contessa's problems seem much smaller. She began to make her way towards the center of the garden, thinking it would be nice to sit and listen to the splash of water for a moment. As she walked, the wind blew through the trees, rustling the nearby leaves. In fact, Contessa mused that the wind sounded almost like a blissful sigh as it moved through the plants.

As Contessa rounded the bend in the garden path, she understood why this comparison had occurred to her. Her favorite perch on the edge of the fountain was already occupied by Gregor and Kristoff, who were sitting very close together indeed. Gregor's hands were fisted in the lapels of Kristoff's coat, rumpling the fine fabric and pulling him in close. Kristoff, for his part, seemed equally enthusiastic, one hand cupping Gregor's face and the other brushing through his hair as their lips pressed together.

Contessa took a step back and gasped softly, but the noise came out louder than she intended. Gregor pulled back, and even in the dim light, Contessa could make out the look of horror on his crimson face. Kristoff sprang to his feet and took a few strides towards Contessa, his palms outstretched placatingly.

"Wait, please. Please don't think poorly of Gregor," Kristoff begged. "This was all my doing, I swear."

Contessa shook her head. "I...I don't think poorly of either of you. I was just caught off guard."

Kristoff relaxed a touch, but Gregor continued to look mortified, burying his head in his hands. Kristoff continued, "I'm sorry. I shouldn't have cornered Gregor while he was working. Please forgive me, it won't happen again."

Now that Contessa had recovered from her initial shock, she had the wherewithal to arch her eyebrows at Kristoff's promise.

"Alright, well, it may happen again," Kristoff conceded as he sensed that Contessa was not going to faint in horror at their actions, "but I will ensure it does not happen in a place where you might unwittingly wander by us."

Contessa raised her chin but couldn't help the upward twist of her lips as she responded, "See that you do."

"With that, I should be going," Kristoff said, straightening his rumpled jacket. He sketched a dramatic bow to Contessa before striding off down the garden path. Gregor didn't look up during this entire exchange but remained seated on the fountain with his hands concealing his face.

Contessa sighed before making her way to the fountain and settling herself on the edge next to Gregor. As she sat, Gregor parted his fingers so that his round blue eyes could peek out between them. Contessa remained silent, patiently waiting for Gregor to speak first.

Eventually, he let his hands drop and looked up at Contessa. He opened and closed his mouth a few times before saying, "I wasn't avoiding my work or anything, Mrs. Woodrow, I promise."

Resisting the urge to shoot him a disbelieving look, Contessa said, "With the way you and Julia keep things running around here, I would say you probably could use a night off."

Gregor nodded and looked down at his twisting hands.

"I'm more concerned about Kristoff's relentless pursuit of you. If he made you at all uncom—"

"I was the one to kiss him, Mrs. Woodrow."

"Oh. Well. In that case, I suppose there is nothing more for us to discuss," Contessa said, about to make her way to her feet, but Gregor stopped her.

"Please don't think poorly of me, Mrs. Woodrow."

Contessa settled herself back down on the fountain edge and cocked her head at Gregor. "I wouldn't think poorly of you for stealing a kiss after work. We're all adults here, Gregor."

Gregor relaxed in his seat next to her, some of the redness draining from his face. "Very wise, Mrs. Woodrow. No wonder Mr. Woodrow seems to get on with you so well."

Contessa suppressed a snort at Gregor's politeness. Still, as she pictured the way her father's face would purple with rage at what she had come upon in the garden, she could understand Gregor's hesitance. It served as a perfect reminder that her father hadn't always been right about everything. Pushing to her feet she said, "On that note, I think I will be heading to bed. I came out here to clear my head, but I sense that you need the refreshing air more than I do."

Gregor nodded. "Goodnight, Mrs. Woodrow, and thank you."

Chapter Eight

Contessa spent the next day fretting over what she would say to Mr. Woodrow when she saw him. As she sat in the garden struggling to focus on the newspaper in front of her, she came to realize that she didn't know exactly what she'd been offered when he'd implied they should cooperate.

Mr. Woodrow had vaguely suggested that joining forces might be beneficial, but he hadn't been clear what he wanted. It seemed illogical to think he might be proposing the daughter of one of his victims help his gang in their violent pursuits. However, he seemed to be aware the plight of the children in the factories had struck a nerve with her. He was going about helping them in his own way, but perhaps with Contessa's aid, they could do more.

Besides, being part of Mr. Woodrow's work might get her access to solid proof of his crimes.

As Contessa readied herself for dinner, she still hadn't settled on exactly what she was going to say to Mr. Woodrow regarding his proposal. It was a supremely uncomfortable feeling for somebody who was used to having a plan, but she found this a more difficult issue than she had faced in the past.

However, as Contessa entered the dining room that evening, it appeared she would have a temporary reprieve. There was only one place setting at the table. Mr. Woodrow didn't materialize as Contessa finished her meal either, and she breathed a sigh of relief, although it was accompanied by a pang of disappointment in her chest. She had to admit that her nights spent over a chess board with Mr. Woodrow were much more diverting than evenings spent alone in the empty house. Once again, Contessa lamented the lack of good reading material. Maybe she should learn to embroider after all.

After a cup of tea, Contessa ended up heading to bed early, if only for the pleasure of Julia's company as she readied her for sleep. Contessa had continued to ask Julia bits about herself, and Julia had begun questioning Contessa about herself in turn. Julia lingered over Contessa's hair just so they could converse a bit longer.

When Julia eventually left, Contessa climbed into the crimson fourposter bed and turned down her lamp. In the darkness, she pondered the silhouettes of the roses adorning her wallpaper. The flowers made her think of Gregor, of how smitten he seemed with Kristoff. It made her wonder what it would feel like to kiss somebody like that.

♟♜♙♚♟♚

Contessa jolted awake to a banging noise. She sat bolt upright, head whipping side to side in search of danger.

Her thoughts cleared as the noise came again and she realized it was simply somebody knocking on her door, if rather insistently. Contessa pulled on her dressing gown before padding over to the door and cracking it open. When she peeked into the hall, her jaw dropped in shock, and she immediately threw it wide.

Standing in the hallway was Mr. Woodrow, dressed in shirtsleeves and looking rather the worse for wear. His hair stood out at all angles, and he swayed slightly where he stood, holding on to the doorframe for support. Most shockingly, his shirt was splattered in something dark. In the dim light of the hallway, Contessa couldn't be completely sure, but she thought it was blood.

"What happened?" she gasped. She might know the answer, but she was more concerned with why he had chosen to show up at her bedroom door in this state.

"Don't worry, most of the blood isn't mine," he responded, trying to sound nonchalant even as he gritted his teeth.

Before Contessa could respond, he swayed again where he stood. Contessa found herself reaching out automatically to steady him, her hands landing on his firm shoulders.

"I do need some assistance, though," he said, taking an unsteady step forward. Contessa moved to his side and let him lean on her as they made their way to the bed. He was much larger than her, so it was an awkward affair, but they made it until he could sit on the edge.

"The wound is on my back," Mr. Woodrow said tightly. "I don't know how bad it is because I can't see it."

"I thought you said most of the blood wasn't yours," Contessa pointed out.

"Most of it, not all of it," he countered, his hands moving to the top button of the shirt to undo it.

Contessa's face suddenly grew hot, and she floundered. "What about Gregor? He's the one with the medical kit. I only know the basics."

Mr. Woodrow's fingers paused but remained hovering over the

button at his neck. "I happen to know that Kristoff took Gregor out for the evening. If you'd rather me tend to my wounds myself, though, I can leave."

Contessa didn't argue with that, with the assistance he had needed to get to the bed, she doubted he could get far on his own at this point. The fact of the matter was, she had her sworn enemy injured in front of her, giving her the option to do nothing. She could let him suffer alone and possibly die from his injuries.

She was already shaking her head. If he was going to suffer for his crimes, it was going to be after a fair trial, not bleeding out on her bed while she watched.

"I'll help you as best I can, although it might not be much."

Mr. Woodrow nodded and resumed unbuttoning his shirt, the top of a muscled chest coming into view. Contessa ripped her gaze away from him, trying not to stare, but it seemed she didn't know where else to look. She decided to busy herself with lighting the lamps so she would be able to inspect his injuries properly.

By the time she was finished, Mr. Woodrow had completely removed his shirt and angled himself on her bed so his back was to her. She was unsurprised to see his pale skin was not smooth, but dotted with thin white scars, and even a pink one that looked like it may be more recently healed. Most noticeable right now were the series of deep scratches running across his left shoulder blade and down to his mid back. They were still oozing, but it appeared he hadn't been lying about most of the blood on his shirt not being his.

Contessa picked her way closer and perched herself on the edge of the bed next to him. He bowed his head so she could get a better look, and she leaned in to inspect the wounds. This close, she could smell the sweat and blood that clung to him, as well as something darker and more earthy. She found herself inhaling deeply.

Brushing those thoughts from her mind, she focused in on the task before her. In the deepest wound, she thought she caught sight of something glimmering.

"Is it possible there are pieces of glass in these wounds?" she questioned.

"It's possible," he conceded. "I think Gregor has some tools in his kit you could use to get it out. He should have left it downstairs."

He directed Contessa to where the kit would have been left, and she scurried from the room to retrieve it. She was grateful for the moment alone to clear her head after the shocking turn her night had taken. Mr. Woodrow was now shirtless in her bed, although it wasn't in the context she'd thought it would be when she'd married him. Perhaps more surprising was the fact that she was voluntarily helping him.

She hurried back up the stairs with the leather case clutched in her hands. When she pushed through the door back into her bedroom, she found Mr. Woodrow had laid down on the bed. He was on his stomach with his hands folded under his forehead so Contessa would have good access to his injuries. She found she was glad of the positioning, for at this angle, she couldn't look at his face. Contessa could simply treat the injuries before her without having to think about who the torso belonged to.

Contessa settled herself on the edge of the bed, opening the kit and laying out the tools. She found a pair of pointed tweezers and a long needle that would serve her purposes admirably.

With her tools selected, she turned back to Mr. Woodrow. Blood trickled from his wounds and dripping onto the already red comforter, making it nearly black. Contessa leaned in and placed her hand on his side to steady herself as she selected her starting point. At the contact, Mr. Woodrow jumped. The movement caused the muscles in his back to tense, driving the glass deeper into his skin. He grunted in pain and Contessa jerked her hand back.

"I'm ok. Your hands are just cold." Mr. Woodrow's voice came out muffled from being facedown in the pillow.

Looking at the project before her, Contessa knew he had a lot worse than cold hands coming.

"I'm going to touch you again. Try to hold still," she directed.

As Mr. Woodrow nodded into the pillows, Contessa slipped off her dressing robe and set it on the covers beside her to collect the shards of glass. The cool of the air chilled her skin to goose bumps, and she felt strangely exposed even though Mr. Woodrow couldn't see her from his current position.

When Contessa placed her hand on him again, Mr. Woodrow did a better job of not moving, but she could still see tension across the top of his shoulders, causing the muscles there to cord and bunch.

She began with the shallowest of cuts, picking out the most easily visible fragments first. Mr. Woodrow hissed into the pillow but remained still. The muscles under her hand twitched with the effort. As she began to reach for deeper fragments of glass, she needed a better view. She scooted closer to see until the side of her hip was pressed flush against Mr. Woodrow's ribs. She was overly conscious of his body heat seeping through her thin nightdress, and soon she found she was no longer chilled.

As Contessa finished cleaning the first cut, the silence in the room was thick, broken only by Mr. Woodrow's breathing, which was so measured that Contessa was sure he must be counting his breaths to manage the pain.

Before Contessa began working on the second wound, Mr. Woodrow said into the pillow, "Could you...talk?"

"Talk?" she echoed in confusion.

"Just... to give me something else to think about," Mr. Woodrow said haltingly.

Contessa furrowed her brow before an image came to mind—her mother perched on her bedside when she was ill, singing the sweetest melodies to distract young Contessa from the feverish ache in her bones. The songs told of princesses or knights, and Contessa became so engaged in them that the pains eased until she drifted off to sleep.

Contessa didn't have a singing voice that would calm anybody, so as she picked the first shard of glass out of the next wound, she blurted out the first thought in her head.

"My mother used to sing to me to distract me when I was sick."

"What kind of songs would she sing?" Mr. Woodrow asked through gritted teeth.

Contessa plunged ahead, too distracted by the delicate extraction of a particularly tricky piece of glass to think how odd it was to be telling stories of her mother to the man who was responsible for her death.

"Made up songs about dragons and heroes. They always made me feel better and lulled me off to sleep."

The jagged piece of glass finally pulled free of Mr. Woodrow's skin with a wet sound, and he let out a soft groan as she dropped the crimson-stained shard onto her dressing gown. Contessa rambled on as she investigated to make sure she'd removed all debris from the second cut.

"She was always singing around the house, as she embroidered or brushed my hair. Everybody always paused in what they were doing to listen, her voice was that beautiful. I swear the very sun seemed to shine brighter as she sang."

Contessa ensured the second cut was cleared. Mr. Woodrow's muscles trembled under her touch, and a slight sheen of sweat formed on his back with the effort it was taking him to hold still. She unconsciously ran her hand over his uninjured shoulder, trying to soothe him into relaxing.

Now it was time to move on to the largest cut, across the thick muscle of Mr. Woodrow's upper back. There were several small fragments of glass embedded in the edges of the gruesome wound, with one large shard protruding from the center, glistening red with blood.

"She sounds lovely."

Contessa had been so concerned with examining the task before her that she'd lost the thread of the conversation.

"She was," Contessa murmured as she used the tweezers to remove the smaller pieces of debris.

"You must take after her," Mr. Woodrow grunted into the pillow.

Her hand froze in midair, the tweezers poised above the largest shard as she processed what Mr. Woodrow had said. To buy herself time to respond, she grasped the glass and gently began to pull at it.

In response to her actions, Mr. Woodrow twitched and let out a choked grunt before going limp. It seemed that the pain of the process had finally become too much, and he had fallen unconscious. He must have been delirious during their entire conversation. It would explain that last odd comment.

With Contessa's attention now completely free to focus on the task before her, she set to work on the last shard. She ended up having to employ a needle to dig out the base of the glass while tugging with the tweezers in her other hand. After long minutes, a piece of glass the length of her little finger came free of his back with a wet squelch.

Mr. Woodrow's back now clean of debris, Contessa pulled some ointment and a piece of cloth from the kit beside her and set to cleaning and bandaging the wounds. Her work wasn't as neat as Gregor's, but by the time she'd finished, the cuts were no longer oozing blood.

Contessa admired her handiwork for a moment before realizing the predicament she was in. Mr. Woodrow was unconscious in her bed, and he was too large for her to possibly move on her own, much less without disturbing his injuries.

With a sigh, she bundled up the glass in her ruined dressing gown and brought it over to her dressing table. With Mr. Woodrow's body no longer warm against her side, she began to shiver. She grabbed the blanket from the foot of the bed to wrap around her shoulders. Before she moved away, she paused, contemplating Mr. Woodrow's bare torso laid across the coverlet. She hesitated only a moment before folding the quilt over, covering him up.

Then she made her way to the window seat and settled herself there to wait through the long night until Mr. Woodrow awoke.

♟♟♜♛♝♞

Contessa woke to find she could barely move her head, her neck impossibly stiff after spending the night dozing in the window seat. She was momentarily confused as to why she was propped against the cool glass that overlooked the street before she remembered the events of the night before.

She jerked away from the window and looked towards the bed, half expecting to find it empty. Instead, Mr. Woodrow occupied the same spot he had last night. During the night, he had rolled onto his side, so he faced the window where Contessa sat. His face was pillowed on his hand, and his mouth hung slightly open. The entire effect would have been less than intimidating, had the coverlet not slid down around his waist as he slept. In the dim light, the shadows under his muscles were exaggerated, accentuating his wide shoulders and thick chest.

Contessa swallowed, pulling the blanket tighter around herself even though she felt uncharacteristically warm. She had to remind herself not to be embarrassed by the situation. They were technically married. She'd seen as much of his body the night before, but she'd been too distracted by the blood and the glass to take in what the rest of him looked like.

The thought brought Contessa back to last night, and she remembered that Mr. Woodrow was still wounded. She pressed to her feet and padded over to the bed. She expected the creaking of the floor to wake Mr. Woodrow, expecting somebody of his profession to be a light sleeper, but he didn't stir.

As she drew closer to the bed, she could make out a dull purple circle under his good eye. It made her think of how he was already out in the morning before she came down for breakfast, even though she was a habitually early riser. He often went to his office after their nightly game of chess. Perhaps it was no wonder that he slept like the dead.

When Contessa sat down on the side of the bed, the movement jostled Mr. Woodrow enough to finally make him stir. When his eyes fluttered open, they looked momentarily wild, darting around the room as his shoulders tensed. His gaze landed on Contessa after a moment, and his shoulders relaxed although he still looked wary.

"I just came over to check your bandages, see if they need to be changed."

Seeming to remember why he was here, he shook his head and pushed himself to sit. His wince was slight but unmistakable.

"No need. Gregor should be back by now, and I can have him take a look. And if he's not, I will have to have a talk with Kristoff about not getting in the way of my employee's work."

Contessa nodded. Gregor would be far more help than she was.

"Thank you for your help last night. I would be in sorry shape without you," Mr. Woodrow went on, cocking his head as he spoke, like he was as confused by her actions as she was.

"You're welcome, Mr. Woodrow."

He made a face as he swung his feet to floor.

"You don't have to call me that you know," he said, his voice tight with discomfort as he stood.

"Mr. Woodrow?" Contessa asked, taken aback. "What else would I call you?"

"You can just call me Nate. Everybody else does," he paused as he considered for a moment. "At least, that's what people call me to my face."

It seemed odd to call her husband by such a nickname, but then again, this whole situation was turning out to be rather odd.

"Alright Nate," she tested the name out. "Then I would prefer it if you wouldn't call me Mrs. Woodrow as well."

Nate picked up his soiled shirt off the ground and examined it as he spoke.

"Then what should I call you? I can't very well go back to calling you Ms. Cook."

Seeming to decide the shirt was not worth salvaging, Nate threw it over his shoulder.

Contessa chewed her lip. "Well, then you can call me Contessa."

"You're calling me Nate, not Nathanial. That hardly seems even," Nate countered. "What about a nickname? I think Connie would suit you nicely."

Contessa's breath hitched, and she folded her arms over her chest.

"Do you not like Connie? If not that, then maybe Tessa?"

She shook her head. "No, I like Connie. It's just...that is what my mother always called me. Very few people call me that anymore." She met Mr. Woodrow's curious eyes as she spoke, and she expected to be filled with rage at the memory of her mother. Instead of the normal fury rising up in her chest, there was a hollow sort of sadness in the space her heart occupied.

"It's a lovely name. It suits you."

Contessa nodded. "Then Connie it is."

"Well, thank you, Connie," Nate said as he turned to go. "I'm going to go find Gregor before he gets busy preparing breakfast."

He made his way to the door but paused on the threshold for a moment. He turned his head back, not fully looking at her.

"I'm sorry about your mother."

The words were so soft Contessa wasn't sure she heard them correctly, but they almost knocked her off the bed as Nate disappeared around the corner. If she'd been perplexed by her emotions yesterday, the events of the last eight hours were enough to make her feel as if she were drowning.

She sat on the bed for a long time before she rang for Julia. As she contemplated, her eyes roamed over the rumpled and bloody sheets. It reminded her of her question to Mr. Woodrow the prior night. If they were fighting for justice, then why must so much blood be spilled?

Chapter Nine

The seat across from Contessa's was already filled when she entered the dining room for dinner that evening. She jumped when she walked in to find Nate, even though she'd spent all day thinking about him, replaying his words in her mind. She nodded, not sure what she wanted to say despite all her ruminating and sat down to dinner. She was halfway through dutifully spooning her portion of split pea soup into her mouth when Nate broke the silence.

"Is the color of that dress more to your liking?"

Contessa froze with her spoon halfway to her mouth, momentarily dumbstruck by his attempts at conversation. She glanced down at her sleeve, which was indeed an icy blue of a simple cut, mercifully free of lace and bows.

"Yes," she answered simply before pushing her spoon into her mouth without another word. Nate didn't attempt to press her for more of a response, but she could feel his sharp eyes on her through the rest of her meal, even though she pointedly avoided looking at him. In fact, she avoided looking at anything in particular, choosing instead to vacantly stare at her plate and chew her food without tasting it.

"I want to do something to help," Contessa blurted out, the thoughts that had been bubbling in her head finally bursting forth. The troubles of London might have been more complicated than she'd originally thought, but she was done sitting on the sidelines.

Nate looked up hopefully, opening his mouth to respond, but Contessa cut him off before he could speak.

"It doesn't mean that I'm on your side, though, and you would do well to remember that."

"What if I'm on your side?" Nate asked.

"I know for a fact that you aren't."

Nate's good eye narrowed, but he didn't press the matter.

"I'll make some arrangements then. See how you might be able to aid some orphans without brushing up against anything too...unsavory."

Contessa nodded and pushed to her feet, the events of the night before and the lack of sleep finally crashing down on her and making her feel drained. She turned to leave and head to the sanctuary of her bedroom, but before she turned into the hallway, Nate spoke behind her.

"It's a shame your mother hasn't gotten to see what you've grown into."

Contessa stopped but didn't face Nate as she asked, "Oh, and what am I?"

"Whatever you want to be."

Contessa left the room without responding, but she was glad Nate hadn't been able to see her reaction as she blinked hastily.

Apparently, the arrangements Nate had to make for their newly developed partnership were involved, because Contessa didn't see him at all the next day. She couldn't decide whether or not she was glad about it, and when she tried to discern her feelings on the matter, she only succeeded in giving herself a headache. This seemed to be a theme for the day, as Contessa only managed to spin her thoughts in endless circles. Even she had lost sight of her goals.

Contessa didn't fetch the newspaper from Gregor for her afternoon reading in the garden. It seemed Gregor had noticed the break in her routine, and when she entered the dining room for dinner, the paper was neatly folded at her usual place. On top of it was a letter sealed with green wax embossed with scales. She furrowed her brow but ate before heading upstairs to read both the letter and the paper.

Sitting on her bed, Contessa cracked the seal open to find that this note from her father was just as short as the last. All it said was that he was anxious to see her at the executions tomorrow. Contessa hadn't known there were executions scheduled, but she'd been too distracted to read the paper today. She had no way of knowing if Nate planned on attending tomorrow. Still, since he had watched the last executions, it served to reason he would do the same tomorrow.

On the other hand, maybe they shouldn't attend tomorrow. Contessa shook the thought from her head immediately. Of course, she would follow her father's instructions. Her main goal was still to bring criminals to justice, even if she was doing what was necessary to help the people of London in the meantime.

Contessa would make sure they attended the executions tomorrow and hear the information her father had for her. Maybe it would mean she could be free of this marriage soon and return to her father's house. However, as Contessa lay down to sleep, she knew going home wouldn't mean she could put everything she'd learned behind her.

♟♟♜♝♞♞

It seemed Contessa shouldn't have worried about the plans for attending the execution, for no sooner had she finished her breakfast than Gregor announced he was going to pull the carriage around. Nate entered the dining room just as Gregor left, looking solemn in all black and holding a smart top hat in his hands. It made Contessa wince at her own attire, a canary yellow dress bedecked with a series of oversized bows. It seemed outright disrespectful to wear such a garment to an execution, but she hadn't thought to request a different outfit when Julia dressed her that morning.

Nate broke her from her thoughts by clearing his throat.

"You know, you can stay here if you'd prefer."

Contessa blinked.

"Oh, no it's alright. It would not do for a wife to make her husband attend such an event alone."

It was the first excuse Contessa could come up with for her insistence on attending. She knew Nate could tell she didn't enjoy watching people hang. He tilted his head and looked at her with something like softness—if his face had been capable of such an expression—before turning to lead her out to the carriage.

As the carriage lurched forward and clattered through the streets towards the main square, Contessa watched Nate's hands twist his hat in a white-knuckled grip. She nearly asked him why he insisted on attending the executions when they obviously caused him such distress. However, as she opened her mouth, the image of his white, sweat-soaked face from the last time flashed before her eyes, and it suddenly felt like much too personal of a question for a man she'd already gotten to know better than she'd ever intended to.

They remained silent the entire ride, even as they pulled up to the square and Nate stepped down out of the carriage. This time, though, instead of letting Gregor help her out of the carriage, Nate turned back and offered his hand as Contessa stepped down. It was a small thing, but it made the idea of the coming horror a little more bearable than it had been last time, when she'd felt as alone as humanly possible.

They wove their way towards a spot in the rear of the square, not too close to the looming scaffold, but giving them a clear sightline to the proceedings. Contessa avoided looking towards the front of the square where the police officers stood lined up at attention. Still, in the brief glance she spared them when she arrived, she couldn't help but notice that Joseph stood in the place of honor next to her father. His words about being on the wrong side played unbidden in her head. She tried not to think about what he would say about her offering to help Nate.

Contessa also couldn't bear to look at the rest of the assembling crowd, who once again dressed more like they were attending a party than anything else. The ones who were solemn hung back or peeked out of shuttered windows. Contessa stared straight ahead at the scaffold in the center of the square. Its stark height only served to add to Contessa's growing sense of foreboding. She always dreaded the hangings, but this time was worse than usual, a gnawing sensation in the pit of her stomach growing until she felt like she was facing the gallows herself today. Heart pounding in her ears, she resisted the urge to rock from foot to foot and search around frantically for some sort of threat.

Taking deep breaths, Contessa tried to calm herself with thoughts of her father's firm hand when it came to security. He would have dealt with any threats to the execution—unless there was something different this time. He had insisted it was important for her and Nate to be here. Her mind raced with possibilities.

Contessa was ripped from her anxiety by a firm hand on her shoulder.

"Connie, what is it?"

Contessa jerked in surprise as she glanced at Nate, who was looking her up and down like she was unwell. Giving how she felt, he might be right.

"I...I don't know." Contessa's voice came out thinner than ever before. "I feel...afraid."

Nate's good eyebrow shot up, and Contessa was just as startled as he was at her admission.

"You can go wait in the carriage," Nate offered. "You don't have to watch, and I'll come join you afterwards."

Just as Contessa became sure this was a good idea, she was struck by the sudden need to not be alone.

"No," she said, much of her usual firmness returning to her voice. "No, you have to come with me. We need to leave."

Nate hesitated, his brow furrowing even further. Not having the patience to wait for him to make up his mind, Contessa grabbed his hand and began forcibly towing him through the crowd. This seemed to make Nate's decision for him, and he didn't resist, instead trotting to catch up with Contessa as she marched across the square. Now that she was moving, some of the tension in the pit of Contessa's stomach eased, but she couldn't stop her eyes from darting this way and that, still on high alert.

What felt like ages later but was only a few moments, the pair emerged from the crowd at the edge of the square and turned to make their way towards the carriage. No sooner had Contessa let out the breath she'd been holding and dropped Nate's hand, there was the earsplitting bang of a gunshot.

Contessa's hands flew to her ears as she whirled around to find the source of the noise. She turned just in time to see the hangman tip over face first on the scaffolding, a bloody bullet hole exactly in the middle of his forehead. People instantly began screaming and pointing at the spot where Contessa and Nate had been standing not a minute earlier. Before Contessa could spot the gunner, a firm grip on her elbow yanked her around the corner.

Nate continued to tug on her arm even as Contessa stumbled over her skirts, pushing through a door and yanking her through behind him. The sounds of screaming and chaos in the square were dulled as Nate slammed the door behind them and threw the bolt.

As soon as they were alone in the darkness, Nate swore colorfully. It was the type of language that was supposed to offend ladies like herself, but Contessa didn't blush as she echoed similar sentiments in her own head.

"Where have you brought us?" Contessa asked when he paused for breath.

Nate seemed to compose himself at the reminder of her presence and took a steadying breath.

"It's a storeroom. I've used it as a hideout before."

Contessa vaguely thought about trying to figure out what storeroom this was so she could track it down later, but that train of thought quickly took a backseat in her mind as Nate began swearing again. He clearly was beyond worrying about admitting to criminal activity at this point.

"Are you hurt?" Contessa ventured.

"No, but this is bad."

Now that Contessa's eyes had adjusted to the darkness, she could see Nate plunging his hands into his hair in frustration.

"That gunshot came from right where we had been standing, and I'm the first person people would want to implicate in the disturbance of an execution. Especially when they thought the people being executed were Lions. It's like somebody..."

"Tried to frame you," Contessa finished for him, her mind racing again. "My father wanted..." She kept herself from finishing the thought...that her father had wanted to make sure he was at the execution that day. She shoved the suspicion aside to turn back to the issue at hand.

"Do you think we were seen there?" she asked.

Nate let out a sound almost akin to a growl.

"I'm not exactly hard to recognize. People will be willing to testify against me, and I don't exactly have an alibi."

"You would if you were seen somewhere else," Contessa suggested. "Right now, we should go somewhere very public and pretend as if we don't know what's happened. It could sow enough doubt that whoever framed you would have to risk looking like a liar in court."

Even as Contessa spoke, she had to wonder why she was doing this. Of course, if Nate had been seen at the crime scene, then so had she. She didn't want to be implicated.

"We need to be seen somewhere with lots of high society people that any accuser wouldn't want to cross," she continued.

"Strolling in the park?" Nate suggested.

"No, we need something more high profile." Contessa wracked her brain before another announcement from the newspaper the day before presented itself to her. "There is a public ball at Snowberry Hall. It's far enough from here that it wouldn't seem suspicious, but close enough to get there quickly. Although if we take the carriage, it will be obvious we are just arriving and haven't been there the whole time. Maybe—"

"That much, I do have a solution for," Nate cut in, already striding further into the darkened space. She trailed behind him, struggling to keep her skirts from snagging on the cramped shelves and crates in the darkness.

By the time Contessa caught up with Nate, she could hear the dull scraping of something heavy sliding across the stone floor and just make out Nate's broad shoulders flexing as he shifted a huge flour barrel. Before Contessa could ask what they needed that much flour for, Nate bent down and opened what appeared to be a hidden panel in the bit of wall.

"Is that..."

"A secret tunnel, yes. I'll explain later, but right now, time is of the essence."

Contessa snapped her mouth shut but added another topic to the long list of questions that needed answering when they got home —if they managed to make it there without being arrested, that was.

As Nate stepped into the tunnel, he reached back to her, and it took Contessa a beat to realize what he wanted. Her fingers wavered in midair for a moment as it struck her that this was not just the choice to take her husband's hand. This was the choice to help him evade arrest—an arrest for something that, for once, he hadn't done.

"It's dark inside, and I know the way," said Nate as way of explanation when he noticed her hesitation, his hand drooping slightly as if he were about to withdraw it.

Before he could return his arm to his side, Contessa reached out and grabbed it. A moment later, when Nate had shut the panel behind him, she was glad to be holding onto him. She couldn't see more than a few inches in front of her, and while she didn't fear the dark, it would have been disconcerting if she didn't have the warm roughness of Nate's hand to ground her.

She had no more than a moment to contemplate the blackness before Nate pulled on her hand and they began hurtling through the tunnels at breakneck speed. The pace at which Nate turned invisible corners and navigated the few steps up and down, warning Contessa of the upcoming obstacles, made it clear he was no stranger to this particular passage. She would have speculated more had she not been so focused on keeping her footing.

As quickly as they had traversed the tunnels, Nate stopped, causing Contessa to run headlong into his back. It was like crashing into a mountain, and Contessa caught the briefest whiff of sweat and earth before righting herself and smoothing her dress. She was pleasantly surprised by how fast they had arrived, getting to the ball in nearly half the time they would've if they had gone through the streets.

Nate didn't comment on their collision, instead standing stock still as if listening for something.

"This panel should let us out in one of the rear hallways of Snowberry Hall," he whispered. "I don't think I hear anybody out there, so we should be safe to go in."

Light seeped in through a hairline crack as Nate pressed some hidden panel to open the wall. They were greeted by the distant sounds of music and merriment but heard no voices in the immediate vicinity. Nate pressed the panel open, and they slipped out into an empty hallway, forcing Contessa to blink rapidly in the sunlight streaming in through the high windows on the opposite wall.

She only had a moment to let her eyes adjust before Nate was marching down the hall towards the laughter and voices in the ballroom.

"Better be seen as soon as possible if this is going to work," Nate grumbled, about to lead them around the corner into the open ballroom.

Contessa darted after him, grabbing his elbow.

"Wait! We need to look like we've been here for a while and have an excuse for why we're suddenly appearing out of a back hallway."

Nate looked quizzical.

"And what excuse could we have for skulking around a back hallway that wouldn't raise even more suspicion?"

"Not all skulking means you've committed a crime," Contessa snapped. "Act like you've been kissing me."

Nate purpled for a moment before giving her a single jerky nod. Seeming to catch on to what Contessa was getting at, he tugged at his cravat, making it look crinkled and askew.

"You should mess up your hair and..." Nate chewed on his words for a moment, "giggle or something."

Not one usually prone to giggling, Contessa found herself surprised by how easily a high-pitched laugh bubbled up in the back of her throat. Perhaps it was the hysteria of the whole situation, or perhaps it was how embarrassed somebody as notorious as Nathanial Woodrow seemed by the prospect of stealing a private moment with his wife at a ball.

Taking advantage of her momentary girlishness, Contessa leaned herself into Nate's side, and they ducked around the corner into the ballroom. It was too easy to relax into the arm he threw around her waist, and another giggle burst past her lips. Nate, for his part, gave her what appeared to be his best try at a devilish grin, but it sat rather oddly on his face and came off as a grimace.

They found the ballroom crowded and lively, and Contessa worked on weaving them through the chattering crowds in as visible a way as possible. Suddenly, she was grateful for the prominent color of her dress, as everybody she passed spared her a glance. The room grew momentarily quieter as the musicians in the corner finished their song, and the couples on the floor bowed and curtsied to each other.

Suddenly struck by an idea, Contessa tugged Nate towards the emptying space in the middle of the floor.

"We're going to dance," she announced, directing them as close as she could get to the center of the room.

Agreeable to all her suggestions so far, Nate seemed to have reached his limit as he balked.

"That can't possibly be a good idea. Don't you remember... You know neither of us can dance."

"But everybody watches the dance floor, and they're sure to remember we were here if we dance. And not to worry, the worse we dance, the more memorable it will be," Contessa stated as she positioned them across from each other.

At that moment, the musicians played the opening notes of a gavotte, and Nate mumbled under his breath, "This is about to be the most memorable dance in the history of London."

As it turned out, Nate may have been right. Only through sheer adrenaline and a steel will did both Nate and Contessa manage to stay upright for the next several minutes. While the waltz at their wedding had been far from graceful, at least it had been short and slow. Their combined inexperience with dancing was magnified tenfold with the livelier dance, and the matter was further complicated by the fact they now had to navigate around the other couples occupying the dance floor. Owing to the amount of minor collisions they caused, Contessa had no doubt everybody in the ballroom had noticed them by the time the musicians brought the dance to a close.

Somewhat breathless, Contessa offered Nate a polite curtsy at the conclusion of the dance. Nate surprised her by taking her hand and pressing a kiss to the knuckles, but she realized such a gesture would probably be expected for a married couple out for an afternoon of merriment. Still, the rough feeling of the scar across his lips brushing her skin came as a shock and she almost jumped. Then the moment was over, and he led her to the side of the dance floor.

"Now that we've thoroughly embarrassed ourselves, can you promise me we will never do that again?" Nate grumbled, producing a handkerchief to blot his now damp brow.

"Believe me, I took no pleasure in it either, but I'm sure anybody here will be able to testify that we were dancing at the ball this afternoon," whispered Contessa, so as not to be overheard, as she fanned herself with a hand. She glanced around, finding there were indeed several influential socialites in their vicinity.

Still, Nate looked uncomfortable in the crowd, shifting from foot to foot and fussing with his cravat as if it was strangling him.

"I think we've been here quite long enough to make an appearance," he grumbled again.

"Indeed, it is rather warm in here," Contessa said for the benefit of anybody who might be listening. "Perhaps it's time to go home and rest."

As they wove their way through the crowd and pushed out of the exit, Contessa's heart sank. There was a line of carriages in the circular drive of the public ballroom, but of course, their own black coach was nowhere to be found. Nate seemed to have the exact same realization and let out a sound halfway between a sigh and a growl.

"I'm not entirely sure my feet can handle a walk home in these shoes after that dance," Contessa admitted.

Nate looked down towards where her feet were hidden by the hem of her dress and frowned.

"Damn impractical things," he muttered. "Come with me, I may have a solution."

He led Contessa to the edge of the drive where it met a side street. It was deserted except for a small group of children rolling a ball between themselves. Nate leaned on the wall and shoved his hands in his pockets, suddenly looking the picture of casual ease, the exact opposite of his demeanor in the ballroom.

He let out a low whistle, and the heads of several of the children popped up. The instant she spotted him, a round faced little girl sprang to her feet and skipped over to them.

"Nate!" She squeaked as she approached. "Whatcha doing round these parts? You haven't visited in ages!"

"I know. I've been busy. You've gotten big while I've been gone, though, Poppy. Not letting John push you around too much I hope?" Nate answered with easy familiarity.

The girl, Poppy, responded with a wide smile, revealing missing front teeth. "No, sir."

"That's my girl," Nate praised. "You think you could do me a favor? Gregor is with our carriage over by the town square. You think you could fetch him for me?"

The girl nodded vigorously, bouncing on her toes. "You got it Nate! I'll be back with him right quick!"

Poppy took off down the side street at a headlong sprint.

Nate finally turned back to Contessa, who had been watching the whole exchange in fascination, feeling oddly like an outsider. Now that he was looking at her, she cocked her head and raised an eyebrow.

"You probably don't want to know," Nate offered by way of response, rubbing the good side of his face wearily.

"Oh, I've decided there are a good number of things I do want to know after the day we've had," Contessa said, folding her arms.

"That's fair enough, but can we at least wait until we're at home and can do it over a glass of whiskey?" Nate conceded, looking exhausted.

"Alright, but don't think I'm going to let this drop."

"I wouldn't dream of it."

Silence fell as they returned to the drive to wait for Gregor and the carriage. It seemed Poppy was good to her word, and it wasn't long before there was a clatter of hooves and the familiar coach pulled into the drive, Poppy perched next to Gregor on the driver's seat. As it came to a halt in front of Contessa and Nate, the girl hopped down and gave them another wide grin.

"As promised, Nate!" She gestured proudly to the carriage.

"You've become quite the fast runner." Nate fished a copper piece out of his pocket and flipped it to the girl, who snatched it deftly out of the air. Poppy pocketed the coin and disappeared around the corner, presumably to rejoin her group of friends.

Contessa and Nate made to enter the carriage, and Gregor immediately opened his mouth to bombard them with questions. Nate held up a hand to silence him.

"Save it until we're home, Gregor."

As the horses clattered over the cobblestones to the safety of the house, the thought dominating Contessa's mind was which of her questions she wanted answered first.

Chapter Ten

When they arrived back at the house, Gregor attempted to fuss over Contessa and Nate like an overbearing mother hen, but Contessa wasn't having it. At some point, Nate would have to explain to him how they had gotten away safely, but for now, it seemed Gregor could tell they were breathing and without major injury, so that would have to be enough. Now was the time for a frank conversation with her husband.

Nate seemed to be of like mind, dismissing Gregor in a way that would have been firm had it not been interspersed with assurances they were safe and he would explain later. Gregor glanced at Contessa, and his eyes lit with understanding. She was overdue on a lot of explanations. Once Gregor had reluctantly retreated in the direction of the gardens, Nate led Contessa to the back of the house. Contessa was almost shocked when they stopped in front of the locked door to his office, but it was hardly the oddest thing that had happened today.

Nate produced a key from a hidden pocket on the inside of his waist-coat and used it to open the door, gesturing for Contessa to lead the way inside. She looked around as she stepped past him, getting her first good look at the space while not fearful of being discovered. It looked much like it had when she had been there last, though without the wicked knife on the desk. In the sunlight shining in from a small window, Contessa could now see the room was painted in a pale blue, the shelves filled with all sorts of trinkets from globes to pen stands. Contessa couldn't help but notice that these too were noticeably empty of books.

A clinking of glass drew Contessa's attention, and she turned to find that, true to his word, Nate was pulling a decanter of whiskey off one of the shelves and pouring a healthy amount into two cut crystal glasses.

"I normally save this for special occasions but," Nate shrugged one shoulder as he passed her a glass, "today feels like as good a day as any to celebrate being alive."

"As well as out of prison," Contessa commented as she plucked the glass from his fingers and gave it a sniff. It smelled richly of cloves and oak, and Contessa gave an appreciative hum.

"I'm likely only going to stay out of prison due to your quick thinking. There were quite a few people that could testify we were at that ball. Influential people that somebody wanting to frame me wouldn't want to cross in court." Nate swirled his glass thoughtfully, watching the amber liquid slosh against the sides as he spoke. "Although they probably wouldn't come forward just to defend me. It's probably your presence as the chief's daughter that saved my skin."

Contessa hummed noncommittally as she perched herself on the wooden chair across from the desk, keeping her focus on smoothing her skirts. She ignored the implied question in Nate's comment. If he was hoping to coax some admission as to why she'd helped him, he was going to have to be far more direct.

Seeming to sense Contessa's reticence, Nate sat himself on top of his desk as he continued, "You know, you probably wouldn't have been implicated if I had been framed for the disturbance at the execution. Nobody would want to testify against the daughter of the chief, even if you had been at the scene of a crime. The same notoriety that would have saved you is exactly what I have to thank for not being in custody right now."

"Are we sure you were being framed?" Contessa deflected. "We had to assume the worst in the moment, but it could have all been a coincidence."

Nate shook his head.

"No, it's all too much to be sheer happenstance. The paper said the Talented being hanged were from the Lions, but I'd never seen those people before in my life. I originally thought it was a mistake, but..."

"Careful, it might sound like you are admitting to being associated with the Lion gang," Contessa commented with an arched brow.

Nate fixed her with a flat stare, his eyes penetrating as he asked, "Are we really going to play this game still, after what we've just been through? Dancing around facts we both know is getting exhausting, and I have a hard time believing you're going to turn me in for it when you just helped me escape arrest."

Contessa shifted in her seat. "Well, that was for a crime you didn't commit. Who is to say I might feel differently when you are actually guilty?"

"Your father seems to have no such scruples," Nate snorted into his glass.

Contessa opened her mouth to argue that they had no way of

knowing her father was behind the set up but then snapped it shut again, remembering her father's insistence that Nate attend the executions. She pursed her lips, and her inner turmoil didn't go unnoticed by Nate.

"I'm glad to see you're no longer set on defending your father," he commented. "Although I imagine it must be hard to try to impress a father who would so thoroughly disapprove of you if he truly knew you."

"What is that supposed to imply?" Contessa snapped, her cheeks growing hot. Helping Nate was causing her enough turmoil without him rubbing the salt of her betraying her family in the wound.

Nate blinked.

"Your father has made it his life's mission to wipe out the Talented," he said slowly.

"And what of it?"

"But..." Nate's brow furrowed. "You're Talented. You must have had to hide it from your father your whole life."

Contessa blinked once, then again. Then she shook her head, as if that could force Nate's words to make sense.

"How could you possibly think I'm Cursed?"

"Only the Royal Police call us Cursed," Nate snorted derisively, "but I know because I'm Talented, and I could sense it on you the moment I saw you."

Contessa stared at Nate silently, hoping she would detect some hint of a lie on his twisted face, but she found he only looked as confused as she felt.

"That's why I asked to marry you," Nate continued, as if all of this should have been obvious. "I wanted to give you a chance to get away from your father before he found out and you were endangered. It wasn't an elegant solution, but it was the best thing I could come up with on short notice. I assumed you agreed to marry me because you knew you needed to get out of your father's house."

Contessa shook her head dumbly, mind feeling dull as a spoon as she tried to process his words.

Nate sighed and scrubbed his face with a large hand. "That would explain the hatred I felt rolling off you when we were first married. I must have truly seemed like the Beast everybody calls me for asking to marry somebody I had never even spoken to."

This finally snapped Contessa out of the trance that seemed to have overtaken her.

"You think that's why I hate you?"

Nate drew back as if Contessa had slapped him.

"Of course. If you thought I wanted to marry you without even knowing you just because of how you looked—"

"Your shallowness is the least of my concern when I'm married to an actual murderer!"

Nate chewed on his lips looking hurt, but still appeared rather confused.

"People have died in the attacks of my gangs before, yes, but only those that enslave children or worse. I've never murdered anybody in cold blood before, though."

Contessa didn't know she'd jumped to her feet.

"That's not what it looked like when my mother bled out in my arms with three slashes cut across her face!"

The glass slipped from Contessa's fingers and shattered on the floor, shards going everywhere and liquid splattering the hem of her dress. The crash seemed unnaturally loud in the total silence following Contessa's shouting.

"You think I murdered your mother?" Nate asked quietly, as if he was explaining this fact to himself more than asking her for confirmation.

Contessa was still trembling, but she managed to make her voice firm as she spoke.

"*That* is why I agreed to marry you. So I could be the one to bring down my mother's killer from the inside. And then everything got all turned around, and I've ended up helping you, and I don't know how I can live with myself for it." Contessa's eyes burned but she refused to let herself cry.

Nate looked as if he had been turned into a statue, and the silence stretched long as Contessa tried to swallow down her tears. She clenched her fists at her side to try and control her shaking, but to no avail.

"I didn't murder your mother."

Contessa swallowed until she could speak again.

"Why would I believe that?"

"Because I don't cut slashes into people's faces."

There was silence again as Contessa stared.

"Why don't you sit down, and I can explain," Nate said, his voice the gentlest she'd ever heard it, as if he were approaching a wild animal.

Contessa sank back down onto her chair. Her legs shook so hard they wouldn't have held her upright for much longer anyways.

Nate shifted so he faced her fully from his perch on the desk, one long leg folded in front of him as the other dangled down towards the floor. He took a long gulp from his glass before he began.

"I grew up working in the factories with the rest of the orphans on the street. I assumed my parents had been killed in the Inquires, but I never knew. Either way, my own Talent started to display itself when I was about twelve, and I knew I wouldn't be able to hide it forever. So, a group of other factory workers—some Talented, some not—made a plan to run away. To live on the streets where we thought we would have a better chance of hiding our Talents from the authorities and where we would be free of the brutal working conditions. Kristoff was one of the boys who escaped with me. When we were finally free, I started to lead the band of children. You see, I can use my Talent to sense people's intentions and feelings.

"For a while, I used it to gamble for money to feed us, and I always won because I could tell when people were bluffing. Eventually, we started running bigger cons, and I began investing our earnings in endeavors I could sense would be successful. That's how I made my fortune, and the Lions formed from that original group of escaped factory children.

"As we became more successful, we started going back to get the other children out of the factory. I used my abilities to sense Talented children among the workers, and we tried to get them out before they, too, were discovered and hanged. During the escapes, though, several of the Lions started getting more and more violent. They killed the foremen and factory owners for revenge for the way they treated us, and they began leaving the slashes on their victims' faces.

"Eventually, I confronted them, telling them it was our mission to free the workers, not to get revenge. There was a huge fight, and they ended up leaving the Lions to go join other gangs, but by then, people had already associated that signature with us. Other gangs have used the slashes ever since to push responsibility for their crimes onto us. I've never tried to stop it, because the fear associated with the Lions gives all our members a certain degree of protection."

Contessa didn't realize she'd been holding her breath while Nate spoke until she tried to speak and found herself breathless. She panted for a moment before asking, "So, my mother..."

"I'm sorry," Nate said, his eyes full of sympathy, "I didn't even know I had been blamed for it. It could have been any one of the rival gangs who likes to frame us for their violence."

It couldn't possibly be true. Her world was being turned inside out, and she no longer knew which way was up.

"You didn't kill my mother, and I'm Cursed."

"Talented." Nate corrected her patiently, apparently willing to let her repeat her questions again and again until she believed the answers.

"What is my Talent?"

Nate shook his head as he responded. "I'm afraid I don't know. My Talent doesn't work like that. It's far more general, sort of an extra sense that gives me vague intentions. For example, I could sense you hated me, but I had no clue as to why. I can also sense the presence of a Talent, but never what it is. I've learned to hone my skills over time, so I can sense lying or fear, but I'm still far from being able to read minds."

"I guess that would explain how you were able to make such strategic investments and amass wealth so quickly," Contessa mused absently. The shock faded, instead being replaced by a pleasant warm numbness. She seemed to be experiencing some sort of acceptance of the truth without absorbing any of the facts into her reality yet.

Nate, apparently, could use his Talent to sense her state and offered gently, "This has been a lot to process. Why don't I get Gregor to make us a pot of tea to settle your nerves?"

At the glare Contessa shot him, Nate held up his hands placatingly and amended, "Not that you're hysterical or anything. It's just been a long day, and the whiskey hasn't seemed to have the desired effect."

Contessa, content that she didn't appear to be somebody in dire need of having their nerves settled, pursed her lips and nodded her assent.

Nate slid from the desk and ducked from the room with a quick assurance that he would be back as soon as he found Gregor.

Grateful for a moment to collect herself, Contessa slumped in her chair and buried her face in her hands. She tried to start at the beginning of their conversation, picking through each comment and organizing each bit of new information, desperately trying to reconcile all this new content with her present world view and failing miserably. She abandoned that pursuit almost immediately in favor of making a mental list of questions she still needed to ask Nate. While this task was much easier, she hadn't made it through more than two questions before a bell chimed, echoing loudly through the house.

Contessa shot upright in her seat, frozen. In the entire time she'd been living in the house, not a single visitor had rung the front bell, and the sound startled her. No sooner had the echoing faded than the bell chimed again, somehow managing to sound more urgent even though the tone was the same.

Contessa sprung to her feet and strode through the house, picking her skirts up to walk faster. All she could think of was that, after all the trouble they had gone to, the police were coming to arrest Nate for the disturbance at the execution anyways. While the question of how she felt about Nate's guilt in light of the new information echoed unanswered in her head, she was sure she would let him be convicted of something he hadn't done when she'd gone to such lengths to get him an alibi.

Picking up her pace, Contessa slid around the corner into the front hall, hoping that if she was the one to answer the door, she could have a chance to use her influence to talk the officers out of making the arrest. She was already forming arguments in her mind when she yanked the door open, only to draw up short as she found her father standing on the front step, completely alone.

Contessa would have expected him to bring reinforcements when arresting such a notorious man, but she didn't have time to ponder further as her father instantly grabbed her wrist and yanked her onto the front porch. His nails bit into her skin, and Contessa barely managed to suppress a yelp of surprise as she stumbled onto the stoop.

"What part of 'be at the executions' did you not understand?" he demanded.

When Contessa had regained her balance, she looked up to find her father's face purpling under his neat moustache, and she schooled her features into neutral surprise as quickly as she could manage.

"Well, Mr. Woodrow wanted to go to the public ball, and I thought it might be a good opportunity to gain his tru—"

"You thought?" Her father's grip on her wrist tightened even further, and Contessa ground her teeth as her father continued. "This wasn't the time for thinking, Contessa. This was the time for doing as you were told. I could have had you home and your mother's murderer at the gallows in a week, but then I found out you were at a public ball today. *Dancing* of all things."

Her father's voice was a low hiss, but Contessa's eyes still widened at the fact he would talk about such things so openly. His rage was making a vein in his temple throb, reinforcing the idea he wasn't thinking rationally.

"I didn't want to draw Mr. Woodrow's suspicion by being too insistent," Contessa tried to reason as she attempted to pull her wrist from her father's grasp, but he seemed beyond reason.

"I thought you had the iron will necessary to pull this off, but when the time came, you were nothing more than a cowering damsel."

At this, Contessa did manage to wrench herself out of his grasp and was opening her mouth to say something she was sure to regret when Nate ducked around the door.

"There you are, darling! I just returned from making our tea when I found you had disappeared. I was afraid you had gotten bashful on me."

Nate stepped onto the stoop and put a hand on Contessa's waist, pulling her a step closer to him and away from her father.

"How nice of you to visit," Nate commented to Chief Cook, wearing a broad smile that made his features appear less disfigured. "I know Connie here misses you terribly, it must do her good to see you."

Her father stiffened at the use of the familiar nickname, and he offered a single sharp nod, keeping his lips set in a firm line.

"Contessa and I just got back from an afternoon of dancing," Nate continued in a voice so convincingly friendly that Contessa now understood how he had conned his way into such wealth. "Nothing like a little revelry to remind me how beautiful my wife is and make me want to hurry her home."

Nate pulled Contessa a few inches closer to him as he spoke, and she allowed the familiarity, hoping it would hide the fact she was still trembling with rage. She allowed him to back them towards the still open door, trying to seem natural even as her father stood so stiffly that she could have been convinced he was made of stone.

"I must insist on continuing to monopolize my wife's evening, but I'll be sure to have my man bring her around to your house for tea this week," Nate continued to explain easily even as he led them back inside the safety of the house. "It was so kind of you to pay a visit."

Contessa caught one last look at her father's dumbstruck face before Nate quickly shut the door between them. Now that she could no longer see her father, Contessa's rage quickly faded, and she felt deflated. The panic that had been propping her up when she answered the door left her all at once, and now she felt like a puppet whose strings had been cut.

Nate's arm around her waist tightened, making Contessa realize she'd been making him support some of her weight in her sudden exhaustion. She regained her footing and stepped away from him, instantly regretting the loss of warmth and support.

For his part, Nate hurriedly smoothed his clothes, seeming surprisingly embarrassed by the situation, considering Contessa had already seen him without his shirt.

"I'm sorry about that," said Nate. "I could sense your rage across the house, and I thought it would be better to interrupt before you accidentally incriminated yourself. Wouldn't want you to spoil all the hard work you put into making us appear innocent."

Contessa nodded dumbly, but Nate was still looking at her like he expected some sort of answer, so she said the first thing that came to her mind.

"I'd like to go to bed."

Nate blinked.

"Oh, yes. Of course. Today has been quite eventful. Nothing of what we have discussed can't wait until morning. I'll send Julia up."

Contessa nodded again, offering Nate a quiet thank you.

Before Contessa turned to head up the stairs, Nate raised his hand halfway, and Contessa was unsure if he meant to pat her shoulder or grab her hand. Before she could decide, he let it drop back to his side again.

"We can figure things out in the morning. Get some rest, Connie."

On her way up the stairs, Contessa couldn't help but feel comforted by the use of her old nickname.

Chapter Eleven

Contessa considered how wise a woman her mother had been when she told her there was nothing like a good night's sleep to set things right. Already halfway through a large breakfast, Contessa was feeling much more herself, and her mind was already methodically replaying each minute of the day before and scouring it for important bits of information.

Still, one discovery kept circling to the front of Contessa's thoughts, no matter how hard she tried to think of other things. Nate hadn't killed her mother. Her father's skeptical voice played in her head, telling her that a Beast like Nate wouldn't hesitate to lie if it meant he could manipulate her more easily, but the voice grew softer and softer as she contemplated. Instead, Nate's soft apology from several nights ago grew louder in its place, and Contessa felt Nate's innocence was the puzzle piece she'd been missing throughout their marriage. Still, she had so many questions lingering in her mind that Contessa only managed to stay to finish her breakfast through extensive self-discipline.

Contessa was saved from her own impatience just as she was serving herself a second bowl of porridge by the entrance of Kristoff and Nate. Their arrival was signaled before they rounded the doorway by Kristoff's bombastic laugh, and Contessa was momentarily curious what Nate could have said that was so funny.

Immediately upon catching sight of Contessa, Kristoff crossed the room to her and snatched up one of her hands in both of his.

"My dear Mrs. Woodrow, I owe you my deepest gratitude," Kristoff said as he bowed over her hand with a flourish.

"What for?"

"I hear that it was your quick thinking that saved Nate here from arrest yesterday," Nate continued, releasing Contessa's hand and throwing himself into the chair next to hers. "Normally, it's my job to keep him out of too much trouble, but I'm glad you do such a good job in my stead when I'm not there."

Nate, meanwhile, sat himself down across the table from Contessa with none of Kristoff's easy grace and frowned.

"And how, Kristoff, are you supposed to be the one keeping me out of trouble when you're the one making the trouble in the first place?" Nate asked as he forked four pieces of toast onto his plate.

"Ignore him," Kristoff said with a wave of his hand. "He's just grumpy I insisted he get a good night's sleep after yesterday's excitement when he would have rather been running around the city trying to get more information on who set him up."

"But we already know it was my father who tried to frame you, right?"

Nate had just torn into a heavily buttered piece of toast and was forced to chew quickly, spraying crumbs onto his plate, until he could swallow and answer. "Yes, but he couldn't very well use his own officers to pull off an illegal operation like that. He must have had help from outside the law."

Kristoff thumbed the revolver at his hip as he cut in. "When you're lucky enough to be as influential as Nate here, you have a lot of enemies. The trick is to figure out who hates you so much they would work with law enforcement to take you down. My money is on the Rattlesnakes. They've wanted to see the Lion's fall ever since Two-Faced Thomas became one of Caleb's lieutenants."

Contessa's mind still stuck on one thing as she interrupted. "You are saying my father is cooperating with the gangs? But...he hates the gangs. It doesn't make sense."

"If what you told me last night is true, and he thinks that I murdered his wife, I'm surprised it took him this long to come to this," Nate said with a grimace. "If he was willing to marry his own daughter off to a man he considered a monster just to bring me down, then he must be desperate."

A voice in the back of Contessa's mind told her to defend her father, but then she pictured the way his nails had dug into her wrist the night before, and she bit her lip.

"Speaking of the setup that is your marriage," Kristoff interjected, and Contessa imagined she saw Nate flinch out of the corner of her eye. "I heard you found out about your Talent yesterday. Any idea what it is?"

"Yes, apparently everybody knew about it but me," Contessa shot back. "And before you start grilling me, I think it's my turn to ask some questions. There are still many things left unanswered after last night."

Nate gestured for her to continue, and Contessa pursed her lips as she considered where to start. She ended up turning to Kristoff and asking, "If Nate is Talented, and the gang formed from a group of Talented factory children, what's your Talent?"

Kristoff chuckled. "I'm afraid my only talent is being a gifted sharpshooter, and that's not any sort of magical ability, just years of practice. I ended up here by following through on Nate's daring plans."

"But you've dedicated your life to rescuing Talented children?"

Kristoff shrugged. "Nate used his Talent to save me many a beating when we were in the factory, sensing what foremen were in a bad mood and which would be lenient with us if we asked for an extra bit of food. I realized then that Talents could be used for good, a realization which has been reinforced time and time again over the years. I mean, look at Gregor's garden. How could the Talent to make plants grow so beautifully be born of ill, and why should Gregor have to worry about hanging just for making flowers bloom?"

Contessa blinked, envisioning the garden she read the paper in every day in a new light. Gregor was not at all what she pictured when she thought of a violent gangster using their unnatural abilities for personal gain, but perhaps she'd been misled. Perhaps her own Talent would be something just as lovely.

"So, what do you do besides free Talented children from work in the factories?"

This time, it was Nate who answered. "Very quickly into our mission, we learned that freeing the children is the easiest part of the operation. The problem is figuring out what to do with them after they're free. The Lions give them a sort of...home...to grow up in. We give them the skills they need to survive on the streets, and as they get older, they run jobs for the money to feed the little ones—normally, small things like pickpocketing and learning to deal rigged hands at the gambling tables. Although, occasionally, they'll run bigger cons on people who we feel have wealth that could benefit from—redistribution."

Contessa scrunched up her face at the thought of children having to deal crooked card games to feed themselves, and her face didn't escape Kristoff's notice.

"Perhaps we should focus on how we feed the children and give them a family, instead of the illicit activities."

Contessa shook her head. "It's not that. It's just...sad."

"The kids have the best life we can give them," Nate interjected softly. "They all take care of each other, and the older ones look out for the younger ones like their own siblings."

Contessa glanced across the table and met Nate's eyes, wondering if he could sense she'd always wanted a younger sibling of her own. Shaking herself from that thought, Contessa pushed on.

"So, say I were sympathetic to your cause," Contessa started, and she thought she saw a flash of happiness in Nate's eyes. "Where would I fit into this whole operation?"

"Where would you want to fit in?"

Contessa glanced back down at her uneaten toast and resisted the urge to begin shredding it with her fingers as she thought out loud.

"I doubt I'm a person who should be helping run cons, for too many reasons to list right now. But I do think I'd like..." Contessa pictured little Poppy running to fetch the carriage. "I'd like to meet the children. See what I might be able to do for them."

"That can be arranged," Kristoff said with a dazzling grin. "Rhosyn will be thrilled to meet you. She's jealous I've gotten to meet the woman who's been giving Nate here so much trouble, and she hasn't gotten a chance to congratulate you yet."

Contessa opened her mouth to ask who Rhosyn was but then paused, hearing an odd ringing sound.

"We could go this afternoon if you're feeling up to it. I have to stop by the warehouses anyway for business, and I could bring you..." Nate trailed off as Contessa waved her hand at him for silence, trying to hear the ringing better.

It became clear in a matter of seconds, as Nate and Kristoff looked on in confusion, that the ringing Contessa was sensing wasn't a noise at all. Still, the sensation of vibration in Contessa's skull persisted as she looked around for the source of the disturbance. Her heart beat louder in her chest as she failed to find any sort of reason for the buzzing in her head, until her eyes landed on Kristoff.

Without her mouth asking permission from her brain, Contessa said, "I think you should leave, Kristoff."

"And here I thought you enjoyed the pleasure of my company, but—" Kristoff started, clapping his hand to his chest in exaggerated offense. Contessa cut him off before he could finish his thought.

"I'm serious. You need to leave right now."

Kristoff glanced over to Nate incredulously, but Nate was looking at Contessa, his sharp eyes narrowed.

"I think you should listen to her. Leave, and we'll catch up to you later."

To his credit, Kristoff pushed to his feet without complaint, even as he continued to look supremely confused, and headed for the door.

"Not the front door," Contessa blurted without thinking once again.

Kristoff paused for the barest of moments before Nate interjected again. "Let's go to my office. We'll get out that way."

Nate led them out of the side door to the dining room, and Kristoff strode after him towards the back office. Gathering her skirts, Contessa rustled down the hallway behind them, confused as to why they were going to the office and still oddly unshakable in her conviction that Kristoff should already be gone by now.

As Contessa rounded the doorframe to the back office, she found Nate and Kristoff braced against the solid desk, inching it across the wooden floor with a heavy scrape. For all the desk's substantial size, the two men slid it several feet across the room in a matter of moments. Nate fell to his knees in the spot the desk had just occupied, feeling the floorboards for just a moment before pressing some unknown notch, causing a panel in the floor to spring up. Contessa's mouth hung open as Nate swung the panel open to reveal a tunnel identical to the one they had taken to the ball the day before. Kristoff didn't seem nearly as surprised by this revelation and hopped down into the tunnel without a moment's hesitation.

"Go. We'll meet you at the den this evening," Nate assured him before slamming the panel closed and plunging Kristoff into darkness.

No sooner had the panel clicked shut when there was a *bang* from the far end of the house, as if a door had been slammed open hard enough to rattle the walls, followed by shouting voices.

"Help me move this back into place," Nate hissed, already bracing a shoulder against the desk and sliding one end of it back into position.

Contessa braced her own hands on the end closer to her and shoved with the entire weight of her body, and it began to scrape across the floor, albeit much slower than it had when Kristoff and Nate moved the desk together. The wooden legs stuttered across the floorboards at an agonizing pace as pounding footsteps grew louder and Contessa began to be able to make out the voices now echoing through the house.

"London Royal Police here for Kristoff Mainsworth. Show yourself!"

The voices sounded as if they were just around the corner when the desk finally slid back in place over the trap door. Nate and Contessa straightened up and dashed out into the hallway towards the source of the commotion, shutting the door behind them as subtly as possible. The latch had barely clicked when a stampede of Royal Police rounded the last corner into the back hall, led by none other than Joseph.

"Halt!" Joseph shouted, as if Nate and Contessa were not already standing completely still in the hallway of their own home. Contessa resisted the urge to raise her hands in surrender while simultaneously suppressing the desire to give him a hostile glare, knowing it would not help with whatever sort of trouble they were in. The animosity in his returned gaze made her heart shudder with loss. She could find none of their former friendship in his expression.

"We have reason to believe that you are harboring one Kristoff Mainsworth," Joseph barked, "Turn him over immediately or face charges as accomplices!"

"Mr. Mainsworth?" Nate asked with a confused tilt of his head. "Why, I haven't seen him in almost a fortnight. What led you to believe he's here? Don't tell me he broke in!"

Joseph hesitated, deflating a bit, as if he had expected Nate to throw a punch and was disappointed by his casual denial. Still, Joseph puffed up his chest and continued with renewed bluster. "He was seen entering your house early this morning. If he has left, you have to tell us where he has gone."

"I assure you, it was just my lovely wife and I sharing breakfast this morning. We had no company. Isn't that right, Connie?"

Contessa was so busy watching Joseph's face drain of color at Nate's words that she almost forgot she needed to speak as well.

"Oh, of course," Contessa nodded. "Although, we would be happy to let you look around."

Nate's shoulders tensed next to Contessa for the barest of moments at her suggestion, quickly falling back into casual ease, almost as if Nate was more comfortable facing down the police than sharing dinner with his new wife. Come to think of it, he probably was.

Joseph signaled to the men standing dutifully at his back.

"Search the entire house. Look for open windows or a back door he might have left through."

Contessa fought to remain relaxed as the stomping of boots spread through the house, battling the feeling that her space was somehow being invaded, even though she was used to officers stomping through her home at her father's house. Instead, she put on a cold smile and offered sweetly, "Why don't I show you through the house, Joseph. Help you on your search."

With that, Contessa brushed past Joseph towards the front of the house, feeling him trail reluctantly. Contessa led the way to the living room, determined to show Joseph through the house and get him out of there.

They rounded the corner, out of sight of where Nate was casually hindering the search of the other police officers by attempting to be helpful. Joseph cornered Contessa immediately.

"Where is he hiding him? If you tell me, then I won't have you charged as an accomplice as well." Joseph's eyes were fanatical as he interrogated her. "We'll charge him either way. Make up evidence if we have to."

Contessa's face heated. "You lecture me about right and wrong while you spit in the face of justice and a fair trial?"

Joseph's expression twisted in fury, and for a second, he looked just like her father the night before.

"You've been here too long. The Beast has poisoned your mind. Confused you."

Contessa trembled with rage. "I'm not confused. I'm thinking for myself. Maybe you should consider who really has the poisoned mind here."

Joseph looked at her for a moment longer, all color drained from his high cheekbones, before letting out a sort of choked grunt, turning on his heel, and striding from the room.

The rest of the inspection went quickly, Joseph directing the team to comb the house in such a manner it seemed as if he could barely stand to be breathing the same air as Contessa. Nate even let the officers into his back office, and Contessa held her breath as Joseph tore through the drawers, even going so far as to tap at them to check for false bottoms, but he came up empty-handed. Not even a single piece of paperwork.

At last, Contessa accompanied the group of officers to the front door, having no concrete evidence that Kristoff had even entered the house in the first place.

As he walked out onto the front step, Joseph turned to look back over his shoulder to where Contessa and Nate stood in the doorway and said, "I'll tell your father you send your regards."

The way he said it made it seem like a threat, but Contessa squared her shoulders and simply said, "See that you do."

Joseph marched down to the street where the officer's horses waited for them, and Contessa shut the door and slumped with her back against it, letting out a breath as if she'd been holding it the entire time Joseph had been in the house. Perhaps she had.

She glanced up at Nate, who was staring down at her with his good brow creased. Contessa squinted up at him and pushed herself back up into a more dignified posture.

"You're looking at me as if you want to investigate me too," she commented. "Not the reaction I was hoping for considering I just saved our skins again."

Nate cocked his head as if he hadn't heard her.

"How did you know the police officers were coming?"

"I didn't betray Kristoff if that's what you mean," Contessa snapped, but Nate seemed unperturbed.

"I know that. He already told me he was afraid he was spotted at a break-in last night. What I want to know is how you knew the police would be ambushing him here this morning?"

Contessa glanced down and smoothed her already neat skirts.

"I didn't know. I just had...a feeling, like a dog before a storm."

"Was it the same as when we were at the executions yesterday?"

Contessa blinked, thinking back to the sudden panic she'd felt standing in the crowd yesterday. The way her heart suddenly started pounding in her ribcage just as it had today. She nodded silently as she gazed up at Nate, who was beginning to look as if he had successfully put together his puzzle.

"Have you had things like that happen before?" he asked.

"Not since I was a child. It faded as I got older, but I was always a scared child, thinking something bad was going to happen," Contessa admitted, trying not to think about the buzzing feeling and pounding heart that had caused her to run downstairs one night, only to find her mother lying in a pool of blood.

"Fear is rarely so accurate," Nate commented.

Contessa squinted at him.

"What are you saying?"

"I'm saying we may have just figured out what your Talent is."

She opened her mouth to retort that being afraid was hardly a talent, but then she thought of how adamant she'd been that Kristoff needed to leave. Of how sure she'd been yesterday that Nate had to escape the executions with her.

"So, my Talent is being able to sense when people are in danger?"

"It may be. We'll need to test it out. Find out what it's limits are and how exact it can be."

Contessa nodded even as she pursed her lips. "I feel as if I have been shortchanged with my gift if I just have a sense of impending doom, when other people get to fly."

"You would be surprised." The good corner of Nate's mouth

pulled up in a wry smile, "Flashy, impressive abilities don't always turn out to be the most useful. My ability seems mild at first, but I've been able to put it to good use over the years, and it's allowed me to keep it a secret relatively easily. Not to mention that I could feel your 'sense of impending doom' both today and yesterday. It was very useful in persuading me that you hadn't just lost your mind."

"You would have thought I had lost my mind?"

Nate looked abashed.

"I mean, not exactly. You just have been completely on guard for the past weeks, and it seemed likely you might crack at some point."

Contessa offered Nate a hand gesture of a very unladylike nature that she'd picked up from some of her father's lower ranking officers. Nate let out a low chuckle, and Contessa realized she hadn't heard him laugh before. It was a pleasant sound.

Nate turned to walk towards the back of the house and gestured for Contessa to follow.

"Come on," he said. "Let's go fill Kristoff in on what happened."

"Will he still be hiding in the tunnel below your desk?"

Nate shook his head. "No, he'll have used the tunnel to head to the warehouse the Lions use as their home base. I thought I would take you there so you can see our operation like you wanted."

"So, these tunnels..."

Nate shrugged a shoulder. "When we were younger, I could tell a thief was lying about how he broke into some houses. I got him to show me the tunnel he used. Kristoff and I spent months mapping them all out, and we've been careful to keep the knowledge well guarded. When the Lions eventually formed, I chose to build my house here because of this entrance. I use it to come and go from the Lion's other safehouses without being spotted. It's probably the reason your father has never caught me."

Contessa nodded. It suddenly made much more sense that the

Royal Police had never managed to catch the infamous Beast even though they had a guard on his house for the last several years.

Once they entered the office, Contessa and Nate worked to push the desk back out of the way, and Nate opened the secret panel once more.

He hopped down into the dark entrance without hesitation before turning and offering a hand up to Contessa.

"Are you ready to meet the Lions?" Nate asked.

Contessa held her breath and nodded before reaching to take Nate's outstretched hand. Then she jumped down into the tunnel and the darkness waiting beyond.

Chapter Twelve

Contessa wasn't sure what she'd expected of the Lion's den, but it certainly wasn't what greeted her when Nate ushered her through another hidden panel in a wall. The first thing that struck her, as she blinked to regain her sight in the warm lamplight, was the sound of children laughing. No sooner had Nate stepped into the large open space and shut the door behind them than several children noticed their presence.

"Nate! It's Nate!" a chorus of voices sounded, and instantly, they were surrounded by a sea of upturned and grinning faces.

Nate himself smiled back just as broadly, none of the reserved silence from their meals together in evidence now, as he greeted the children by name and affectionately ruffled a number of bouncing heads. Contessa felt the corners of her mouth pulling up despite herself.

"Alright, alright, let Connie here through. We have business to attend to," Nate said once he had completed his greetings.

Immediately, a hush fell over the group, and Contessa heard a few whispered snippets of "Mrs. Woodrow" and "a proper lady".

Nate distracted her from the flush now spreading across her cheeks by ushering her across the space and letting her get a better glimpse of their surroundings. They were in a vast storeroom of a warehouse, but it wasn't at all the dank and rat-infested place Contessa had envisioned when she thought of the buildings down by the dock. Instead, it was warm and lined with neat rows of child-sized bunks. There were even a few roughly carved wooden toys in sight.

Seated on one of the beds was a girl older than the rest, if Contessa was to judge by her size. For now, all she could see was a mass of red hair as the girl looked down to talk to a small boy beside her.

"Rhosyn," Nate called, and immediately the girl looked up.

Her eyes landed on Contessa, holding a glint that showed even more mischief than Kristoff's smirk. Contessa liked her the moment she grinned broadly, revealing crooked front teeth.

"Nate! You've finally decided you're not too embarrassed of me to introduce me to your wife," Rhosyn bounded up with too long legs and slung a lanky arm around Nate's shoulders with ease. He seemed to be used to the gesture, even though Contessa had never seen him display physical affection before.

"Contessa, this is Rhosyn. She does, well, everything that Kristoff and I can't around here," Nate introduced, extricating himself from Rhosyn's embrace.

"That's me. Nursemaid, universal big sister, and pickpocket extraordinaire, although don't be telling your father that last bit." As Rhosyn spoke, Contessa could hear the hint of the round vowels that marked her as being from the North. "I hear you've gotten our boys here out of two close scrapes in as many days."

"That's why we're here. Can we talk in your office?" Nate said, jerking his head towards a nearby door.

Her "office" turned out to be little more than an adjacent store-room with overturned barrels for seats and an empty box serving as a makeshift desk. Still, the wall served to give them some privacy from the chatter of the dozen or so children in the next room.

"So, give me all the details on what's happened with the execution and the raid on your house," Rhosyn said as she settled herself on a barrel with the stilted grace of a young woman who had recently come into her full height and hadn't yet figured out how to maneuver her limbs. "All I've gotten are jumbled reports from a panicked Gregor and an assurance that you would tell me more from Kristoff on his way through."

"Kristoff has left already?" Nate asked.

"He passed through to let me know he had been compromised and to grab some supplies before heading on to one of the safe houses," Rhosyn explained. "Said he was going to lie low for a while. What exactly was he running from, though?"

Nate quickly recounted the events of the last two days. While he was speaking, Contessa caught Rhosyn stealing a few appraising glances at her, but she tried her best to keep her full attention on Nate's story.

"And now Connie wants to help with the children, so I brought her here to you. You know best what they need," Nate finished.

Rhosyn tapped her chin.

"I want to know more about this Talent of Contessa's, for starters," she said, raising an inquisitive brow towards Contessa.

"That makes two of us," Contessa said honestly.

"I have some ideas on how we might be able to test it out," Rhosyn commented as she leaned back on her stool and shoved her hands in the pockets of her skirt.

"Oh, like what?"

"Like this!"

Faster than Contessa could flinch, Rhosyn had drawn her hand out of her pocket and lobbed something straight at Contessa's face. Just before it struck Contessa's nose, Nate's hand shot out and snatched it out of the air.

"What was that about?" Nate barked as he looked at the object in his hand, finding it to be a wooden ball children would play with.

Rhosyn shrugged but looked apologetic.

"I wanted to see if she could sense it coming before I threw it," she explained.

"I think my Talent gives me advance warning of danger, not faster reflexes," Contessa said, her tone succeeding at sounding delicate even as her pulse fought to return to its normal pace.

"I guess now we know for sure," Rhosyn said.

"Next time, though, can we try to test Connie's powers in a way that doesn't risk breaking her nose?" Nate chimed in, tossing the ball back at Rhosyn, who plucked it easily out of the air.

"I knew you wouldn't let it break her nose," Rhosyn said with a wicked grin. "Your wife is far too pretty for that, wouldn't you say, Nate?"

Nate coughed forcefully. "Of course, she's lovely, but that's not the point."

Contessa's eyebrows shot up, and Rhosyn looked positively thrilled. Noticing their reactions, Nate jumped to change the subject.

"So how do you think Contessa would best be able to help with the children?"

Rhosyn considered Contessa.

"With your Talent, you'd make an awfully useful lookout. You could help us on some of our liberation missions."

Contessa blanched and resisted the urge to stammer inarticulately as she reached for the proper words. Nate saved her before she could speak.

"I think Contessa would rather avoid being so...hands-on with the less savory parts of our operations."

Rhosyn peered at Contessa with narrowed eyes and huffed noncommittally.

"I guess I should let you get yourself acquainted with our herd of little ones then. See what you think you might be able to do to improve their situation."

When the trio reentered the room where the children stayed, they found themselves mobbed again, although this time in a slightly more orderly fashion. Rhosyn introduced Contessa to each child by name, although Nate seemed to know them all already and was quickly drawn off by one child or another who wanted to show him some game they had dreamed up.

As the next child stepped into Contessa's line of view, she caught sight of a partially healed scar cutting across a familiar brow.

"Paul!" Contessa crouched down so she could be at eye level with him. The color in his cheeks was much better than the last time she'd seen him, and he even offered her a small smile.

"You are looking so well. And who is this with you?" Contessa asked, catching sight of a younger girl's face with Paul's same round cheeks peeking out around his shoulder.

"This is my sister, Olivia. Come on, Olivia, this is Mrs. Woodrow, the nice lady I told you about."

Olivia continued to stare but didn't step out from behind the shelter of her older brother. Contessa outstretched a hand towards the girl, hoping to coax her out, but instead the girl jumped back, situating herself more firmly behind Paul.

"Sorry, ma'am. She's still afraid of grown-ups. Not used to everybody being so nice to us," Paul said, "but you're one of the good ones. You and Nate."

At his words, Contessa glanced over to the corner where Nate was entertaining a group of young ones, only to see him completely engulfed in giggling children. He had one perched on his shoulders and pulling enthusiastically at his auburn hair, another had latched onto his leg like some sort of monkey, and he was clutching a third child upside down by the ankles. Contessa would have found it barbaric if the child in question wasn't whooping and laughing as if it were the most fun he'd had in his life.

A throat cleared next to her, and Contessa looked up from where she crouched in front of Paul to find Rhosyn contemplating her with a raised eyebrow. Contessa straightened from where she knelt on the floor, smoothing her skirts as Paul and his sister drifted over to the laughing crowd of children at Nate's feet.

"A lot of them are pretty shy at first," Rhosyn said as they watched Nate hoist another child into the air, the children having decided they all wanted a turn at being swung about. "I mean, I definitely was. It's hard to change your mindset when you're used to being afraid of being beaten all the time."

Contessa glanced at Rhosyn out of the corner of her eye, noticing the way she held her head with confidence, even though she must have been several years younger than Contessa.

"I take it the Lions...liberated you from a factory as well?"

Rhosyn nodded. "I was in the first group they ever went back for... I grew up with Nate and Kristoff as sort of older brothers, and as much as I adore them, it was...sort of a mess. They were good at running schemes and breaking children out, but what do seventeen-year-old boys know about raising dozens of children? So, I've stuck around to help manage the littler ones."

"What about the other children that were rescued with you? Where did they go?" Contessa asked.

"They mostly stayed with the gang. Helped run our gambling operations and go on liberation missions, although they moved out of this warehouse. We've got a few houses full of Lions in the lower city. I do try to get some of them who want a different life out, but it can be hard. Julia, your lady's maid, was one of the older girls living here. Looks like she's adjusted well, if she was the one that did those braids."

Contessa reached up to pat her hair, which Julia had woven several small white flowers into this morning. Contessa had been inclined to comment that they seemed more appropriate for a special occasion than a day in the house, but she was glad she hadn't.

"She's lovely. It's been nice to have her around," Contessa commented honestly.

"I'm sure she loves it, although the girls here miss having their hair braided constantly," Rhosyn chuckled. "I've tried to do it for them, but I'm clearly no good."

Rhosyn gestured at her own mass of unruly curls, most of which had already managed to escape the leather thong she'd attempted to tie it back with.

Contessa smiled. "I would offer to help you, but I'm embarrassed to admit that I can't even do my own hair. My mother always brushed it for me when I was young, and then... Well, then I always had a lady's maid to do it for me."

Rhosyn wrinkled her nose, but there was no real malice to the expression. "All of you great ladies. You'll have to learn to brush your children's hair soon. It'll only be a matter of time until there are a bunch of little Woodrow's running about this place with the way Nate loves children."

Contessa choked on her own tongue. "Our marriage... I mean... that seems highly unlikely."

Rhosyn shoved her hands in her pockets and shrugged as if she didn't notice Contessa's sudden ineloquence. "Tell that to Nate, with the way stares at you when he thinks you aren't looking."

"I think the best word to describe that look is vexation," Contessa argued.

"Yes, and I myself wouldn't want to marry a man that I couldn't vex on a daily basis. But then again, I don't know how these noble marriages are supposed to work."

Contessa squinted at Rhosyn, only to find her eyes twinkling mischievously over her smattering of freckles. Contessa chuckled as she turned her attention back to Nate, who was on his knees having his own hair braided by one of the older girls with a look of the greatest forbearance. As Contessa watched, Olivia began inching out from behind her brother, obviously curious. Nate caught sight of her and held out a hand with a smile. Olivia paused before inching forward once again like a scared kitten. Nate kept his hand outstretched patiently as she slowly reached for it. When her hand finally landed in his, his smile broadened, and Olivia offered him the slightest upturn of her lips, tucking her chin to her chest bashfully.

"I'm glad to see Nate coaxing her out of her shell," Rhosyn commented. "She's been having a hard time adjusting. She has so many nightmares, I've barely gotten any sleep in the past week from sitting up with her, trying to assure her that she's safe. Her brother's escape was rather traumatic—you saw his injury. A couple men were shot, and well, that's a terrible thing for a child to see."

Contessa's throat tightened, and she swallowed a few times to steady her voice before asking, "Do you think if they'd had a good lookout, a fight could have been avoided?"

"Are you, daughter of the Commander of the Royal Police, offering to be a lookout for a liberation mission?"

Contessa opened her mouth and then closed it. If her father, the man who would give his life for king and country, would bend the rules to achieve his ends, maybe the spirit of the law was more important than the letter.

"If it would be only watching for trouble. I don't want to do any breaking in, and I'm not committing any violence," Contessa conceded.

"I wouldn't throw you into a fight, but you know I'm going to have to train you in at least the bare minimum of self-defense," Rhosyn pointed out. "I don't think Nate would ever let me run another mission if anything happened to his lovely wife."

Contessa pursed her lips but didn't argue. Rhosyn, for all her maturity, was committed to romanticizing her marriage of convenience. Contessa got the impression that arguing with the girl would get her nowhere.

"Alright, when would this be starting?" Contessa settled for asking.

"I have some time tomorrow afternoon. Meet me here then and we can get started, and by the King's bloomers, wear something more practical."

Contessa looked down at her full, frilly skirts.

"Gladly."

♟♟♜♟♟♟

Contessa picked her way through the tunnel behind Nate, squinting to make out any obstacles in the flickering light from the lantern he held.

"Watch yourself. There is a little step up here," he shot over his shoulder, not breaking his stride. Despite the jagged floor, he never lost his footing, clearly having traversed these tunnels so often he could have managed in complete darkness. It was probably easier to navigate without having to constantly lift your skirts out of the way.

As Contessa picked her way across the uneven floor, she chose her words carefully. "You seem to be a favorite of the children."

A gruff sigh came from the tunnel in front of her.

"I think the children idealize me a bit too much, just because I organize the gang that broke them free."

"That, and you seem to have a way with them you know."

There was a long pause broken only by the scraping of their feet, and Contessa wished she could see Nate's face.

"I wish I could spend more time with them," came Nate's eventual reply. "I guess I wish I could give them more of an actual family. I remember being their age, and well... We do the best we can for them, but I know it isn't enough."

"Anybody who has seen them with you and Rhosyn would know they see you as family."

Nate's head dipped as he walked in front of her, and she thought he was probably pleased that his face was hidden.

"Is—is a family something you want?"

While Contessa managed by sheer luck not to trip, she knew she didn't school her face into neutrality fast enough to hide her red cheeks had Nate been facing her.

"I hadn't given it much thought," she hedged.

Nate gave a noncommittal grunt but didn't reply. As they walked a little bit farther in silence, something about the flickering lamp made the scene oddly intimate. She thought of Nate holding his hand out to Olivia, and she opened her mouth.

"I guess at one point, when I thought... Well, when I thought my future was going to go differently, I assumed there would be children. I guess I was always so focused on what my father wanted from me—to be quick-witted and well-read. A girl who thought about finding a husband and having a family all the time didn't really fit in that picture."

Nate exhaled in a way that might have been amused. "Funny, I always thought a quick-witted woman would make the best sort of mother."

Contessa ducked her head as they came to the end of the passage, and Nate cracked the trapdoor above them that would lead into his office. He turned back to Contessa to help her up, but she paused. The dim light made it easy to be brave, and she wasn't quite ready to leave it yet.

"Are children something you want?" she asked.

The light from above only shone on the scarred half of Nate's face, making it difficult to read his reaction.

"If I could make a child feel safe, then...yes, I think I would like children," Nate snorted, but there was no mirth behind it. "Although I doubt I make many children feel safe with a face like this. I think they just find me to be a novelty."

Contessa cocked her head. She'd never heard Nate discuss his scar before. It was a looming presence they were both aware of but felt odd to mention.

"Well, I think it shows how brave you are," Contessa defended. "That you fought a rival gang leader to keep your own safe."

Nate shook his head. "That's a nice story that serves to make me a more menacing figure, but that's not how I ended up like this."

Contessa cocked her head, giving him time to continue if he wished.

"It was when Kristoff and I were escaping from the factory we worked in as kids. We sneaked down from the loft where the children slept and were creeping across the production floor when the supervisor spotted us. We were almost to the door, so I pulled over one of the big machines behind us to block his way so he couldn't chase us. When it hit the ground, it broke, and a jagged bit of the metal hit me across the face. I don't remember too much after that, but Kristoff pretty much had to drag me the rest of the way. I wasn't brave, I was just another scared kid." Nate's voice dropped to barely above a whisper. "If we had known Gregor then, he might have been able to patch it up, but we had nothing. We didn't even have a clean cloth to wash it with, and the wound got infected. It eventually cleared and healed itself, but..." Nate gestured vaguely to his face.

Contessa swallowed hard. "Well, maybe it's a mark of how much of a survivor you are."

Nate huffed. "A pretty platitude to be sure, but it has no bearing on somebody who can sense the feelings of those around him. I know people are afraid when they see my face, even if they hide it from their expression. I say let them be afraid if it keeps them out of my way so I can make sure this doesn't happen to any more children."

Contessa looked down, seeing Nate's fist clenching and unclenching at his side. When she glanced back up, Nate's one visible eye was scrutinizing her.

"I'm not afraid of you," Contessa murmured.

"I know," Nate replied. "You never were. When we first met, I sensed rage, even hatred coming off you. But never fear."

In the tight space of the tunnel, Contessa and Nate stood close enough she could see the flickering lamplight reflected in his eyes. Contessa raised her hand, slowly enough that Nate could pull away if he chose to. Instead, he stood perfectly still, not breaking eye contact, as her fingers moved towards his cheek. As lightly as she could, she dragged her fingertips over the ridges of his cheek. Nate's eyelids fluttered, but otherwise, he didn't move at all. Contessa almost asked him if he had feeling in his scar, but she didn't want to disturb the silence between them. She didn't even think she was breathing. As her fingers brushed across his cheek, they traveled to the jagged corner of his mouth, and he let out a sharp exhale, the warmth tickling her wrist. It startled her enough that she drew her hand back an inch, and the moment was broken.

Nate turned towards the trapdoor and hauled himself out before reaching back down to help Contessa up. She did notice, though, that he didn't try to move away from her as hurriedly as he had the time before, as if she were going to scold him if his hand lingered an instant too long.

"Well, you better rest up," Nate commented as they stood awkwardly in the middle of the office, seemingly at a loss for what to do with themselves after the intimacy of their conversation. "Rhosyn told me you are going to start training with her tomorrow. If I know her as well as I think I do, you have quite a day ahead of you tomorrow."

Contessa nodded and bid Nate goodnight before heading up to her bedroom to get ready for sleep. Even as Julia brushed her hair for the night, Contessa could feel the cool ridges of Nate's scar under her fingertips.

Chapter Thirteen

C ontessa stared at the articles of clothing laid across the coverlet in front of her and mused that it was a round-about way of getting what she wished for. She plucked at the gray trousers Nate had dug up for her. She did prefer the color and lack of ruffles, even if the idea of pants made her blush.

There was no point in putting off the inevitable any longer, so she slid on the pants and soft linen shirt. Both were too big, and she had to roll up the cuffs of her trousers a few times to avoid tripping over them. Turning to inspect herself in the mirror, Contessa bit back a laugh. She thought the new clothes would have made her seem like a proper gang member, but it looked like her face had been transposed onto the body of a street urchin. The twist of braids on the top of her head looked preposterous, even though it was one of the simpler arrangements she'd worn recently.

Contessa took a deep breath to brace herself before heading out of her room and nearly jumped at how much freedom her ribcage had to expand. She almost missed the bracing feeling of a tightly laced bodice.

Walking downstairs, Contessa tried to ignore the way the fabric rubbed against her legs with every stride. As she descended the last steps, Nate rounded the corner into the hall, immediately pulling up short and blinking.

"What is it?" Contessa asked, glancing down at herself to make sure the shirt was buttoned. "Did I put them on wrong?"

"No, not at all," reassured Nate, recovering himself. "It's just a different look."

Contessa resisted the urge to smooth her absent skirts. "It's an adjustment. It's strange having so much fabric touching my legs."

Nate tilted his head. "But your skirts have to have ten times as much fabric as those pants."

"Yes, but they aren't nearly as close to my skin."

Nate nodded his understanding and they stood for a moment in silence. Nate seemed like he didn't know where to look until he cleared his throat.

"Shall we be going?"

Contessa nodded, and they headed back to the office to enter the tunnel. As she walked through the hall in front of him, she continued to think about how much less fabric covered her legs and tried not to imagine what Nate could see walking behind her.

♟♟♜♟♛♟

As Contessa approached the doorway to Rhosyn's office, a scraping sound came from inside. As she poked her head around the corner, she found Rhosyn pushing the barrels she used as chairs to edges of the room. She straightened and smiled when she spotted Contessa, blowing a loose curl from her face.

"Well look at you!" Rhosyn said, gesturing for Contessa to come in. "I barely recognized you without all the skirts. It looks like you were hiding a nice pair of legs under all those ruffles, though!"

Contessa knew her father's moustache would bristle at such an improper compliment, but Contessa found herself smiling at Rhosyn's infectious energy.

"Apparently, this is the proper attire for liberation missions, so I better get used to it."

"But you won't be going on any liberation missions until we get you trained up a bit." Rhosyn pointed a stern finger at Contessa. "The plan is to keep you out of the line of fire and just have you signal if any danger is coming, but you never know what's going to happen on a job, and things can change in an instant."

Contessa nodded soberly and stepped into the open circle of floor in the middle of the room.

"Let's start with a few basic self-defense maneuvers," Rhosyn instructed. "The key is to strike where they aren't expecting it and always go for the weak points. Then again, when you're small like you and me, they rarely expect you to strike at all."

Rhosyn's smile was wicked, and Contessa knew she was in for an exhausting afternoon.

♟♜♖♟♞♟♟

Several hours later, Contessa sat slumped against a barrel, all traces of her normally rigid posture gone, her sense of propriety chased away by the intense exercise. She fanned herself with a hand and tried to pick off the pieces of loose hair plastered to her sweaty neck.

Rhosyn, on the other hand, stood in the middle of the room, bouncing lightly on the balls of her feet. The flush on her freckled cheeks served to make her look invigorated, where Contessa was sure she looked like an overripe tomato.

"That was fun, and you did well!" Rhosyn complimented.

Contessa simply narrowed her eyes at Rhosyn and continued to fan herself.

"Seriously, you did better than I would have expected for a proper lady. And you didn't ask to stop as soon as you started sweating."

Contessa pursed her lips but didn't object, even though the first lesson hadn't been particularly productive. She'd only escaped a few of the holds that Rhosyn demonstrated, even though she knew the girl was grabbing her lightly. Contessa would have little chance of actually escaping if a rival gangster were to catch her unawares.

As if she read her thoughts, Rhosyn continued. "The good news is that, with your Talent, you should be able to sense danger coming and avoid combat altogether."

"That's the most encouraging thing you've said so far," Contessa commented.

Rhosyn chuckled and offered Contessa a callused hand to pull her to her feet.

"Do you have time to stay for a bit, or do you need to get back?"

Rhosyn's tone was casual, but a shred of hope flickered in her eyes. She wondered how long it had been since Rhosyn had spent time with a woman close to her own age.

"I'm not in any rush," Contessa replied as she allowed herself to be hauled off the barrel, "I don't normally see Nate until after dinner anyways, so I am at your disposal."

"Good. I have something to show you."

A stack of boxes made a rough scraping sound as Rhosyn pushed them aside to reveal a series of metal rungs in the wall. The ladder led up to a door in the ceiling Contessa hadn't noticed before. Rhosyn led the way up the ladder, Contessa following more slowly. The rungs carried them through an attic space, until Rhosyn opened another hatch and revealed a patch of gray sky.

After easily pulling herself up, Rhosyn reached back to help Contessa, who was currently concluding she was going to need more upper body strength if she was going to continue to spend time with the younger woman. All thoughts of weak arms left her mind, though, when a cool breeze blew across Contessa's face, and she looked out at the view from the roof of the warehouse.

The building was in the industrial district down by the river, which Contessa had known already, but from here, she saw it was on the Southern edge of this section of warehouses. The rooftop had an unobstructed view of the port where merchant ships docked and unloaded. She watched as one vessel set off down the wide river to the sea, a plume of smoke leaving a trail in its wake. Up this high, above the pollution of the city, Contessa imagined she could smell salt on the breeze, even though the ocean was half a day's journey away.

Rhosyn took a deep breath of the fresh air as she settled herself comfortably on the rooftop, leaning back on her elbows. Contessa arranged herself next to the girl, neatly tucking her legs to one side as they watched the harbor together.

They sat in companionable silence for a moment as Contessa surveyed the neat rows of warehouses and factories in the industrial district from this angle, a few smokestacks letting out clouds of smog that faded into the gray sky and blurred the sunshine filtering through the clouds, softening the harsh edges of the city.

It soothed something in Contessa to relax in someone else's presence like this—something she hadn't had since the last afternoon she spent with Joseph before her wedding. With how things were with him now, it seemed possible they'd never have this type of easy companionship again. Finding this sense of peace with Rhosyn now gave her hope that her future might hold more friendship than she had lost.

"I know the lower part of London can be...treacherous," Contessa observed, "but from up here, it almost looks peaceful."

Rhosyn closed her eyes and tilted her face up to the sky.

"That's why I like it on the roof. When handling the kids and running jobs gets to be too much, this is my escape. I come up here and watch the ships come and go. I like to imagine what it would be like to be on one of them, traveling to one of the far-off places they may be heading."

Contessa peered at the girl out of the corner of her eye. "You have an awful lot of responsibility on your shoulders for someone so young."

Rhosyn shrugged. "No one to blame for that but myself. When I was first taken in by the Lions, I told myself that as soon as I could take care of myself, I'd leave to make my own way in the world. But, when the time came, I couldn't do it. I watched all the kids coming in after me, and I knew they needed somebody looking after them, teaching them how to make it on these streets. So, I volunteered to stay, and Kristoff and Nate have treated me like family, so I can't complain. I just...I feel like I owe it to them to pay it forward, even though they would never say that to me."

Contessa watched another ship pull into the wharves, workers scurrying around like ants to bring it to the docks to unload its haul.

"What did you want to do before you decided to stay with the Lions?"

Rhosyn paused, licking her lips.

"I wanted to be a sailor, like my father. I told myself I was going to captain my own ship someday. I guess I take after him and feel a connection to the sea. He was blessed by the sea itself and could read the winds to bring his ships safely to port every time. He was the helmsman of a merchant vessel, and after he predicted a few storms too accurately, well...you can guess what happened next."

Contessa swallowed and looked down at her hands, rearranging them in her lap.

Rhosyn's lips twisted wryly as she continued. "That was a girlhood dream, though, and the world has its own agenda. Nobody has times for fantasies anymore. How about you? What were your childhood plans?"

Contessa pursed her lips. "I'm not sure there was a place for dreams in my father's house. My goals were always to sharpen my mind, convince my father I wasn't too girly to be useful, and help father catch my mother's killer. I guess none of those things worked out, as I'm currently not speaking with my father, am married to his biggest rival, and was totally wrong about who killed my mother."

Rhosyn chuckled, and Contessa herself smiled at the irony of it.

"So now that your old plans have flown the coop, any new dreams?"

Contessa cocked her head.

"You know, I'm not sure," Contessa chewed on her tongue, uncomfortable with the feeling of not having an articulate answer for every question. "I've never had a time in my life where I didn't know exactly what I wanted—or at least what I was supposed to want. It's odd making a new place for myself outside of the forces that always drove me before."

Rhosyn considered Contessa, her green eyes sharp enough that Contessa felt like they could see beyond her words.

"Well, I have a feeling once you do decide what you want your life to look like, there won't be much that could get in your way."

♟♟♜♟♛♟

Contessa pulled up short as she entered Rhosyn's office after a week of training when she saw the barrels in the middle of the room. Twin knives, almost as long as her forearm, gleamed against the knotted wood of the makeshift table. Rhosyn looked up from her work sharpening a similar set of knives and grinned at the stricken look on Contessa's face.

"I thought we'd try something a little different today and put some weapons in your hands. It's good for you to know how to escape if somebody grabs you, but you can only do so much damage with your bare hands. Besides, I highly doubt you want to train in hand-to-hand combat to join the brawling rings."

Contessa stepped closer to the weapons and looked down at them skeptically, even as she knew that Rhosyn had a point.

"Be that as it may, you really think it's wise for me to fight with knives?"

Rhosyn considered her, squinting.

"Well, you don't strike me as the type to be a sharpshooter. And knives are easy to carry without being noticed. I mean, think of how many you could hide under those skirts you normally wear. Not to mention, I'm sure the appeal of a nice thigh sheath wouldn't be lost on your husband."

Contessa looked up to shoot Rhosyn an icy glare, but the girl was undeterred as she continued.

"Speaking of Nate, he's the one who suggested knives for you in the first place. Told me to use these to train you with. If I'm not mistaken, these were his when he was younger."

Contessa looked back down at the blades in front of her, noting their simple design and marks of wear around the handle, where Nate's hands would have gripped them countless times.

"If these were his, what does he fight with now?" Contessa asked.

"Oh, he's still the best knife fighter I know, but I believe Kristoff got him a full new set for his twentieth birthday, so all his knives could match, and these are just a pair." Rhosyn snorted. "It's probably been years since Nate has left the house with less than six knives strapped to him somewhere."

Contessa raised her brows. She'd always found it a bit odd that she never saw Nate with a weapon on him, but now she realized it was a testament to how discreet knives could be if one knew what they were doing.

"Well, these are lovely and all," Contessa commented, reaching down to run her finger down the length of one of the knives but stopping herself before she could touch it. "But I feel like I'm more likely to slice myself with them than harm an attacker."

Rhosyn rolled her eyes in exasperation as she pushed herself up from her seat and walked over to where Contessa stood, picking up the knives she was contemplating.

"That's why I'm going to teach you how to use them. I promise, you're in good hands. I teach all the children how to defend themselves, and I learned from Nate himself. Although, I fancy I'm a bit of a better teacher. He's so comfortable holding a knife I don't think he even knows how to communicate with somebody who hasn't done it before anymore."

Contessa chewed her lip and nodded slowly. Rhosyn tossed the knives expertly, flipping them around in her hands to offer them to Contessa handle first.

"Let's start by figuring out what grip you're the most comfortable with."

After some experimentation with Rhosyn's guidance, Contessa

settled the knives in her hands, left hand holding the blade point forward and the right with the grip reversed, the blade pointing out from the side of her littlest finger. Rhosyn, looked amused as Contessa got comfortable with the grip.

"What? Is this wrong?"

"No, not at all," Rhosyn shrugged a shoulder. "That's just the exact same way Nate likes to fight."

Contessa looked at the blades in her hands, thinking about her husband fighting with them similarly.

"Must be the knives," Contessa said.

"Of course, must be the knives," Rhosyn agreed sagely. Then she settled into a fighting stance in demonstration.

"Remember, the first step in knife fighting is to have fun and be yourself."

♟♟♜♟♛♟♟

The knife slipped from Contessa's sweat slicked palm and hit the ground inches from Rhosyn's foot with a clatter.

Rhosyn, to her credit, didn't flinch. She bent to pick up the blade with a dry comment. "I hadn't thought we'd get to throwing knives until next week."

Contessa covered her face with a hand, thankful she'd managed to make it this far without anybody losing a digit. She let Rhosyn pluck the other blade from her hand, as the younger girl seemed to pick up on her frustration.

"Why don't we stop here for today? We've come far for only having been working together a week, and you're doing well."

Contessa narrowed her eyes at Rhosyn.

"You know I'm not."

Rhosyn scrunched her nose as she replied, "Well, there is a chance I've taught ten-year-olds who have picked this up faster, but I wasn't expecting to turn a proper lady into a street brawler in the blink of an eye."

Contessa snorted at the girl's honesty. "Well, I'm not sure I'm a proper lady. I can't dance or embroider either."

"No matter what you are, you are still making progress," Rhosyn said and tossed Contessa a cloth to wipe her face. "It won't be long until you'll be ready to tag along on a liberation mission. It's not like you need to be a master fighter to be a lookout."

"That's good, because I'm beat," Contessa mopped her face and grimaced at the feeling of sweat crusted on her brow.

"Hmm. Maybe we should take a break from fighting for the sake of your muscles. Do something fun and teach you to crack locks or pick pockets?"

Contessa waved her off as she hobbled over to a barrel and slumped down onto it. "My father already made sure I could pick any lock, and I don't see myself getting much good out of being able to lift purses."

"Wait, your father taught you how to pick locks but gave absolutely no training in self-defense?" Rhosyn folded her arms as she looked at Contessa in disbelief.

"Yes, well, I guess he thought espionage was far more ladylike than brawling."

"Your father looked down on you for being girly and then insisted you still be ladylike? Sounds impossible to please."

Contessa couldn't suppress a choked giggle at how concisely Rhosyn had summed up the struggle of her entire youth.

Rhosyn chuckled. "Well, then let me teach you how to pick a pocket."

Contessa opened her mouth to argue she didn't think she needed to learn how to commit larceny, but Rhosyn cut her off.

"I'm the best there is, and it would be rude of you not to let me show off a bit. Besides, maybe this could be useful in your espionage. You never know when you might need to get an important letter for evidence or something."

While she frowned, Contessa couldn't help being affected by the pleading look in Rhosyn's eyes.

"Fine," Contessa sighed. "Show me some of your tricks, but remember, this is just for fun."

"Good," Rhosyn grinned. "Because I nicked this out of your pocket, and it would be awkward if you didn't approve."

Rhosyn flicked a small golden object into the air, and Contessa's reached out to catch it, bobbling it a few times before finally gaining control of the item. She opened her hand to look at what she'd caught.

"My wedding ring. How on earth…"

Rhosyn looked smug. "I know you put it in your pocket when you train, but you should be careful. It would be a tragedy if you were to lose it."

Contessa wrinkled her nose as she slipped the ring back onto her finger where she hoped Rhosyn wouldn't be able to get to it as easily.

"I don't even know why I continue to wear it."

Now it was Rhosyn's turn to frown.

"What do you mean? You're married. Nate would be put out if you didn't wear it."

Contessa looked up at the younger girl. "Rhosyn, you have to know that Nate and I don't have a traditional marriage. I mean, I'm the daughter of a man who wants to see him dead."

Rhosyn continued to frown as though vexed by the idea that

Contessa and Nate may have ended up married for reasons other than true love.

"Well, maybe if you want to impress him," Rhosyn suggested, "you can use one of my tricks to lift something from his pocket."

Contessa debated for a second whether it would be a better argument to point out that she didn't feel the need to impress him at all, or to mention that she doubted thievery was a particularly endearing form of flirtation. Instead, she decided to let the subject drop.

"Alright." Contessa smiled. "Show me what you know."

♟♞♜♘♙♟

Gregor was just serving Contessa her cup of tea after dinner when she heard heavy footsteps behind her. She twisted in her seat to find Nate's frame filling the doorway to the dining room, his hand fiddling with the knot on his cravat.

"Oh, good. I had hoped I would catch you before you went upstairs for the evening," he said.

Contessa picked up her gently steaming teacup. "Well, then, your timing was impeccable."

Nate continued to stand in the doorway silently, and Contessa raised her brow at him as she blew on the surface of her tea.

"What was it you wanted to ask me?" she prompted.

"Oh, yes. I know we haven't played chess together in a while, since things have gotten so crazy. But, well, I was hoping you would join me for a game tonight. I understand if you are tired from your day with Rhosyn, though."

The corner of Contessa's mouth twitched up. "On the contrary, training with Rhosyn has hurt my pride. I think it would be good for me to spend some time beating you at chess."

Nate's good eye crinkled in what Contessa had come to recognize as amusement, and he gestured for her to lead the way into the living room.

They settled into the rhythm of the game after a few turns, but the air seemed lighter than when they had played in the past. Perhaps it was more enjoyable to play as friends than as adversaries trying to outwit one another. Contessa caught herself at that thought. Friends? She wasn't sure if they had become friends, although it seemed like it might be a nice thing to be, considering they were married. Something about the word rubbed her the wrong way, though. Contessa peeked up at Nate, who was considering his next move, absently chewing on the nail of his thumb.

Catching her looking he asked, "How is training going with Rhosyn? I know she planned to start you with knives this week."

As Contessa watched Nate move his tile into the path of one of her own, she commented, "Well, I think the best that can be said for it is that I managed to come home with all my fingers still attached."

Nate huffed. "I suppose it's only normal you aren't naturally outstanding at it. It would be unfair for you to be fantastic at everything."

Contessa straightened from where she'd bent over the chess set contemplating her next move to find Nate's ears reddened. He snatched up his glass from a nearby table and took a sizeable gulp of the brown liquid within, avoiding eye contact. Something about his expression made her think about what Rhosyn had said about impressing him.

Contessa turned her attention back to the board and made her move.

"I guess you are right. You have to be better than me at something, since it clearly isn't chess." Contessa knocked over his king with her knight, indicating she'd won the game.

Nate scowled.

It's probably for the best we finished anyways. You'll need your sleep if what you're saying about your knife fighting is true."

Nate pushed up from his chair and held out a hand to help Contessa up from her low stool. She took it, but as Nate pulled her to her feet, her tired leg muscles protested, and she stumbled. She threw her arm out for balance, and her hand landed on Nate's waist, her fingers just brushing the edge of his pocket, before she quickly righted herself.

"Are you alright?" Nate asked, reaching out as if to steady her but not quite touching her.

"My muscles just aren't used to this much work," Contessa said, smoothing her skirts as she set herself to rights. "Like I said, I find personal combat quite difficult. Although I will say that Rhosyn and I have found one thing I'm good at."

"Oh, and what is that?"

Contessa held up her prize with a grin.

"Pickpocketing."

Nate blinked at the object in her hand.

"Wait, that's mine. How did you—" He clapped a hand to his face. "Oh, Rhosyn. She's creating a monster. It's like there are two of her now."

Contessa chuckled as she turned her attention to the object in her hand, not having had a chance to get a close look at it before. It was a metal rectangle with intricate engravings, and closer inspection showed a small catch on the side. Contessa pressed it and jumped when a blade the length of one of her fingers sprang free.

Nate huffed and reached for the knife.

"It's just my spare blade," he explained as he took it from her and closed it again. "It's too small to be great in a fight, but you can still stab people with it. Not to mention thugs never expect me to have one more in my pocket."

"One more?" Contessa asked. "Rhosyn said you usually carry six knives, but that seems like a lot. Is that true?"

Nate shifted as he slid the blade back into his pocket and patted it to make sure Contessa hadn't managed to slide anything else from it.

"Six? Well, no. I don't carry six."

"I knew she had to be exaggerating…"

Contessa trailed off as Nate looked down at his feet.

"Wait, you can't possibly carry more than six knives, can you?"

"Well, to be fair, not all of them are very large…"

"How many knives do you carry?" Contessa demanded.

"That's not a very polite question you know," Nate countered.

"Oh, come now. It's not like I'm asking a lady how old she is."

Nate sighed heavily.

"Nine." He paused thoughtfully. "As well as a pistol, if you must know, but I rarely use that."

Contessa looked him up and down several times, trying to place where he could keep them all.

"Even when you're in your own house? Doesn't that seem a bit excessive?"

Nate shrugged. "If they are going to call me the Beast, I may as well have some teeth. Not to mention, it turns out I need to have my guard up even in my own home because my wife is a thief who won't hesitate to grab things from my pocket." He shot her a pointed look, and she held her hands up in surrender.

"But to be honest, I hadn't been carrying this many blades until the past few weeks, but with everything so uncertain…" Nate chewed his bottom lip, and Contessa bit back a question, hoping for him to elaborate on his own.

Shaking himself from him contemplation, he said, "Well, I'm not sure if carrying more knives really makes any difference, but at least the weight of them on my body makes me feel like I'm doing something."

The resigned look on Nate's face only seemed to accentuate the tired circle under his unscarred eye, and Contessa had the sudden urge to reach out and touch his arm in comfort. She gripped her hand at her side and instead contented herself with trying to be useful.

"What's made things so uncertain that you feel the need to be so well armed?" Contessa asked.

"I'm sure you're informed about the controversies regarding the potential succession, with the way you read the papers," Nate explained.

Contessa furrowed her brow. "I mean, of course, but what does that have to do with your...business?"

Nate sighed. "As you would have heard, the people of the lower city prefer Prince Byron for the throne. They think Prince Albert prioritizes parties over the people. They're probably right, considering he's shown absolutely no interest in politics. It doesn't sit well with the people of the lower city who are barely scraping by to see Prince Albert be so...frivolous. I was sure he was going to abdicate, but he hasn't yet. Every day the king creeps closer to his deathbed while Prince Albert remains heir, the people of the lower city get more restless. As talk of violence increased, the Royal Police doubled their watch in the lower city, trying to stem any riots. The streets are crawling with officers, day and night. You can't take two steps without bumping into one."

"Ah, well," Contessa said dryly, "I suppose that would make any criminal activity more difficult."

Nate pulled a face that made it clear he had considered rolling his eyes at her. "It's not just strictly illegal activities, either. We only make a fraction of our money off pickpocketing and bigger heists. Most of the funds the Lions use to function comes from the money we skim at the gambling houses. Now the unrest has scared away most of our casual patrons. We've had to spread out over almost twice our usual area to get enough income to feed everybody."

Contessa pursed her lips thoughtfully.

"Well, why not go back into investing, like you did when you were younger to establish yourself in the upper city?" Contessa suggested.

Nate considered her, his head tilted. "I've thought about it you know, but now that most of the world at least suspects me of running most of the criminal underworld, it's hard to get into straight business. People expect all my financial choices to be crooked. Nobody believes I've just been lucky."

"Well, lucky may be a strong word for it," Contessa pointed out, "considering you used your supernatural perception to guide your investments."

Nate's eye crinkled in amusement. "Well, that too. Although, honestly, I only invested the first time so I could gain status. I keep this house and position so I can appear in circles where I can get leads on our next hit. Most of the men who own warehouses that use child laborers are rich and talk too much for their own good at clubs."

Contessa huffed. "Yes, I'm well aware." She repressed memories of escaping conversations with businessmen twice her age trying to impress her with their wealth, focusing on the topic at hand.

"Well," she ventured haltingly, "if you did ever want to get into honest business again, I might be able to lend my small influence in giving it some legitimacy."

"You know, that's not a half bad idea," Nate mused. "Although it would take time to build credibility. We'd have to come up with a solution for the Lion's income in the meantime."

Contessa bit her bottom lip. "Maybe I could accompany you to the lower city some time and see if I could help some of the gambling houses with their strategies."

"You would want to come to one of the Lions' gambling houses?" Nate asked, taking a step back.

"I've literally run from law enforcement with you," Contessa pointed out. "I don't know why this is that surprising to you."

"Be that as it may, you surprise me nearly every day, Connie."

It may have just been a flicker of the lamplight, but there was a softness in Nate's eyes that made Contessa look down and smooth her skirts.

"Well," she said softly, "if I'm going to be up for a trip into the wilds of the lower city, then I should get my rest."

Contessa moved to retire for the evening, but before she rounded the corner to make her way upstairs, she glanced back to find Nate standing right where she'd left him, looking down at the chess board in contemplation.

Chapter Fourteen

The gambling hall wasn't what Contessa had envisioned. As she stood in the doorway, she was greeted by warm lamplight illuminating round tables crowded together in way that might even be described as cozy. It was a far cry from the dingy gray room where she usually envisioned thugs tossing dice. There was even a fireplace in one corner casting a warmth that was welcome after the drizzle out in the street.

"Is something the matter?" Nate asked from her side, noticing she hadn't moved away from the entrance.

Contessa shook her head as she propped her umbrella against the doorframe. "It's just so...cute."

Nate's eye crinkled in amusement. "You know, we do try to make sure not everything we do projects the feeling of illicit activities. I mean, gambling isn't even illegal."

Contessa narrowed her eyes. "Be that as it may, I'm sure the amount your dealers skim isn't exactly above board."

Nate shrugged a shoulder. "That's not the point. We try to make this a place where people want to spend their time and money. At a dingy dice den, you only get the people that can't stop gambling even if they want to, and they don't have much money to take."

As Contessa and Nate pushed farther into the space, a few youths looked up from their tasks cleaning tables and sweeping floors to raise a hand in greeting at Nate. Several sets of eyes widened as they spotted her, but none of them said anything about her presence.

Nate weaved between the tables towards a small bar on one side, "Unfortunately, our best efforts at making this a place where people want to stay hasn't been great at getting them in off the streets. The most lucrative patrons from the middle city haven't been coming down to the lower city to gamble at all. They see it as a ticking time bomb."

Contessa ran her fingers over the scarred wood of the bar as she contemplated. "Have you considered sending some of your people up to taverns in the middle city as plants? Have them talk the place up? They could even try to bring groups of people down here themselves to make them feel like it's safe."

Nate tapped his blunt fingers on the bar top. "Right now, we only put plants in the other gambling halls in the lower city, but that's not a half bad idea." Nate cocked his head at her. "You're remarkably good at this sort of thing for a woman who grew up on the right side of the law."

"Yes, well, I spent my life being taught how to spot crooked business tactics, so I do know a thing or two," Contessa waved Nate off, not wanting to examine her feelings on such matters too closely. "Why don't we take a look at the outside of the place and see if there is something we can do to make it catch the eye a bit more."

Nate may have replied as Contessa walked towards the front

door, but a high ringing overwhelmed her mind, blocking out any other noise. She was mere feet from the door when she whirled to face Nate, her heart pounding its way up into her throat. She didn't even get a word out before a pair of lethal knives sprang into Nate's hands from somewhere under his clothes.

Contessa lifted a foot to step towards him, but before it could land, there was the sound of wood banging against wood and an arm as thick as a tree branch wrapped around her neck. It yanked her back so hard her feet left the floor.

Blinking away tears from having her windpipe pressed on, Contessa's gaze landed on Nate, who had gone deathly still. His knives were still in his hands, and he had fallen into a low crouch, his muscles bunched to attack. He looked so tense Contessa felt like he should be quivering, but he stood stock still, as if waiting to pounce. Even as Contessa's toes scraped for purchase on the uneven wooden floorboards, she understood what it meant to face down the Beast.

Impatient with her struggling, the arm around her neck gave a sharp tug. Contessa went limp, focusing on taking shallow breaths and regaining her wits.

"Well, this is even better than we bargained for," rumbled the voice close to her ear. "Caleb sent me here to break a few bones and remind the Lions this block belongs to the Rattlesnakes. Instead, we find the Beast himself—and what's more, his pretty little wife."

The man shook Contessa as if they might have been unsure who he was talking about otherwise. Her brain rattled in her skull even as she tried to remember everything Rhosyn had ever said about escaping choke holds.

"Thomas, put her down," Nate said, not moving from his stance, his voice little more than a growl in the back of his throat. "Put her down, and we can figure something out."

Thomas's chest rumbled with laughter against Contessa's back. "Everybody says you're the best knife fighter in London because you've never lost a fight, but I know you better than that. I know you've never lost because, most of the time, you're too coward to fight at all."

By this point, several of the other Lions had come to back Nate up, blades and even a pistol or two in hand, but they waited for Nate to make the first move. They weren't fighting yet, but perhaps they could distract Thomas from his hold on Contessa just enough.

She swung a dangling leg around to try to trip up Thomas and take him to the ground. With the lack of leverage from hanging in the air, he kicked her leg out of the way easily, his boot connecting with a bone in her ankle in a way that made her eyes water.

"Well, if you don't want a fight, I'm more than happy to oblige. I'll just take this pretty little one to Caleb, and you can have her back once you get off Rattlesnake turf."

Nate didn't respond, not moving an inch. His nostrils flared and his gaze met hers briefly, holding an unholy glint that made her wonder how Thomas had the courage to back out the door with her still in his hold.

The cold drizzle hit Contessa as Thomas kicked the door to the gambling hall closed, and she found herself jostled and disoriented as there was a sudden onslaught of rough voices.

"We aren't fighting them after all?"

"Caleb won't be happy if we come back without spilling any blood."

"Who's the girl?"

Thomas brushed them off as he continued to walk into the street, Contessa hanging motionless in his hold to keep him from tightening his grip again.

"We've got something far better than a brawl today. Throw her in the wagon and get her back to Caleb, quick. It won't be long until the Beast comes after her."

Thomas turned her in his grasp, and if her reflexes had been faster, she might have been able to use the movement to escape from his hold, but before she could think, she was once again caged to his chest by arms like bands of steel.

"Now be a good little dove and get in the wagon. We won't hurt you if your dear husband does what he's told and backs down, so you should be fine. He always was a soft one," Thomas leered, giving Contessa a close view of his chipped yellow teeth.

Thomas began to push her backwards into the wagon, and Contessa squirmed, a single thought running to the forefront of her mind before she was shoved into captivity.

What would Rhosyn do?

In her best impression of a street brawler, Contessa reared her head back before slamming it forward with as much force as she could muster. There was a sickening crunch, and Thomas's hold loosened on Contessa for just an instant. Unfortunately, the crunch seemed to have come from Contessa's own face as lightning bolts of pain exploded behind her eyes. She only managed to stumble into Thomas, her hands landing on his thick waist.

Before she could fully process the haze of pain, Thomas had caught her and was shoving her into the wagon, her knees hitting the edge and causing her to topple backwards. Her hands remained clenched in tight fists instead of breaking her fall. Thomas let out a ruthless chuckle as she tumbled to the floor with a thud, slamming the wagon door behind her.

"Oh dear, the Beast's poor little bride has gone and broken her face. I hope he doesn't mind too much."

Indeed, as the wagon lurched into motion, jumping and bobbing over the rough cobblestones of the street, Contessa brought a hand to her face to try to contain the blood dripping from her nose. Still, she brought up her other hand and opened her fist in front of her face to examine the prize she'd slid from Thomas's pocket.

Her heart fluttered in relief as her eyes focused on a switchblade, much plainer than Nate's but revealing a narrow blade when she pressed the mechanism. It would be thin enough to suit her purposes. She pinched her nose tighter and grimaced, even as she celebrated that she hadn't wrecked her nose to distract Thomas only to grab something useless like a handkerchief.

Contessa scooted across the rough floor of the wagon, glad she'd chosen to wear pants today as the material snagged on a few lose nails. As she crouched near the door, she let her hand drop from her face, giving up on staunching the bleeding and letting the blood drip onto her shirt. Getting out of this carriage was the priority.

She leaned in to examine the lock on the door, cursing for asking Julia to put her hair in a simple braid today instead of an elaborate style that would supply her with pins. Still, the blade she'd pilfered would work well enough for raking the lock. A more exacting form of lockpicking would've been difficult in a jolting carriage anyways.

As she examined the lock, Thomas's voice drifted in from the direction of the driver's seat, his rumble carrying over the clatter of the wheels.

"I wonder what Caleb will do with this one. He won't want to give up the leverage over the Lions, but I don't see him giving her back in one piece."

The muffled voice of the driver responded, followed by Thomas's raspy chuckle.

"True. Maybe he'll slit her throat and cut some slashes in her face. He could leave her on her father's doorstep so the Chief could have a matched set."

Contessa's heart jumped into her throat, and she ripped her

attention away from eavesdropping, trying to focus on the task in front of her. Carefully, she slipped the blade into the keyhole and rotated it slightly until she felt the pins lift. She yanked the knife towards her and cursed when she only heard one pin knocked into place. Raking had never been her preferred method of lockpicking, being so imprecise, but there was nothing else to do. She slid the knife back into the lock to try again, only to freeze when the wagon shuddered to a halt.

Contessa braced for the ringing in her ears at the danger that surely awaited her inside the Rattlesnakes hideout, but the world remained quiet. Her breath stilled in her chest in the brief silence before a thud on the roof rattled the wagon, followed by a metallic *shick* and a wet gurgle that Contessa was sure she would be hearing in her nightmares for the rest of her days.

All hell broke loose with sudden shouting and the singing of metal against metal. Contessa swung back to her work with renewed fervor, drawing the blade out of the lock three more times as the sounds of a fight raged outside. She finally felt all the pins fall into place and the door swung open.

The sight that greeted her in the street was one of carnage, the type she'd always been taught to fear from the gangs of the lower city. At the center of the vortex of violence stood Nate, whirling and parrying with his knives in movements so much more graceful than what Contessa was used to from him, as if he was more himself with knives in his hands. The rain had matted his auburn hair down, making it several shades darker where it clung to his face and collar.

As she watched, a mountain of a man aimed a brutal swing of his knife at the side of Nate's head. Before Contessa could open her mouth to scream, Nate had caught the brute's blow on his forearm and sunk the dagger in his other hand into the man's flank. The thug toppled over as Nate yanked his blade free, blood splattering from the knife and falling to the ground where it mixed with the rainwater and ran into the gutters in a crimson river. Before the first fighter even hit the ground, a second charged up behind Nate, but Nate threw up a hand without even looking, slashing the man across the face as he tried to grapple Nate from behind.

Intimidated, the group of Rattlesnakes stepped back to regroup, circling Nate from a distance as he fell back into a crouch in preparation for their next assault. His mouth was pulled up in a silent snarl, and while Contessa had grown used to his appearance, she was suddenly reminded how frightening his scar could appear.

As the men faced off, it became apparent that Nate was severely outnumbered, and the Rattlesnakes glanced at each other out of the corners of their eyes. If they all charged at once, Nate's chances of victory would be slim.

Even if Contessa had thought to strap her own blades to herself that morning, she wasn't going to be much use against seasoned street brawlers. She glanced around desperately, when a distressed whiney behind her grabbed her attention. She spun around to find the wagon she'd just exited, attached to two horses, pawing the ground and whickering at the sudden death of their driver.

Without a further thought, Contessa clambered up into the front of the wagon, hands slipping on a combination of blood and rainwater. As she hoisted herself into the driver's seat, she was forced to shove the lifeless body of the driver aside to reach the reins, trying desperately not to think about the wide gash spanning his throat. Instead, she turned her attention to the horses, tugging them around as best she could. As the wagon slowly wheeled around to face the fight, the circle of thugs tightened around Nate like a noose. He'd managed to position his back towards the wall of a nearby building. She tugged at the reins one more time, trying to point the horses directly at the group of Rattlesnakes in the street.

Just before she snapped the reins, Nate's eyes jerked up to spot Contessa on her perch in the driver's seat. Then, the horses bucked, easily spurred to a charge in their frightened state. The Rattlesnakes looked up at the clatter of hooves, but it was too late. Where Nate managed to press himself into the wall just in time, the horses' hooves hit the first of the brawlers with a crunch, and the wagon jolted over a fallen body with a bump that rattled Contessa's teeth. The rest of the men scattered like pins in lawn bowling, running down the street away from the thundering wagon. Realizing their defeat, they split off into alleyways and ran in different directions, disappearing into the haze of rain. The street went quiet as the pounding of retreating footsteps disappeared. Pulling in the reins, Contessa soothed the frightening horses with some effort, and the cart ground to a halt.

Contessa slumped down in the driver's seat, exhaling. For the first time since stepping out of the wagon, she noticed the cold of the rain pattering against her face, the wet making her shirt cling unpleasantly to her skin and weighing her braid down against her back. The clamminess of her skin only served to make the hot pounding in her nose and the warmth of the blood still dripping onto her lips stand out even more. She ran her tongue over her teeth, gagging at the thought of how much more blood was currently running over the cobblestones of the street.

A thump to her left startled her, and she looked down to find Nate, standing on the ground next to the driver's seat. He looked up at her with wide eyes, his hand braced on the side of the wagon as if debating climbing up to the seat himself.

Without a thought, Contessa clambered to the edge of the wagon and slithered down the side. She barely held on at all as she descended, sliding down so fast she would have fallen to her knees in the street if Nate hadn't caught her under her arms.

He held her in front of him, scrutinizing her face. Contessa could only imagine the state she was in—blood crusted on her lip, her nose swollen and bruised. She might have raised her hands to cover her face if she hadn't been preoccupied making sure the blood splattered across Nate's shirt wasn't his.

"Which one of them... Who did that to your nose?" Nate demanded, his eyes taking on an almost feral cast in the flickering light from a nearby lamppost.

Contessa might have pointed out that whoever it was likely already got what they deserved, but instead, she said, "Oh, that's my fault. I can only blame myself."

Nate's brows drew together as his expression faded from hostility to confusion.

"How?"

Contessa swallowed, then grimaced at the blood dripping down the back of her throat. "Well, I did my best to headbutt Thomas when he put me in the wagon. You all make it look so easy... I think I underestimated how much it would hurt."

Nate's face went blank, and he didn't say anything for a moment.

"It all worked out, though," Contessa prattled on, uncharacteristically nervous before Nate's expressionless stare. "It distracted him long enough that I picked his pocket so I could break the lock and escape."

The corner of Nate's mouth began to pull up, and for a moment, Contessa thought he was about to snarl in anger again. Instead, his face broke into a wide grin, his eyes softening in relief and something akin to wonder.

Before Contessa could gape at him for longer than a moment, she found herself crushed to his chest, his arms around her making her feel blessedly warm in the damp, her face buried in his neck. She would've fretted about getting blood on his jacket if that wasn't already a lost cause.

"I'm not sure why I expected anything less, honestly," Nate mused against her hair.

In response, Contessa wound her arms around his waist, pressing herself into his warmth and wishing she could smell the rain and his skin through her swollen nose.

Chapter Fifteen

The warmth in Contessa's chest began to spread, reaching down to the tips of her fingers, as she swirled the brown liquid in the cut crystal glass Nate had offered her.

As if in response to her thoughts, Nate asked from where he sat at the foot of her bed, "How do you feel?"

"Warm," Contessa answered honestly. "It's a nice change from the wet clothes. Rain can be lovely; it's a shame it is always so cold."

Nate exhaled sharply through his nose as she continued to examine the way the candlelight filtered through the sloshing amber liquid.

"Well, I think you're relaxed enough now. You think you're ready to let Gregor try and set that nose of yours?"

Contessa sighed and placed the glass down on the stand next to her with a clink.

"I'm not sure if ready is the word I would use, but now is as good a time as ever," she conceded as she rested her head back on the pillows and closed her eyes in preparation.

Gregor's voice came from somewhere near the head of her bed. "I'll try to be quick about this. Just hold still and do your best not to fight me."

The bedsheets crumpled in her hands as Contessa balled them into fists to brace herself, even as she tried as hard as she could to relax. She felt Gregor's fingers, surprisingly cool on her face, before he pushed at her nose in a way that made white shine behind her eyelids. Although she managed to stay still, a grunt escaped her lips. She would have been embarrassed by the noise if a warm hand hadn't come to rest on her shin over her dressing gown, a thumb soothing back and forth.

After a few more pushes and a painful click, Gregor declared her nose appeared to be back in place

"I've gotten much better at setting noses since I first started patching up the Lions," Gregor assured her as he stuffed some sort of awful cotton into her nostrils. Contessa tried not to squirm.

"Yours should heal much better than Kristoff's did. His was the first one I set, and I still feel guilty it healed so crooked."

Nate huffed in amusement. "I wouldn't feel too guilty if I were you. I know you think the crooked nose only accentuates his roguishness, and I'm sure Kristoff appreciates that."

"Yes, well..." Gregor cleared his throat and finished packing Contessa's nose in silence before putting some sort of rigid bandage on the outside.

Contessa felt Gregor shift away and she opened her eyes.

"I'll go get you a cold compress to help with the pain and swelling," said Gregor. "After that, all you should need is time and rest."

He slipped from the room to go fetch the compress, but Nate stayed seated at the foot of the bed. She glanced at him from what she knew to be bruised eyes, having caught sight of herself in the mirror on the way into her room.

"Well, how do I look?" she asked, happy that the liquor had gone to her system just enough to numb the embarrassment she felt at her nasal voice.

"Like somebody who just survived their first street brawl," said Nate. "As much as I'm impressed by your resourcefulness, maybe blindly headbutting thugs is ill-advised."

"No more ill-advised than coming after me without any backup," Contessa retorted, burrowing her head into the pillows behind her in an effort to get comfortable.

"I had sent the Lions from the hall to run for backup, but time was of the essence. If they had gotten you back to Caleb..." Nate didn't finish his thought right away. "Well, it was going to be easier to break you out of a wagon than it would have been to rescue you from the middle of a nest of Rattlesnakes. Besides, I knew I could climb over a building and cut them off."

Contessa wanted to press him on the matter, but at that moment, Gregor pushed back into the room, holding a compress as promised. She was untangling her hands from the sheets to reach for it, but Nate beat her to it, thanking Gregor before he slipped back out.

Nate slid up the bed until he was even with Contessa's hip, reaching up to gently press the compress to her bruised face. She hissed at the touch before relaxing into the feeling of cool, soothing the heartbeat echoing in her skull.

"You're going to go through a lot of these," Nate mused. "I remember the first time I broke my nose; the cold was pretty much the only thing that made it feel better. I didn't take anybody's advice about keeping the packing in, either. I hated not being able to breathe through my nose, so it took forever to heal."

"The first time you broke your nose?" Contessa prodded.

"I've broken it three times. My combat training was rather…learn as you go," Nate explained. "It's a good thing I gave up on vanity long ago, because I never seemed to get Gregor to set them in time."

Contessa narrowed her eyes, scrutinizing his nose. She supposed she could see a slight bend, but it was hard to discern under a rope of scar tissue that ran over the bridge of his nose. Seeing her looking, Nate ducked his head.

They sat in silence for a few moments, Nate still holding the cool compress to Contessa's face, and her making no move to take it from him. Instead, she continued to examine his face, comparing the soft expression she saw now to the snarl he had worn in the street.

"You killed a lot of people today," Contessa broke the silence without preamble.

Nate raised his eyes back to hers, his scar worn like a mask that kept his expression neutral.

"I did," was his only reply as he continued to examine Contessa's face.

She said nothing, offering him no reaction, even though she knew he could read her feelings, at least to some degree.

"You killed some people too," he commented.

Contessa inhaled, but still, she didn't say anything.

"How…how does that make you feel?" Nate asked, his voice as halting as his tone was inscrutable.

"How do you feel when you kill people?" Contessa asked in return.

Her eyes tracked the shadow that bobbed in the hollow of Nate's throat as he swallowed.

"Part of me feels like I could say I'm used to it," Nate conceded, "but I think it might be more accurate to say I've learned to keep going. I believe in what I do, and sometimes...sometimes I think how I feel about it isn't even relevant."

Contessa nodded, understanding it from Nate's point of view.

"I watched my father and his men come home wearing other people's blood all the time, and I still held them on a pedestal as heroes because they were making sacrifices to uphold the law," Contessa admitted, unsure if the words tumbling out of her mouth were prompted by the liquor or the pent-up demand of weeks, but knowing she had to say them all the same. "I tolerated murder in the name of the law because I was told the law was right—even though I hadn't evaluated it for myself. If I can live with death in the name of a code that was simply thrust upon me, I can learn to live with it in the name of a cause I chose for myself."

Contessa's gaze was steady over the compress, but there were still feelings crawling under her skin that made it difficult to rest despite her bone-deep exhaustion. Still, as Nate's eyes fixed on hers, she took comfort in the fact she didn't have to explain them to him, that he could feel. He may have even had them himself, which was why she was not entirely surprised when she closed her eyes and he made no move to leave. He stayed perched in his spot, a warm presence next to her hip as she released her mind to let it drift, freed by exhaustion, pain, and alcohol.

She was just about to slip out of consciousness, odd images from the day drifting through her mind, when one suddenly jumped to the forefront. Her eyes sprung open to find Nate was still watching her.

"When I was in the wagon, I overheard Thomas say something," Contessa said. "He said that maybe Caleb would cut my throat, slash my face, and leave me on my father's doorstep just like my mother."

Nate put a hand on her shin, misreading the distress rolling off her.

"We won't let that—"

"No," Contessa interrupted. "I think he killed my mother."

Nate's hand stilled where he had been gently stroking her leg. Contessa wished he would continue.

"The slashes." Nate's voice was deathly soft. "Caleb was the one who started them. The lieutenant that split with the Lions when I confronted him about being needlessly violent."

Cold washed through Contessa's veins, stifling the warmth of impending sleep.

"What do you want to do about it?" Nate questioned.

"I'm not sure," Contessa answered candidly, "but if there ever was somebody I wanted dead, it would be him."

♟♙♖♟♙♟

The sunshine warming her face offered a nice contrast to the cool of the windowpane against Contessa's forehead. She opened her eyes and looked out at the street, watching people walk by and feeling envious of whatever it was they were doing. It seemed that, in the past week of training with Rhosyn, Contessa had become accustomed to a more active daily routine. Finding herself stuck in her room made her squirm.

She realized she was picking at her skirts again and settled them into stillness in her lap. Nate may have preferred she stay in bed today while her nose healed, but Contessa had insisted on getting up and getting dressed, loathe to rid herself of her routine entirely. She'd been tempted to insist she at least be able to go out for a walk as well, but after catching sight of herself in the mirror as Julia brushed her hair, she agreed to stay indoors. While the dark purple streaks outlining the underside of her eyes were unsightly, it wasn't vanity that kept Contessa indoors. She simply wasn't ready to face the questions her appearance would cause and didn't think it was wise to draw attention to herself.

Contessa pushed off the window seat and made to huff in frustration but found it rather difficult to do around the cotton in her nose. Just because she had to stay inside didn't mean she had to lie about in her room like an indisposed lady whose nerves had gotten the better of her. She traipsed down the stairs, unsure of her intentions but adamant she could locate something to occupy herself.

As usual, she found the lower level of the house silent, the dining room spotless as Contessa had been persuaded to take breakfast in her room today. Maybe if she could find Gregor, she could convince him to let her help with some tasks around the house.

As she headed to the back hallway, hoping to see Gregor in the garden, she was greeted by the unusual sight of the office door propped open. Padding up to it, she heard a distinctive scraping noise and peeked around the frame to find Nate sitting at the large desk and running one of his daggers methodically across a whetstone. She spotted the matching knife on the desk and cleared her throat to distract herself from thoughts of why he was cleaning and sharpening his weapons.

Nate's gaze shot up, and he hurried to his feet as soon as he saw her.

"Connie, what are you doing up? You should be resting."

Contessa waved him away, stepping fully into the office.

"It's a broken nose, not a broken leg. And even if I had broken my leg, my mind still works fine and doesn't do well with prolonged inactivity."

Nate settled back into his seat as Contessa perched herself in the spare chair across from his desk. He didn't look pleased with her explanation, but he didn't protest.

"Well," he said, pulling open a desk drawer, "I do have a gift for you while I have you here."

"A gift?"

"Don't get too eager," Nate cautioned. "I doubt it's anything to get excited over, but yesterday brought to my attention that teaching you how to fight with knives won't do you any good if you don't keep them with you."

He pulled a leather bundle out of the drawer and passed it over the desk to Contessa. She turned the items in her hand, finding them to be two sheaths with straps that could be used to attach them to her arms.

"They're just like mine," Nate explained. When Contessa glanced up, she found him shrugging out of his waistcoat. She blushed and looked down at her lap, berating herself for getting flustered at the sight of her husband in shirtsleeves when she'd seen him completely shirtless before. She composed herself and raised her gaze to find him rolling up one of his sleeves. Indeed, he had a long blade attached to his forearm in a similar fashion.

"See, there's a catch here," Nate pointed out a latch on the inner side of his wrist, "and if you press it—"

Contessa jumped as the hilt flew into his hand. Somehow, she doubted she would achieve such elegant results when she tried. Nate twirled the knife mindlessly in his hand a few times, and Contessa followed the blurred silver of the blade through its arcs before he slid it back into the straps on his arm, settling it into place with a muffled click.

Contessa held up the sheaths in her own hand, pressing the mechanism a few times and lifting it close to her eyes to puzzle out how it might work.

"These will go well under a shirt," she mused as she peered in the opening to watch the catch open to free the blade. "Although I won't be able to hide these under the sleeves of most dresses."

Nate blinked and looked her up and down. Today she was wearing a royal blue dress, blessedly free of bows and ruffles, as Julia determined such ornaments weren't necessary for sitting in the house.

"Right," Nate said, eyes settling on her skirts. "I'll have to ask Rhosyn to dig up some for your legs." Realizing he was staring, the tips of Nate's ears went pink, and he looked away to put his waistcoat back on. As he did, Contessa spotted the handles of two more knives in the sides where he could access them easily just by reaching under his coat.

They both settled back into their chairs in comfortable silence, and Contessa let her eyes roam around the room now that she was at leisure to do so without some emergency drawing her attention. It, like the rest of the house, was a rather bare space.

"What do you usually do in this office? You aren't home very much to use it," Contessa asked.

Nate looked around at the empty walls, as if noticing them for the first time.

"I suppose it's mostly a cover for the entrance to the passage. I use it for my comings and goings. I do meet with Kristoff in here, as well, but I think he only prefers to meet here so he gets a chance to see Gregor." Nate's smile was fond. "Otherwise, I'm only in here early in the morning or late at night to do some strategizing on our next job. I just stayed home for today because you were..."

Contessa let the silence stretch as she waited for Nate to finish his thought, but his gaze moved down to the desk where his fingers worried over the whetstone lying there.

"I guess that would explain why the house has no personal effects, if you don't spend that much time here," Contessa eventually mused. "Although, I will admit that the empty shelves in the library upstairs make my heart hurt."

"Yes, well," Nate tugged at his cravat. "I guess I've never really been one for books. I can send Julia out on an errand to fetch some if you like, though. What kind of books do you prefer?"

"Oh, I read everything. Philosophy, history, and I can read in French, too, although my accent is horrendous, so I rarely speak it," Contessa said. "I must admit my favorites are novels about adventures and fairy tales. Not very practical, I know, but they make me nostalgic."

Nate was looking at Contessa with wide eyes, fingers still rubbing over the surface of the whetstone.

"Let me guess, you prefer military strategy and politics?" Contessa prodded.

"Well, I don't..." Nate cleared his throat as his voice came out quiet. "I don't really read."

"Oh, that's a shame. Somebody as clever as— Oh..." Contessa's eyes widened.

Nate looked away again.

"Do you not know how to read? I could teach—"

"I can read," Nate interrupted, his shoulders pulling up towards his ears. "Just not very well. I didn't have the chance to learn as a child, so I started when I was a teenager. I get by, but I've always been too slow to enjoy novels."

Contessa swallowed to dispel the tightness in her chest.

"Considering by then you were on your way to running the biggest gang operation in London, I would say you get by more than well enough," Contessa said gently.

Nate looked up, and his embarrassment softened into a small smile. "Perhaps, but it left me ill-equipped to be married to someone who reads as much as you do."

"That's nothing that can't be easily remedied. Now I just get to build a collection specifically to my taste."

Nate exhaled sharply through his nose. "Good. Now, if I send Julia to get you adequate reading material, will that persuade you to stay in your room and rest at least for a few days while the swelling goes down?"

Contessa pursed her lips. "You are awfully keen on having me do nothing, considering you were the one who wanted me to be trained in self-defense in the first place."

"And embracing the strategic retreat is an essential part of all combat training," Nate pointed out.

Contessa pushed to her feet. "Well as long as you are willing to bribe me with proper reading material, then I suppose I will accept your lesson."

Contessa swept from the room with her head held high, catching the twinkle in Nate's eye before she rounded the corner.

♟♙♜♙♟♙

Contessa stared at the dregs of her tea and debated with herself whether it was too early to go to bed out of sheer boredom when there was a knock at her bedroom door. Grateful for having something to do, she leapt to her feet and yanked the door open to find Nate blinking down at her.

"Oh, if you are already going to bed for the evening, I don't mean to intrude," he commented, finding her dressed in her nightgown and dressing gown.

"Nonsense," Contessa stepped back and ushered him into her room. "If I go to bed now, I'm likely to end up staring at the at the ceiling pondering how I've done nothing with my day."

"Well, good thing I brought something to distract you then." Nate produced an object from behind his back and offered it to her.

Her lips parted in a smile before she could even take the book from his hand, recognizing the embossed cover instantly.

"Julia has good taste," she commented as she ran her hand over the colorful dragon on the front.

"Well, you did say you like fairy tales. I have heard it's meant for children, but I—Julia thought you might like it."

Contessa perched herself on the edge of her bed, letting the book fall open in her lap, her fingers tracing over the words of familiar stories.

"I've always disliked people who say fairy tales are only for children. If the point of them is to escape into our imagination, then wouldn't adults who are so painfully aware of the weary ways of the world need them most?"

"A sound argument," Nate responded. "Although not one a person hears a lot."

Contessa flipped to a page and found herself looking at the title of one of her favorite stories about the girl who tricked a dragon out of its gold by winning in a game of riddles. A wave of nostalgia so painful it made her eyes water rolled over her, and before she consciously made the decision to speak, words were coming out of her mouth.

"You know, my mother used to read these exact stories to me before bed every night when I was small. She even turned the tales into songs to sing me to sleep sometimes. Even though my father said the stories were frivolous, he always stood in the doorway and listened to her read to me.

"When she died, he wanted to take all the fairy tales off the shelves in our library. He tried to get rid of everything that reminded him of her, saying it was too painful to see bits of her everywhere he went. I wouldn't let him get rid of this book, though, and I kept it in my own room. Even though I followed his advice and mostly studied politics and languages, I always had these stories to keep me company when I missed my mother the most."

When she finished, she looked up to find Nate leaning against the corner post of her bed thoughtfully.

"You seem to take after your mother in many ways."

"People say I look like her, with the blonde hair and pale skin and all. But everybody agrees that I have my father's cold disposition."

Nate shifted to face her more fully as he said, "Well, maybe that has more to do with your being around him for most of your life than anything else. I think you're more like your mother than many people might realize."

Contessa swallowed heavily but didn't respond, not trusting her voice to be steady.

"You probably even got your Talent from her," Nate mused.

Contessa started.

"I... My mother wasn't Talented."

Nate shrugged. "It may have been a small Talent, or something subtle like yours that she didn't even know about. Talent usually runs in families, though, and it would be highly unusual for yours to come from your father considering his position on the matter."

Contessa's eyes fell on the page in front of her, and she could practically hear her mother's voice, impossibly beautiful, spinning the words into a song. She remembered how everybody stopped what they were doing to listen when she sang, as if they were bewitched.

"It's possible," Contessa conceded.

There was a long silence, broken only by the clatter of wheels on pavement as a carriage rumbled past outside.

"Well, I'll leave you to your reading," Nate made as if to go.

"Wait." Contessa licked suddenly dry lips. "If you want to stay, I could maybe read out loud."

Nate's look was inscrutable as he paused.

"I mean, I know you said you don't read to enjoy stories, but I thought that maybe if somebody read them aloud to you, you might find them interesting," Contessa continued, uncharacteristically nervous.

"I would love that."

Contessa relaxed, situating herself more comfortably on her bed and flipping through the book to find an appropriate tale.

Nate settled himself onto the seat by the window, crossing one ankle lightly over his knee, looking much too large for the narrow bench. Contessa contemplated telling him that he could sit on the bed with her, but she turned back to the book in her lap.

"Oh, let's start with this one," Contessa said as she flipped the next page. "It's about a princess that must save a king from a curse that turns him into a serpent."

"Sounds delightful," Nate murmured, leaning his head back on the window and keeping his gaze fixed on Contessa.

Contessa tried to ignore the weight of his eyes on her as she began to read. She soon fell into a familiar rhythm, and she read until the candles had all but burned out.

Chapter Sixteen

"I brought you a visitor."

Contessa looked up from the book she was reading, using her thumb to hold her place in today's tome of mythology. She found Gregor peering around the door to her bedroom, a tentative smile on his round face. She raised her eyebrows and nodded for him to let them in, unsure who it might be. It wasn't like Nate to have his presence announced.

A head of curly red hair peeked through the doorway.

"Rhosyn! What are you doing here?"

The girl offered a cheeky grin.

"I thought you could use a little change of pace. The nose looks good, though."

Contessa touched her fingers lightly to the bridge of her nose, testing it since the bandages had been removed a few days prior. It was still bruised, but the deep purple marks had faded to a sallow yellow.

"I'm glad I'll be able to go outside soon without garnering

unwanted attention. Why don't you come in and sit down." Contessa moved the pile of books off the window seat next to her and rearranged her skirts to make room. She gestured to the small table near her habitual perch. "Help yourself to some tea."

Rhosyn moved into the room, picking her way around the stack of books at Contessa's feet to take a place next to her on the bench. On the top of the pile was the book of children's tales she had been reading to Nate every night for the past week. He had continued to bring her all types of history and poetry, but he seemed to enjoy hearing the same stories that had lulled Contessa to sleep as a child, so she continued to read him those.

"You look so different dressed like this," Rhosyn's words brought Contessa back from her thoughts. "It was so easy to forget you were a proper lady when you were wearing trousers and sweating in the back room with me."

"I'm not sure this dress makes me a proper lady," Contessa commented drily, picking at the lace on her sleeve. "It makes me feel like a porcelain doll."

Rhosyn reached out a hand and tentatively ran a finger over a ruffle on today's periwinkle ensemble as she mused. "I suppose it would be different if I had to wear one every day, but your clothes are so beautiful. I can't even remember the last time I wore a dress myself. They get in the way of rolling around on the floor with children."

"Who's with the children right now if you're here with me?"

Rhosyn glanced up with the sly grin of a fox who had spotted a chicken coop.

"I talked Kristoff into watching them so I could have a day off, and he talked Nate into joining him. When I left, they had children climbing all over them like monkeys."

Contessa covered her smile as Rhosyn let out a devious chuckle.

"I swear, those two can face down an alley full of armed thugs without fear, but they are intimidated by a dozen little ones."

Contessa picked up her teacup and sipped delicately to hide the grin threatening to spill across her features at the memory of Nate playing with the children.

"Well," she put down her teacup with a light clink, "we better make sure you have a great day off so the men will not have subjected themselves to chaos for nothing. I think I might have an idea."

Half an hour later, the entirety of Contessa's wardrobe was spread across her bed, a garish heap in a cacophony of colors making Contessa wonder just what dressmaker Nate had asked to create her clothing. Still, Rhosyn stared at them all with wide eyes as Julia laced her into the ruffled number she'd selected. The pastel pink clashed violently with her copper curls, but she didn't seem to care as she admired herself in the mirror, executing a small twirl as soon as Julia had finished.

"Is this how it feels to be the delightful Mrs. Woodrow?" Rhosyn teased as she twisted to see herself from all angles.

Contessa's chest warmed as she watched the woman smooth her skirts, trying to make them lie gracefully. Watching the joy she took in trying on a dress reminded her just how young Rhosyn was to have the lives of so many depending on her all the time.

"It doesn't look quite right on me somehow, though," Rhosyn commented, tilting her head as she frowned at herself in the mirror.

"Well, of course it doesn't," Julia piped up. "We haven't even touched that lovely hair of yours yet."

Julia ushered her over to the seat in front of the vanity table, even as Rhosyn continued to look dubious.

"Good luck," she said as she helped Julia remove the leather band fighting valiantly to keep the stray curls from her face. "I doubt my hair is going to be as easily tamed as Contessa's over there. Hers is just so smooth."

Rhosyn looked wistful, but Julia wasted no time in waving away her concern.

"Yes, and it's so smooth it would lie flat on her head if I didn't tend to it every day. I know just how to deal with your hair too."

Indeed, it wasn't long before Julia had begun to coax Rhosyn's hair into a thick copper braid twining around her head like a crown. Rhosyn tried to twist and turn to catch a glimpse of the curls cascading artfully in the back, but Julia scolded her to sit still.

"Are you sure your ability to do hair isn't a Talent, Julia?" Rhosyn asked in wonder. "Perhaps a gift to bring beauty to those around you?"

Julia wrinkled her nose as her fingers continued to deftly weave the strands together.

"Oh, it's definitely not a Talent," Julia said around the hairpins she held in her mouth. "It took a lot of time to figure out how to do most of this. I subjected you and all the other girls to having your hair pinned and repinned several times a day to practice. I'm sure I made your scalps ache."

"You were amazing at it, even then. There was a reason we never complained about letting you style our hair." Rhosyn's eyes caught Contessa's over her shoulder in the mirror. "Speaking of Talents, how's testing yours going? I'm surprised Two-faced Timothy was able to grab you if you could sense him in advance."

Contessa grimaced.

"Apparently, I don't always get more than a few moments warning, and it's vague at best."

Rhosyn chewed on her bottom lip in contemplation.

"Have you and Nate tried anything to sharpen your sense? Like having him surprise you or anything? I know he said he had to practice to get his Talent as attuned as it is."

"You know," Contessa started, "I have been thinking about that while I've been stuck here for the past few days, and it occurs to me that it is still possible to surprise me. I don't think my Talent alerts me unless there is actual danger."

Rhosyn drummed her fingers on the dressing table in thought.

"That is certainly a good theory. Although that means it would be hard to test your Talent, considering I'm not willing to actually try to stab you in the name of experimentation."

"Pity," Contessa commented over the rim of her teacup.

"You know what this means, though?" Rhosyn asked as Julia put the finishing touches on her hairstyle. "We're going to have to bring you on real missions to develop your Talent more. Kristoff and I are planning a liberation mission for next weekend. The Lions could use a spare lookout."

Contessa set down her teacup carefully.

"I doubt Nate would be pleased with the idea of me being in a fight when the last one didn't go as well as we could have hoped."

"Nonsense," Rhosyn retorted, admiring the feather that Julia had worked into her braid. "We all heard about your stunt with the carriage. Winning in a street fight is more about resourcefulness than technique most of the time anyways."

Rhosyn stood from the seat, turned to face Contessa where she sat in the window seat, and put her fists on her hips in an exasperated manner that looked odd in her current clothing.

"Besides, you're Nate's wife. Tell him you'll make his life miserable if he doesn't let you come along."

"That's not exactly..." Contessa tried to come up with an adequate explanation for why she would not be doing that.

Rhosyn wasn't to be deterred and flounced over to where Contessa sat, flopping down next to her in a rustling pile of lace.

"We can plan it so you're not really in any danger, reassure Nate you'll be perfectly safe. I'll help. You have to admit that it sounds much more exciting than staying at home all day."

Contessa helped Rhosyn adjust her skirts properly on the bench to buy time in responding. Rhosyn had a direct way of attacking issues that caused Contessa to feel like she was mentally treading on very thin ice. Indeed, during her period of rest, she had plenty of time to reflect on what Rhosyn had asked her last time they were together. What did she really want? The answer had come to her in a single word.

Purpose.

Her former goal of bringing the Beast to justice had been shattered in the most unexpected of ways, but now she was granted the chance at a new purpose in giving factories full of children a better life. It may not have been the purpose she envisioned for her future, but it was the one she chose for herself.

"Alright," Contessa said. "But I'm going to enlist your help in working with Nate to create a suitable plan of attack."

Rhosyn sprang to her feet and whirled around the room a few times, and Julia chuckled at her antics even as she looked tempted to warn Rhosyn not to disturb her hair. Rhosyn stopped, her eyes bright in the orange light from the low sun coming in through the window, reminding her of the time of day.

"Do you want to stay for dinner?" Contessa asked abruptly. "It would be a shame for you to have gotten all dressed up and not have a chance to show it off."

The women descended the stairs to head to the dining room, and Contessa smiled at the way Rhosyn still managed to gallop down the stairs in a gown. Upon entering the dining room, they pulled up short at the unexpected sight of Nate, standing beside a table already laid with food.

"You two have certainly had a fun afternoon," he commented, looking Rhosyn up and down. She shamelessly twisted this way and that to show off her outfit.

"It was my turn to spend a day in the upper city while you got to play with the rascals for a change," Rhosyn retorted. "It seems you managed to survive unscathed."

Nate didn't appear to be the worse for wear, except for his hair, which stuck up at odd angles as though it had been pulled at by small hands.

"I like children." Nate shrugged one shoulder as he lifted the cover off a serving platter on the table to investigate what was beneath. "I only left because Gregor came to relieve me. Said he had prepared dinner and put it on the table for us and didn't want me to miss it."

Rhosyn snorted.

"You know that's just a cover for Gregor and Kristoff wanting to play with the children together," she pointed out.

"Naturally."

"It looks like Gregor made plenty for all of us," Contessa added, gesturing to the table. "Why don't we enjoy his offering while they have some fun."

The trio didn't get more than two bites into their soup before Rhosyn broke the companionable silence.

"Contessa's going to come with us on the next liberation mission."

Nate coughed on his mouthful of soup and hastily took a drink of water to clear his throat.

"And when was this decided?"

"Just this afternoon," Contessa jumped in, giving Rhosyn a look that indicated there might have been better ways to broach the subject. The woman just shrugged and turned back to her soup.

"We thought that, considering my Talent only displays itself when there is legitimate danger, there's little point in trying to hone it at home," Contessa explained. "My Talent can only really be developed on the job, as you put it."

Nate ran a hand through his hair, which somehow only managed to make the unruly tufts stand up further.

"I suppose you have a point," he admitted. "But can you at least promise me you will not try to use your face as a weapon against men twice your size again?"

Contessa nodded, taken aback by Nate's quick acceptance of their plan.

"We figured we would station her nearby, but out of harm's way where she wouldn't necessarily have to do any fighting if things go awry," Rhosyn said around a mouthful of bread.

"When do things not go awry, Rhosyn?"

Rhosyn glared at Nate. "Well, maybe now with Contessa standing watch they won't."

"What we need to figure out," Contessa interjected, "is how I should signal you if I sense a problem. I was thinking maybe flashing with a mirror, but that wouldn't work while you're inside."

Nate shook his head.

"That would take too much time to be useful. Last time, you only had a few seconds warning of danger. We'll have to rely on my ability to sense your fear as a warning."

Contessa frowned, but Rhosyn spoke before she could question Nate.

"That would make it hard to keep her out of any potential fight. She would have to stay close to us. You've admitted that you have a limited range on sensing people."

"Yes." Nate fussed with the napkin in his lap. "Although I can sense certain people from farther away than others. If I've become particularly...attuned to their emotional signature."

Rhosyn's brows shot up even as Contessa tilted her head in curiosity.

"You're saying you could possibly position me farther away if you were attuned to me?" Contessa clarified.

"We live in the same house," Nate hedged, abandoning his napkin in favor of twisting his fork over and over in his fingers. "I'm already quite accustomed to your presence."

"So how far away were you planning to put her?" Rhosyn interjected, as direct as always.

"I was thinking on the roof of the building next door."

Contessa blinked. Rhosyn let out a low whistle.

"And I thought your range on Kristoff was good." Rhosyn sounded impressed. "You're sure you'll be able to tell if she senses something from that far away?"

Nate's eyes briefly flicked to Contessa's, and he nodded.

Rhosyn immediately jumped into an animated discussion about how they should go about gaining access to the warehouse next to the factory. Contessa listened with half her attention, sighing in relief when she was reassured she would not have to climb up the outside of a building. The other half of her attention remained fixed on Nate, who kept glancing at Contessa out of the corner of his eye.

It wasn't until later, after Rhosyn had excused herself, saying she should get back to the children so Kristoff and Gregor could have some privacy tonight, that Contessa asked what she really wanted to know.

"How far away can you sense my feelings from?"

Nate sighed and leaned back in his chair, although from the

expression on his face, it was clear he knew this question was inevitable.

"I start being able to feel you about a block away from home."

Contessa's spine straightened, but she didn't say anything.

"At that distance, it's still vague. I don't get distinct feelings until I'm much closer, but I can still tell you're there. It's part of how I was able to track the wagon so easily last week."

Contessa nodded slowly, even as she asked, "But while you are in the house?"

Nate flushed. "I try not to eavesdrop on your emotions, if that is what you mean, but yes, I could sense your moods clearly if I wanted to."

Contessa spent a moment neatly folding her napkin and placing it back on the table.

"Your Talent sounds like it might be difficult sometimes," she eventually responded. "Feeling my own feelings is quite enough for me without constantly having somebody else's moods in my head while I'm home."

Nate offered her a smile.

"I suppose it does get annoying, especially when I'm near somebody in a particularly foul mood. The worst is when I'm unprepared and I come across somebody drunk...but your feelings do not bother me." There was a long pause and Nate took a deep breath. "This house was so empty for so long, it's been a strange reassurance to feel you about. Having somebody here... Well, it finally feels like a home."

Contessa swallowed and found there wasn't much she could say in response to such a statement. Instead, she pushed back her chair and stood up, reaching out a hand to Nate across the table.

"Come on. Let's go upstairs and read," she invited. "If I'm not mistaken, tonight's story is one with a dragon."

Chapter Seventeen

Of the many things Contessa worried about during her first liberation mission, being hopelessly bored wasn't one of them. She'd spent the past hour and a half lying flat on her belly on an unforgiving rooftop, periodically peeking her head over the edge to watch the sparse traffic on the street below. Her bones creaked as she rolled her shoulders and ankles, trying to relieve her stiffness. While she ached to stand up and stretch her muscles, she didn't have it in herself to risk being spotted.

Contessa extended her neck over the side once more to check for traffic and found the streets in the industrial district almost completely empty in the darkness. Although she hated not being able to spot any threats on the street as easily, she breathed a sigh of relief now that the sun had set and taken the heat of day with it. She could still feel the sweat crusted on her neck and back from her time lying so uncomfortably with no shade. Honestly, she didn't think she had sweat as much in her entire life as she had in the past months.

Her attention was drawn from the itching sensation of dried

sweat in the small of her back by the sight of faint shadows moving in the street. She risked edging forward to get a better view and relaxed when she determined that it was, in fact, the Lions. Not only were there five of them, as Nate had told her there would be, but they all had black fabric obscuring their faces. Contessa spotted Nate by the width of his shoulders and his stomping gait. It didn't help that a number of unruly curls had escaped one Lion's head covering and briefly shone a bright copper in the thin moonlight.

The group stole towards the back door where they paused for a moment while one of them worked the lock. Contessa took the opportunity to crawl on her belly to the edge of the roof that looked over the alley between the two buildings. Here she had a better view of all the entrances and exits, as opposed to the street. In a moment, the group slipped inside, and Contessa was left to wait in the oppressive silence. She tried to calm her breathing and watch carefully, both with her eyes and senses. With her mind on such high alert, she worried that she wouldn't be able to sense a change at all if her Talent was triggered. She focused on her heartbeat to distract her from that thought, choosing to trust that Nate would be able to sense the difference between tension and true panic.

Contessa began to wonder how long this operation would take, feeling like they had been gone too long. They already knew how to get the children out of the room where they were locked in to sleep without alerting the skeleton guard kept there at night. She was just reassuring herself that quietly corralling a group of children would be no quick feat when she felt it.

Even as the ringing in her ears grew so loud it nearly drown out her own frantic breathing, Contessa cast about wildly for the source of the threat. She spotted six large figures sneaking down the alley and the telltale glint of moonlight on sharpened steel. Contessa thought about projecting her panic as loudly and clearly as she could, unsure if that was even possible but hoping it was helpful. To her momentary relief, the figures stopped outside the door the Lions had entered through, flanking it, clearly setting up an ambush.

Contessa bit her bottom lip so hard she tasted blood, unable to do anything but wait and hope the warning she was able to pass to Nate was helpful even if wildly vague. Maybe if he knew there was a threat to look for, he would be able to locate and avoid it on his own. He had spent so many years surviving attacks without any warning at all.

A movement on the other side of the building caught Contessa's eye, and she squinted to get a better look. Her hand flew to her mouth as she stifled a sigh of relief. She spotted the Lions and a small herd of short figures creeping out the front door of the factory in the opposite direction of the ambush.

They had gotten her warning, so why was the ringing in her ears only intensifying? Contessa scanned the small group again and counted those present once, twice. Nate was missing. She could only see four hooded Lions among the smaller silhouettes, and she couldn't spot Nate's broad form among them. None of the enemies had gone inside the factory, so it seemed unlikely he had gotten caught or injured. It made no sense why he wouldn't be escaping with the rest of the group.

As if in direct answer to her thought, the back door opened with a crash, and Nate jumped into the ambush in a flurry of shining steel. In the noise of the resulting chaos, the Lions and the children bolted down the street away from the distraction that was Nate and his knives. Contessa couldn't see well in the darkness, but he seemed to be holding the enemies off admirably, although she knew six against one wasn't good odds even for someone as skilled as Nate.

Contessa reached for the catches that would release her own blades before immediately abandoning the idea of jumping into the fight herself. She would be more of a liability than an aid. Still, she cast about for a way to help Nate when her eyes fell on a coil of rope on the roof a few feet away. She sprang to her feet and snatched it up before darting over to the exit from the roof. Grabbing the handle, Contessa nearly dislocated her arm as she yanked, only to find the door would not budge. She shook the door violently and checked the handle to make sure it wasn't locked, but it appeared to simply be jammed. She threw her body into her efforts to open it, all while the backdrop of grunts and steel reminded her she had no time to lose.

Seeing no other option, Contessa strode to the edge of the roof and looked towards the ground. It was only a three-story building, and she reasoned that even if she fell from this height, she would probably survive, albeit with broken legs. Not giving herself a chance to consider it further, Contessa looped her rope over her shoulder, turned around, and lowered herself off the edge of the roof. She thanked every God that might be listening for the small, barred windows that gave her footholds as she scrambled down the side of the building with every bit of haste she could muster.

Contessa held her breath as she descended most of the way. The next time she looked down, she was a manageable drop from the ground. Contessa landed on her backside with a jaw-rattling thump. Still, she shot to her feet, fueled by adrenaline, and was grateful when a snarl from around the corner indicated Nate was still on his feet and in the fight.

With all the speed she could manage, Contessa unraveled the rope and used fumbling fingers to tie one end of it to a drainpipe running down the side of the factory. Then, she darted across the small alley between the factory and the warehouse, holding the end of the rope so it ran across the narrow passage.

Ducking around a corner still holding the rope, Contessa closed her eyes and tried to think. She needed Nate to lead the combatants over here to enact her trap, but she doubted he could infer that much from the odd mix of concern and determination he must feel coming from her direction. So instead, Contessa did the only thing she could think of to draw his attention. She panicked.

Her breathing grew fast even as Contessa imagined the ringing in her ears. She imagined the way she'd felt when Two-faced Thomas had grabbed her around the neck. Her mind even brushed up against the memory of her mother's blood running over her hands.

The response was instantaneous. A roar echoed through the alley from around the corner, followed by the thundering of multiple pairs of boots. Contessa managed the barest of looks around the corner, seeing Nate charging down the alley with four men hot on his heels. In seconds, he had crashed past her hiding spot.

Contessa pulled on her end of the rope, bringing it to knee height. It was ripped from her hands as Nate's pursuers careened into it, crashing to the ground in a heap. Nate skidded to a halt and looked around to find his attackers on the ground and Contessa unscathed apart from the rope burn on her palms.

Still, the heap of men started to move, one of them struggling to his feet. Nate wasted no time in leaping at him, executing a headbutt of the type that Contessa had been envisioning when she'd attempted the maneuver. The big man staggered, and Nate's fist, still closed around the handle of his knife, connected with his jaw. The man dropped as if he had been struck by lightning, but two of the others struggled to their feet. The fourth still lay on the ground, and Contessa was briefly distracted by the sight of jagged bone protruding through his skin.

The urge to vomit was pushed to the back of her mind as Nate took on one man while the other caught sight of Contessa. Blanching, she fumbled with the catches at her wrists, almost dropping her knives as they sprang free. She tried to settle into her stance as the man approached, and he grinned as they both caught sight of the end of her blade quivering as her hands trembled.

Then the man's head snapped back as Nate leaped on him from behind, wrapping his forearm around the thug's thick neck. Nate squeezed mercilessly until the man went limp against his arms and then lowered him to the ground.

The resulting stillness in the night air was unsettling after the chaos of the fight. Nate's head covering had been ripped off during the fight to reveal his face. He was panting and staring wide eyed at Contessa across the alley scattered with enemies.

Contessa swallowed heavily, trying to ease her pounding heart.

"The others..." she started.

Nate swore.

"We need to meet them at the rendezvous point, I told them to wait for me there." He stepped forward and grabbed Contessa's wrist, tugging gently as if he could sense she was rooted to the spot as her adrenaline faded. "Come on, we have to get out of here. The noise will have garnered unwanted attention."

Contessa let Nate pull her behind him as they darted along the streets of the industrial district. She was still out of breath from her fight and was grateful as Nate motioned her into a building after a few blocks, leading her to the hidden door Contessa recognized as connecting to the network of tunnels. Nate opened the passage to reveal Kristoff, pistols already drawn and ready to shoot, but he waved him off.

"Relax, it's just us," Nate reassured as he pulled Contessa into the passage and closed the door behind him. The space was lit dimly by a lantern held aloft by a Lion Contessa didn't know, and she could just make out Rhosyn trying to quiet and reassure seven harried-looking children.

"Come on," Nate ordered. "It's not far to the den. Let's get these children to safety and then we can talk."

Contessa wearily peeled herself off the door she hadn't even realized she was leaning against and followed the small crew down the passage. It only took a few minutes to reach the entrance to the den, as Contessa supposed she could have expected considering it was also in the industrial district.

As they stepped into the den, they were immediately greeted by the chatter of other excited children, as well as Gregor, waiting with a medical kit in hand in case there had been any injuries. Everybody's attention turned to the new influx of children, and Contessa slumped back against the wall with a sigh. She was feeling oddly light and ridiculously tired at the same time, the adrenaline still in her system causing her heart to thunder even as the world around her seemed bright and fuzzy.

A warm hand on her elbow steadied her.

"Are you alright?" Nate asked as Contessa leaned mindlessly into the strength of his arm. He put his other hand on her other elbow, no doubt sensing her need for support.

"Yes, I'm not injured," she reassured. "I'm just..." She looked around the scene vaguely as if that were an explanation for the chaos of the past half an hour.

Nate nodded and Contessa was once again glad she didn't need to come up with adequate words to express her feelings.

"You probably saved my life you know," he said quietly.

"You would have escaped somehow," Contessa commented, suddenly aware of how intensely Nate was looking at her, his eyes appearing golden in the candlelight.

"Maybe," he acquiesced. "But what you did was still incredibly brave, remarkably resourceful, and so...ridiculously you." Nate's voice was low, but Contessa could still hear him clearly.

"Well, I couldn't just stand by and watch while you got hurt," Contessa responded, her voice equally low. It occurred to her that Nate had gotten very close while they spoke, enough that her breath stirred the lose hairs around his face. He was near enough to kiss. With a jolt of surprise accompanied by a spreading warmth, she realized she would like very much for him to kiss her. His lips were just so close.

He took a sharp breath in, and Contessa knew he could sense the direction of her thoughts, and neither of them moved away. If he could sense what she wanted, then why wasn't he kissing her already? Would he just hurry up and—

Taking matters into her own hands, Contessa leaned forward and pressed her lips to his. He froze for a moment, before his fingers came up to cup her face and he kissed her in return.

His mouth moved slightly asymmetrically, and she could feel the hard ridges of his scar against her upper lip, but all she could think about was how warm and close and solid he was. His fingers tentatively brushed her hairline and Contessa inhaled his scent of sweat and woodsmoke. It drew her in, and she found her hands fisted in his shirt, holding him as close to her as possible. Nate didn't seem to mind, tilting her head back to kiss her more thoroughly, his fingers less tentative as they cupped her head, holding her still as he explored her mouth.

A sudden whoop of joy brought Contessa to the present, and she pulled back sharply, leaving Nate looking stunned. She glanced over his shoulder to find Rhosyn looking at them, practically jumping up and down and clapping her hands.

"Kristoff, Gregor, I told you!" she yelled, grinning.

"About damn time!" Kristoff swaggered up behind Rhosyn and clapped a hand to her shoulder.

"Pay up," Rhosyn demanded, and Kristoff dropped a few coins into her waiting hand.

Nate, coming to himself, closed his eyes, dropped his head to the wall over Contessa's shoulder with a thud and groaned. Contessa couldn't help herself. Maybe it was the adrenaline still fizzing in her bloodstream or the joy of the kiss, but she looked up to the ceiling and laughed.

Chapter Eighteen

The sweat at the nape of Contessa's neck had dried, and she scratched at it where it crusted a few loose locks of her hair to her skin. To be honest, the itching was a welcome distraction from the tense silence Contessa and Nate were sharing, standing at the bottom of the stairs. The giddiness of their earlier kiss had faded on the trip home, and now they both looked down at their shoes, seemingly unsure of where they stood with each other.

"Do you suppose it's too late for me to run myself a bath?" Contessa mused, trying to make conversation. She knew Julia would never complain about helping her at any hour, but it still felt rude to call for a bath in the middle of the night just because she was reluctant to go to bed still crusted in dust.

"I doubt Julia would mind being woken up if it meant she got to hear we had made it home safely," Nate responded.

Contessa nodded and looked down to contemplate the dirt on her boots, still reticent to ring for Julia at this hour.

"If you prefer..." Nate started. "If you prefer, you could use the tub in my chambers. It's much larger and more comfortable than the one in yours."

Contessa's gaze shot up.

"I didn't mean— I'm sorry," he stammered. "That must seem far too forward."

Contessa sighed and reached out, gently grasping Nate's wrist between her fingers. She could feel his pulse hammering even as he swallowed heavily.

"Nate, I would hardly worry about seeming too forward. We've been married for months."

Nate twitched in her grasp, but he didn't pull away.

"You know that's not what I mean," he said.

"I know, but a decadent bath sounds like just what I need right now. Lying on that roof was not kind to me," Contessa explained as she began to tug Nate up the stairs.

He followed her lead before turning the opposite way down the hall from her own room to lead her to the door at the end. Contessa let herself look around his bedroom as she walked, smiling at the slate painted walls and a wide painting of the sea above the bed. A dusty pair of boots lay haphazardly at the foot of the bed, and a black waistcoat draped over the back of the chair, indicating this room at least was more lived in than the rest of the house.

She only had a moment to appreciate it until Nate led her through another door to the bathroom. The color scheme from the bedroom was echoed here with creamy white and blue wallpaper, but Contessa's attention was drawn to the massive cast iron tub dominating the far wall of the room.

"And to think I've been making do with the small bath down the hall while you have a tub big enough to swim in right here," Contessa teased softly.

Nate had the decency to look abashed.

"I will admit that while I haven't given much thought to this house, the bath is one of the few comforts I've indulged in," he explained with a self-conscious shrug. "Nothing quite helps with bruises and aches like a warm soak."

Contessa walked up to the large basin and ran her fingers over the smooth white coating on the interior of the tub, feeling it cool against her hand.

"Well, then I'll have to give it a try."

Nate let out a noise halfway between a cough and clearing his throat behind her.

"I'll just go down the hall and fetch your nightclothes and dressing gown," he said, already beginning to back out of the room. "So you have something to put on when you are finished."

"Wait—" The word leaped from Contessa's mouth before she'd decided what she was going to ask for.

They both froze in place, and it was Contessa's turn to swallow thickly.

"Will you help me take my hair down?" Her voice was soft but clear. "I need to wash it after tonight's excitement."

Nate didn't respond but took a few measured steps forward, and Contessa turned around and closed her eyes. His fingers landed on her scalp gently at first, investigating just how to go about unwinding the braided twist Julia had concocted to keep her hair out of the way. Contessa didn't offer any instruction, just enjoyed the touch of his hands as he began slowly uncovering and removing pins. She let her eyes flutter closed, and her breath left her in a soft sigh. Eventually, the braid uncoiled itself, falling down her back, and Nate ran his fingers through it slowly, almost reverently, to unwind the strands. He continued to stroke her hair past when Contessa was sure the braid was untangled, but Contessa didn't say a word. She was sure her hair was plastered to her head oddly, with all sorts of strange bends and twists from its confinement, but Nate seemed fascinated by it, nonetheless.

After far too short a time, Nate removed his fingers and stepped back.

"There." His voice was bordering on hoarse. "You should be able to wash it now."

He made to back out of the room once more, and for the second time this evening, Contessa found herself saying, "Wait."

She licked her lips as Nate looked at her expectantly.

"Stay," she asked again. "It doesn't have to be— Just...stay."

Contessa wasn't sure what feelings Nate might have been sensing from her, but apparently, they convinced him. He hesitated for only a moment before nodding.

Contessa turned back to the tub and began fiddling with the knobs, testing the temperature until the water ran hot enough it would soothe her muscles. Without turning around, she stood and began methodically removing her shirt. Layer by layer, her clothing fell to the floor with soft swishes. When she moved to unlace her pants, Contessa chanced a glance over her shoulder to find Nate staring determinedly at his feet. The smallest smile curled her lips as she returned to undressing. By the time she was finished, the water in the tub had reached a level she was sure would cover her, and she stepped in, sinking into the warmth with a sigh.

She fanned her hair over the edge of the tub, sliding all the way down to her neck in the water, finding her toes still didn't reach the far end of the tub. Contessa giggled and wiggled her feet, causing little ripples to slosh against the side.

"You weren't exaggerating about how large this tub is. It almost feels like a waste to fill this thing up just to bathe somebody of my stature," she commented.

At this, Nate glanced up, finding her almost completely

submerged in the water. He took one step forward, as if he didn't even realize he was doing it.

Contessa wet her lips one more time before continuing.

"You know, this tub is big enough for both of us." Her voice was steady even as her heart pounded. "No doubt you could use a bath, too, after today's scuffle."

Nate was so still Contessa was sure he wasn't even breathing.

"Connie," was the only word he managed in reply.

"Nate," she echoed, meeting his eyes.

His fingers creeped up to his neck, untying his cravat slow enough to give Contessa time to change her mind if she wished. Instead, she busied herself with a bar of soap she located on the side of the tub, beginning to clean herself. She heard the soft rustle of Nate removing his clothes, but she didn't look up, his self-consciousness seemingly mitigated by having her otherwise engaged.

She jumped when she heard a clang, making the water slosh over the side of the tub. Glancing up, she saw Nate looking sheepish as he placed another knife on the tile more carefully. He unstrapped several more from his upper arms. When he reached under his shirt to pull out two more knives, a laugh bubbled up in Contessa's throat. The sound echoed in the tiled room, chasing away any awkwardness. Nate chuckled, too, as he divested himself of the rest of his weapons and one small pistol tucked into the back of his pants.

When he was unclothed, Nate stepped towards the tub, hesitating at the edge. Contessa scooted forward, continuing to clean herself, giving Nate room to step into the water behind her. The only noise in the room was the water sloshing against the sides of the tub as Nate lowered himself down behind her. Without saying a word, Contessa shifted back so that Nate completely surrounded her.

He hissed when her back touched his chest, and his fingers gripped the edge of the tub so hard his knuckles turned white.

"It's all right, Nate," she soothed, putting one hand over his and relaxing his grip.

"Connie, you know you don't have to..." he started, trailing off as she brushed her fingertips over his knuckles.

"I know," she said. Contessa felt Nate's breath on the crown of her head, and the gentle press of what might have been lips. "Do you want to help me wash my hair?"

She offered him the bar of soap over her shoulder, and he plucked it from her fingers. She sighed as he used his cupped hands to pour water over her scalp. He went about washing her hair as methodically as he had unbraided it, and Contessa let herself drift in the sensation of warm water and firm fingers. She unconsciously pressed back into his chest, enjoying the slick heat of his torso against her and the way his arms surrounded her. The soap wasn't her usual soft and floral variety, but it smelled like Nate's skin had when he'd held her earlier, and that was enough.

When Contessa's hair was fully rinsed, she reached back to take the soap from him before announcing, "Your turn."

She maneuvered around to face him, such a dramatic move making water slosh over the sides and onto the floor, but neither of them was paying much attention to that. Being able to see each other's faces renewed the tension in the room as she began to work the soap through Nate's hair. He kept his eyes closed, and Contessa took the opportunity to examine him—the way the water droplets trailed across his lips and down his chest. She watched in fascination how the muscles of his abdomen tensed when she touched him, and her mouth went dry when her gaze drifted down past his waist to see what was partially obscured by soapy water.

Once Nate's hair was clean, Contessa dropped the soap and let her fingers trail from his hairline, down to his face, tracing her thumbs over his cheekbones. She leaned in close enough she knew he could feel her breath.

His hand shot out of the water and grabbed one of her wrists, halting her.

"Tell me you want this," he said hoarsely, his eyes snapping open.

Contessa blinked.

"I know you can feel how much I want this," she whispered, but he just shook his head.

"I need to hear you say it." His serious gaze allowed no room for argument. "Connie, I married you against your will. If I laid a hand on you without hearing you say in the clearest of terms that you wanted it, it would make me the monster that everybody already says I am."

Contessa nodded and began stroking her thumbs across his cheekbones once more.

"Nate, I've spent my whole life doing things because it was what other people told me I should want. But being around you has shown me how to decide how the world is for myself. You have allowed me to think about my own desires. And you might be the first thing I've let myself want, not because anybody else says I should, but because I want you. I want you more than anything."

Nate blinked at Contessa once, twice, then surged forward to kiss her for the second time that night.

Nate's lips traced over hers with enthusiasm. When he shifted to try to angle their lips more firmly together, his nose bumped hers, and there was a hiss of pain and a few giggles about how it was still healing. Then they were kissing again, and it was warm and slick and utterly perfect.

When Nate stood, he picked Contessa up and out of the tub before she had a chance to move, causing a veritable tidal wave of water to spill over the bathroom floor. Contessa didn't have time to assess the damage however, as her mouth became otherwise occupied with tracing the hollow of Nate's throat. She reveled in the noise he made when her teeth grazed his collarbone and repeated the motion just to hear it again.

Nate finally laid Contessa back on his bed, pausing for a moment as he looked down at her. Droplets of water still clung to their skin and hair, but Contessa was too consumed with the way Nate gazed at her to care. She had thought she might be shy, but instead, she basked in the fire glimmering in Nate's eyes, her skin burning just as hot. Then Nate was on her again, his fingers mapping every inch of her skin even as she tried to touch as much of him as she could in return.

He pulled back to look her in the eyes as his hands drifted lower, and a soft noise caught in her throat as his fingers trailed through the damp curls between her legs. He smiled as he found a spot that made Contessa squirm, and when she began making soft, desperate noises, he caught them in his own mouth, quieting her with kisses.

When Contessa thought she couldn't take it anymore and that she would dissolve into a puddle of joy and sensation, she retaliated. Her own hand brushed down Nate's stomach, through the trail of hair from his navel to grasp him. It was his turn to make a broken noise as his fingers stuttered where they worked between her legs.

"Now Nate," Contessa murmured into his neck. "Please."

Not being one to deny her, Nate propped himself on his elbows over Contessa, one hand cupping her cheek as he finally slid home. Tears pricked at the corner of Contessa's eyes at the sheer rightness of it—of being with somebody she wanted so desperately, even before she admitted it to herself. Of him being hers, and her being his.

Nate shuddered over her as her feelings washed over him, and he began to move. He was heartbreakingly gentle, stroking Contessa's face, her hip, her hair, until he found a spot that made Contessa squirm anew. As Nate's movement grew more sure, Contessa was delighted to find he made love the way he fought—powerful and raw around the edges in a way that did nothing to detract from his grace. Soon Contessa felt as if she might fly into a million pieces, bucking beneath Nate as she chased the feeling of tightness in her belly. She knew he could sense her desperation as he let out a strangled moan, ending in her name.

"*Connie...*"

It was all it took for her to tumble over the edge, pulling Nate with her with the intensity of her pleasure. It was long moments before Contessa came back to herself, cracking her eyes open to find Nate looking at her with pure adoration, undercut with a current of something more primal. Finding her looking, he smiled and rolled to his side, tucking her into his chest. Then it was just the two of them, with only the quiet night serving as a witness to their delighted explorations, contented sighs, and whispered promises.

♟♞♜♝♛♛

The sun filtering red through Contessa's eyelids woke her, and she bit back a groan at how tired she felt, despite her habitual dawn awakenings. Her eyes fluttered open to find a pair of squinted hazel eyes reflecting the same sentiment. Still, she offered a smile, suddenly shy at the new experience of waking up next to somebody else. Nate reached up and traced her cheek with his fingertips in response, featherlight, as if he were unsure if he was still allowed to touch her now that the sun had risen.

Paradoxically emboldened by his hesitance, Contessa nuzzled into his hand and pressed a soft kiss to his palm.

"You're still here," Nate observed.

"Oh," Contessa said, wondering if she'd misread the situation.

Now that she thought about it, she hadn't asked Nate if she could sleep in his bed. "I can go back to my room. Julia will probably be missing me—"

Nate effectively silenced her by throwing an arm over her waist and pulling her close.

"Don't go back," he reinforced. "You hate that room anyway."

"This one is more to my liking," Contessa pulled back from his chest so she could speak clearly. "No gaudy flowers, and a much more pleasing color palette." Contessa pushed on Nate's shoulder so he laid on his back and she rolled on top of him, propping up on her elbows so she could get a good look at him in the morning light. "Not to mention that you're here, and it turns out you are much better company than I ever could have hoped for."

Nate nodded and they fell silent, listening to the sounds of the city waking up as Contessa attempted to push strands of hair out of Nate's face only for them to stick out in every conceivable direction.

"Are you sure you're fine with my being here?" Contessa eventually whispered, focusing on the strand of hair she was twisting between her fingers instead of meeting Nate's eyes. "I know you can tell how I feel about you, but I know I'm not the only one of us that didn't exactly marry for love. I don't want to assume too much."

Nate grabbed the hand that toyed with his hair, stilling it, before bringing it to lay flat on his chest. His heart beat against her palm.

"Despite my ability to sense feelings, or maybe in part because of it, I've never been skilled at expressing my own emotions," Nate started. "I guess it's hard to put words to what I already intuitively know about other people. But I can say confidently that I want you here, actually being my wife and not just putting on a show of it.

"For so much of my life, I've felt damaged. I've been trying to tamp down my anger by helping others like me, but I still felt like shattered glass. Like if I let somebody try to pick up the pieces, they would cut their fingers on my jagged edges. But then we were getting married, and you looked at me, so lovely and so full of rage that you nearly knocked me off my feet. It was the first time I realized that maybe—maybe sharp things could be beautiful too."

Contessa blinked rapidly. Using the hand that wasn't pressed to Nate's chest, she reached up and traced the lines on the scarred side of his face. He shuddered slightly but didn't close his eyes.

"You are beautiful you know," Contessa admitted, as she let her fingers drag to Nate's eyelid, rough and permanently squinted. "Can you feel this?"

"No," Nate whispered. "Sometimes I can feel a light prickling, and occasionally, it burns, but most of the time...nothing."

Contessa craned her neck up and kissed the raised corner of his mouth, feeling its now familiar roughness against hers. She felt as if she should be sad her husband was once a broken boy who had suffered so much, but nothing could quell the happiness that he was here now, in her arms where she could make sure he knew he was loved.

In response, Nate wrapped his arms around her waist and buried his face in her hair.

"I'm glad you don't pity me," he said into the top of her head. "I don't need it when I have a beautiful wife, a worthy cause, and close friends."

Contessa smiled into his shoulder, and they lay in silence for a moment before Contessa felt a deep groan rip from Nate's chest.

"Speaking of close friends, I just remembered that Kristoff said he would be coming for breakfast. We have some things to discuss after last night's adventures."

Contessa attempted to sit up, saying, "Well, I better go get dressed. I can hardly entertain company as naked as the day I was born."

Nate hindered her efforts at escape with his firm grip on her waist. "We can let him wait a little bit. He's probably just flirting with Gregor, seeing if he can distract him into burning the bacon."

"Be that as it may," Contessa giggled, finally worming her way out of Nate's grasp, "I happen to want bacon this morning, and I would be quite put out if it did end up burned."

Nate gave a long-suffering sigh and reached over to ring for Julia, who bustled in mere moments later with today's dress in her arms. She didn't seem remotely surprised to find Contessa naked in Nate's bed. If she had any significant thoughts on the matter, she limited them to a cheerful comment about how she would have to teach Nate how to properly brush hair if Contessa didn't want to wake up with it so dreadfully out of sorts.

Chapter Nineteen

The bacon wasn't burned, but instead perfectly chewy, the way Contessa preferred it. She eyed the heaping plate of meat as she and Nate rounded the corner to the dining room, finding herself hungry from the eventful night behind her.

She was distracted from the mouthwatering smell of bacon by Kristoff jumping out of his seat and rounding the table to grab her in an embrace so tight it lifted her off her feet.

Kristoff ignored her undignified squeak, instead proclaiming, "At last the lovesick couple has come to their senses and Rhosyn, Gregor, and I can stop trying to discreetly hint that perhaps your being married isn't such a bad thing."

Contessa immediately tried to put her dress to rights upon being set down, hiding the heat on her cheeks.

"You are making a lot of assumptions considering you only saw us kiss last night," Nate grumbled with no real venom as he made his way to his seat.

"Well, I've never known you to be in bed past dawn, so there must be some explanation for you making your guest wait on your company," Kristoff retorted.

"I would apologize for the lack of courtesy, but it doesn't seem to have stopped you from enjoying your breakfast," Contessa remarked as she slid into her seat, nodding to the half-eaten plate of food already sitting in front of Kristoff's seat.

Nate huffed through his nose and passed Contessa the porridge.

"You know I can never resist Gregor's...cooking," Kristoff defended with a twinkle in his eye. As if on cue, the man in question rounded the corner carrying a pot of tea, with a few strands of his normally smooth hair notably out of place.

"Alright, we understand," Nate said as he scooped a hefty amount of marmalade onto his toast. "We're all hopelessly improper. Can we move past that and focus on what it is you are here to discuss?"

Kristoff clapped a hand to his chest in mock offense. "Can I not just be here to enjoy the company of my closest friends?"

"You could be," Contessa remarked, "but considering we were attacked last night and have yet to discuss it, that seems unlikely."

Kristoff's expression grew serious, but he pointed a finger at Contessa gravely. "That is indeed something we need to talk about, but don't think you are going to distract me from my celebratory mood forever."

"It was the Rattlesnakes," Nate jumped in without prelude. There was a long silence only broken by the clatter of Contessa's spoon as she set it down.

"How can you be sure?" Contessa asked.

"I saw their gang tattoos on their forearms."

Contessa furrowed her brows. "Well, that is convenient. It seems counterintuitive to ink your allegiance on your skin for everybody to see when you're in an industry that values secrecy."

"It is," Kristoff cut in with a wave of his fork. "That is why the Lions don't do it. I actually do have a Lion tattoo, though, but it is in a place I don't usually display to just anybody."

"Kristoff, focus," Nate cut in. "We need to figure out how they knew where and when to ambush us."

"Not to mention why," Kristoff offered. "They've tried to stop our operations from expanding into their territory before, but they've never tried to hit us on a liberation mission. It doesn't seem like Caleb would want to copy our recruiting tactics, either. He doesn't have the disposition to deal with children."

"They didn't seem too happy with the Lions the last time we encountered them," Contessa commented as she forked some bacon onto her plate. "At this point, they might be hitting us wherever they can to send a message."

"If they knew we would be there, they would attack us anywhere they could at this point," Nate said. "Which brings us back to the question of how they knew where we would be in the first place."

"Where did you get the tip on this warehouse?" Contessa asked.

"I eavesdropped on the owner of the business at the Standard Club," Nate said with a shrug. "He said he had just opened a new factory in the lower city and was having trouble hiring security with the current political climate. It made me think it would be a prime target."

"Is it possible Caleb has somebody who would be running in these same circles that could have heard this same information?" Contessa ventured.

Kristoff shook his head. "I doubt it. Caleb doesn't play the long game like that, but he would not be above cutting a deal with somebody powerful."

Contessa stirred her porridge as her mind skipped through the possibilities.

"You know, we never did figure out what gang was cooperating with Chief Cook at the executions," Kristoff pointed out. "He certainly wants us gone and already knows about our...recruiting practices."

Contessa opened and closed her mouth, then turned her attention back to her porridge. She felt naïve now for having lain the information about Nate stealing the children away from the factories at her father's feet, although her intentions had been good at the time.

Nate reached out and laid a hand on her knee, palm up, under the table. Contessa set her own hand in it and spoke.

"Be that as it may, I have a hard time believing the Rattlesnakes and my father could maintain any sort of alliance. They're the second most hated of the gangs in London, and the feeling seems to go both ways. I mean Caleb..." Contessa swallowed. "Caleb may have killed my mother."

"Your father likely still thinks it was me, though," Nate said, running his free hand through his hair. "Do you think if you talked to him, you could convince him otherwise?"

Contessa licked her lips and thought about how hard her father had grabbed her wrist the last time she'd seen him. She envisioned him calling her a cowering damsel.

She shook her head.

"I don't think he would trust me at all, not after I foiled his plan for framing you for the scene at the execution. He is angry beyond reason."

"Well, it was a thought," Kristoff sighed. "I suppose suspicion won't get us very far anyway. I'll have some men try and tail Caleb's lieutenants and see if they can spot any meetings with potential informants. Although I still have to figure out who replaced Two-faced Thomas after his unfortunate incident."

Contessa tried not to picture how she'd shoved Thomas's limp body out of the driver's seat of the carriage.

"For now," Kristoff continued, "we have slightly more important matters to attend to. I should go see the children we liberated last night and welcome them to the Lions, and I think you two have things you'd rather be doing."

Contessa thought about saying that of course they would be going with Kristoff to see the children, but she shut her mouth when she saw how Nate was looking at her. He obviously had plans for them upstairs, and she was of no mind to object.

♟♜♖♞♛♟

Contessa shivered pleasantly as Nate traced nonsensical patterns over her back with calloused fingertips. She was lying on her stomach, chin propped on overlapping hands, contemplating the painting over the bed with no real focus. For a rare moment, she let her consciousness drift in the comfort of the solid presence of Nate, propped up on one elbow beside her, and the warmth of the afternoon sun drifting through the window.

"It seems decadent to be in bed in the middle of the afternoon," Contessa observed, her eyelids fluttering as Nate's fingers walked up and down her spine.

"Well, we don't usually live decadent lives, so I think we've earned an exception."

Contessa hummed in agreement and fell back into a comfortable silence, letting her eyes drift open again to land on the painting of the sea once more.

"I love the ocean," she commented with no real intent, reveling in the opportunity to talk for no other reason than the pleasure of each other's company.

"I've never been," Nate responded. "Although, the painting is nice."

Contessa flopped onto her back to look at Nate, squinting.

"You've never seen the ocean? It's not even a day's travel from here."

The sheets rustled as Nate shrugged. The movement pushed the blankets dangerously low on his hips, and Contessa let her eyes wander.

"I've never left the city really. There wasn't a good reason and always so much to do."

Contessa cocked her head.

"To be fair," she conceded, "I haven't been since I was a child. My mother used to take me for a few days every summer. My father never saw much point in it."

Nate was silent for a few moments, each absorbed in their own thoughts as the faint sound of a song over crashing waves drifted through Contessa's memories.

"We should go," Nate said abruptly.

"Go to the beach?" Contessa echoed as she was pulled back out of her contemplations.

"Yes. We never did go on a honeymoon you know. It would be a good chance to get to know each other better."

Contessa rolled onto her side to face Nate, resting a hand on his ribs and offering a smile.

"We already know the important things about each other," she pointed out.

"True." Nate reached up a hand to trail his fingers through Contessa's hair, which was now so hopelessly tangled that Julia would surely spend an hour getting it back in line. "I know you're brave and intelligent and wonderful. But I want to know all of the unimportant things too." Nate leaned in as he spoke, pressing a kiss to her cheekbone.

"I want to know your favorite season..."

He kissed her nose.

"What kind of soup you prefer when you're ill..."

The corner of her mouth.

"If you're secretly ticklish..."

Contessa felt herself grinning and acquiesced, nipping at Nate's own smiling lips.

"Well, when you explain it that way. When were you planning this trip?"

"Next week?"

Contessa blinked.

"That's certainly quick."

Nate shrugged again. "I've found that when I put the important things off, they never get done. Anything worth doing is worth doing now."

The bubble of lightness that had been forming in Contessa's chest for the past weeks grew, the new freedom making her positively effervescent. A feeling that she finally had a modicum of control over where she went and what she did—that she wasn't just a pawn in somebody else's game. Contessa could choose to go away with her husband next week, without having to justify herself to her father, to anybody.

"Next week it is."

Chapter Twenty

Contessa placed her queen on the chess board with a clink and smiled despite herself. Across the table, Nate growled at losing once again, but there was no menace to it. Contessa could see the amusement sparkling in his eyes.

"That was even quicker than usual," he commented, draining the last of his whiskey and wiping his mouth with the back of his hand.

They had taken to playing again each night, but the games were more enjoyable without thinly veiled threats being lobbed at each other. The games went slower now that they actually conversed, and Nate had managed to distract Contessa almost to the point of victory a few times, but she always scraped through in the end.

"Well, I decided not to toy with you tonight, since we should be getting to bed early. We're planning to leave for the cottage early tomorrow."

Contessa smiled at the thought of the cottage by the sea Nate had described. He had managed to persuade an acquaintance into letting them use his summer home for a few days, and Contessa pointedly didn't ask how Nate had managed this.

"Toy with me?" Nate demanded with false belligerence, "I don't let you toy with me."

Contessa stood, looking down and smoothing her skirts to hide the smile on her face as she replied.

"You can keep telling yourself that if that's what it takes for you to sleep at night."

Contessa only made it a few steps before there was a quick rustle behind her and Nate grabbed her by the waist and hoisted her into the air. Contessa let out an indignant squawk.

"Oh, I think you're the one who's not going to be sleeping tonight," Nate growled in a way that made Contessa's insides warm. He tried to toss her over his shoulder, but as he loosened his grasp to turn her around, Contessa managed to slip out of his grip using a trick Rhosyn had taught her.

"Using my own moves against me now, are we?" Nate asked, the good side of his mouth twisting up and giving away how pleased he was as he advanced on her. Contessa backed up against the railing of the stairs, offering her own coy smile.

She didn't resist as Nate caged her in with his hands resting on either side of the banister, leaning down to kiss one ear before playfully biting at it in a way that made Contessa yelp in surprise, even as her own hands flew up to grip his collar.

This had become part of their routine, too, and while Contessa thought it might be an adjustment to live like this after so long in her own world of relative isolation, she found she didn't miss going to bed alone in the rose room one bit.

Contessa was distracted from her fingers' work undoing Nate's necktie by an unmistakable clatter from down the hall. Nate obviously heard it, too, stilling immediately, shoulders hunched around Contessa to shield her from the hall.

"Nate!"

A familiar voice rang through the house, following the sound of pounding footsteps. Hearing Kristoff might have been reassuring if not for the uncharacteristic panic rising in his voice.

"Nate! Down by the port...the mob..." Kristoff seemed as if he was trying to start three sentences at the same time and failing at all of them as he skidded to a halt in front of Nate.

"A mob? What mob?" Nate's voice was steady but held none of the levity of just a few moments before.

"People are rioting in the lower city. Demanding that Prince Byron be put on the throne," Kristoff managed between pants, leaning to rest his hands on his knees. "The king—he died."

"Where was the mob at?"

"They were on Bennet's Hill headed down towards the docks, which—"

"Will lead them past the den." Nate swore colorfully, two strides already taking him halfway down the hall towards his study. Contessa and Kristoff rushed to follow, and she felt as if she were a dinghy foundering in the ginormous wake of Nate's frigate as he barked over his shoulder.

"Kristoff, take a horse and go to all the safehouses in the lower city. Warn everybody and make sure everyone is accounted for. Gregor can help too. I'll head to the den to help Rhosyn. I can bring everybody back here if worst comes to worst."

"Once everybody is warned, I'll bring help," Kristoff agreed before turning down the hall to the kitchen, presumably to find Gregor.

Nate had already braced his shoulder against his desk and was pushing it out from over the trap door when Contessa rushed to help.

"Hopefully, the children will be alright, but be ready for chaos when I get back if I need to get them out of there," Nate grunted as the desk finally gave way.

"Of course, I'll be ready for chaos, I'll be bringing the children back with you," Contessa pointed out, already working on pulling the trapdoor open.

There was a beat before Nate bent down to help her, and Contessa looked up at him to find him blinking and still for the first time since Kristoff had barreled into their home.

"You're coming with?"

"Why wouldn't I?"

There was only half a second pause before Nate was bending down to push the trapdoor the remainder of the way open.

"You have your knives on you?"

Contessa tilted her wrist, the cuff of her dress falling back to reveal the catch of her hidden sheathe.

"You've succeeded in teaching me a few things at least."

Nate gave a sharp nod before levering himself down into the tunnel, not bothering to climb down the ladder. Contessa peered over the edge, hearing the slap of Nate's boots hitting the stone floor. He rose from the crouch he'd landed in and reached up both arms, indicating for Contessa to jump down. She slid off the edge, although not nearly as gracefully as he had. She was surprised she didn't knock the wind out of Nate when he caught her, but there was just a sharp exhale before she was placed on her feet and then pulled down the now familiar passage in the direction of the den.

As they traversed the passage at breakneck speed, a prickling began creeping up the back of Contessa's neck that had nothing to do with the sweat breaking out at her hairline and under her arms. The heat creeped into her ears and transformed into a ringing, getting louder and louder with each passing step. She didn't need to say anything to be able to tell that Nate felt the danger rising in her senses. It was apparent he knew by the way his shoulders drew further and further up towards his ears as the ringing grew to a screaming in Contessa's skull.

By the time they reached the hidden entrance to the Den, Contessa was about to vibrate out of her skin with the force of the sensation. The roaring was no longer just in her head, but coming through the door, as well. Nate shouldered it open forcefully and swore loudly when a wave of heat hit them. Contessa caught a brief glimpse of the far wall drenched in fire, the flames beginning to lick across the bunk room before Nate's hand yanked on her shoulder. She was wrenched down to her knees where the air was clearer with a suddenness that shook her teeth. There was no time to recover before she began to crawl, following Nate into the blaze. He was crouched low, prowling through the wreckage. He called out for anybody in the warehouse but got no answer. He led them through the blaze to the front door, Contessa hot on his trail even as her dress snagged and ripped. Splinters dug into her knees as she crawled across the floor. Despite the suffocating heat of the inferno, it wasn't hard to pick a path to the already wide-open front door as the fire had yet to touch almost half of the building.

Contessa and Nate made it out the door into the marginally cooler air of the night, Contessa coughing the smoke from her lungs. The street was empty, but the brightness of the glow indicated that more than one building was suffering the same fate as the den. Shouting could be heard loud enough that the heart of the riot couldn't have been more than a few streets away.

Nate reached back to help Contessa to her feet and farther from the burning building. She waved him off, pointing into the street, trying to speak but not getting the words out around the hacking that was making her eyes water.

Nate's gaze traced to where she was pointing, to a crumpled figure on the cobblestones. In the shimmering light from the blaze, Contessa could just make out a flash of red hair spilled across the pavement. Nate was at Rhosyn's side in a flash, rolling her gently onto her back. Contessa's heart started again where it had stilled in her chest as the woman groaned in response.

"Nate, Nate..." Rhosyn gasped. The one eye Rhosyn had managed to open all the way was darting around in panic, the other limited to a squint by swelling and a fresh bruise blooming over her cheekbone.

"Rhos, what happened? Where are the children?"

"They took them, Nate. The fire started and I was trying to get everybody out and they just appeared," Rhosyn babbled, her breath coming in quick pants. "I tried, but there were too many of them, and they had the little ones. I couldn't..."

Rhosyn broke off in a choked gasp of pain and distress, a shudder wracking her body in a suppressed sob. Contessa reached to take her hand and found Rhosyn's brass knuckles still wrapped around her fingers. Blood smeared itself on Contessa's wrist as she eased them out of the girl's hand so she could hold it properly.

"Nate, I tried..." Rhosyn gasped out, her good eye squeezing shut, the faint glimmer of tears clinging to her lashes.

Contessa rubbed her thumb over Rhosyn's knuckles to soothe her.

"Who was it, Rhosyn? Who took them?" Contessa tried to ask gently but her voice came out rough after the smoke and the coughing. She paused as Nate shifted beside her, reaching over Rhosyn to grab a scrap of paper lying on the ground at her side.

"Men. Thugs. It all happened so fast—" Rhosyn struggled to

answer but trailed off when she was interrupted by a growl low in Nate's throat.

"You were set up. Those bastards set the fire on purpose." The loose piece of paper trembled in Nate's hand, starting to crumple in his white-knuckled grip. Peering over Nate's shoulder, Contessa could just make out a short line of messy script and a crude drawing of a rattlesnake.

"We're going to get them back, Rhos." Nate's voice was as hard as stone. "We'll show them what it's like to fight the Lions when it's not an ambush, four on one."

"Actually, it was five on one." Rhosyn's hand still shook in Contessa's, but she managed a twitch of the corner of her mouth. "Stop trying to short me the credit I deserve."

Nate laid a hand on Rhosyn's shoulder.

"Kristoff and Gregor will be here soon. Then we can get you patched up so you can show them why they should fear you in a fair fight."

With Nate supporting her shoulders, Rhosyn managed to make it to a sitting position, hiding her wince admirably. Contessa looked over her shoulder in the direction of the shouting masses where more trails of smoke were rising, making the outline of the moon hazy and dim in the night sky.

"Do you think you can walk?" Contessa asked, turning back to Rhosyn. "I think we should try to move away from all these fires."

Indeed, the air was growing thicker with smoke by the minute, and Contessa's eyes were starting to burn and water.

Rhosyn nodded.

"My legs are fine. They mostly just did a number on my face and one side."

Contessa and Nate each took an arm and levered the girl upright. She did seem steady on her feet for somebody that had been nearly unconscious a few minutes ago, although she was hunched to one side, instinctively guarding her flank as Nate helped her stagger down the street. A clatter of hooves interrupted them as they made it to the end of the block. Gregor and Kristoff's horses skidded to a halt in front of them.

"We got here as fast as we could—" Kristoff started.

"We were too late," Nate said. Kristoff and Gregor looked like they were about to barrage them with questions, but Nate stopped them, holding up the hand that wasn't wrapped under Rhosyn's shoulders.

"Rhos is hurt, and that's what we need to worry about right now. Get her home and fix her up. We'll need everybody in fighting shape soon enough."

Kristoff scrambled down off his horse to help Nate lift Rhosyn up.

"Connie, you go with Gregor. The horses can't take all of us, so I'll meet you back at the house."

In a flurry of movement, Contessa found herself perched in front of Gregor on a horse, her position mirroring Rhosyn's with Kristoff. Contessa had just a moment to look back at Nate standing in the street before Gregor kicked their horse into a trot. The light of the fires behind him silhouetted his frame, and for just a moment, his eye's caught the light just right, glinting gold in his hard face. As they pulled around the corner and out of sight, Contessa thought there was still a reason her husband was called the Beast, and the Rattlesnakes were about to find that out.

While not usually uncomfortable with silence, the current quiet hung thick and heavy in Contessa's head, making her want to pace back and forth or pick at her fingernails—maybe even scream in frustration. Instead, she contented herself with squeezing her fists so tight her nails dug into her palms.

Across the room, Kristoff seemed to be faring similarly. His elbows were propped on his knees, and his head was in his hands. His face was obscured, but Contessa was sure his expression looked as lost as she felt.

The only noise came from the sharp intakes of breath coming from Rhosyn as Gregor prodded her bruised side, checking for broken ribs. It seemed she'd been right about most of the damage being restricted to her face. In the brighter light, it looked even worse. Dried blood from a split lip decorated her chin, and a bruise across her hairline joined her black eye.

The noise of the front door opening broke everybody from their reverie. Contessa recognized Nate's heavy footsteps coming down the hall, and she sprang to her feet, her need to move finally breaking free. She met him in the doorway to the sitting room, freezing, unsure of her intentions. There was a wildness in his eyes Contessa didn't see often, and the smell of smoke still clung to him. Contessa didn't know whether to embrace him or step away, but Nate made her choice for her. His hand cupped the back of her neck, and he bent his head to press his forehead to hers for a moment, inhaling deeply. Contessa closed her eyes, feeling his breath on her face, grateful at least to know he was safe and fighting. After a moment that felt far too short, Nate straightened and stepped around her into the sitting room.

"It was Caleb," he said without preamble, tossing the scrap of paper from the street onto the low table in the middle of the room. Kristoff jumped to his feet and snatched it up, only looking over it briefly before swearing and throwing it back down. Curious, Contessa stepped forward to see what it said.

Give up the Beast if you ever want to see the brats again.

Below was an address and the symbol of a snake.

"I'll go at first light," Nate declared, slumping heavily into a chair and smearing soot all over the upholstery in the process. At least it wasn't blood this time.

"You can't actually be planning on giving yourself up to Caleb," Kristoff protested.

Nate huffed in flat amusement.

"Of course, I'm not, but I have to at least pretend to get the children back," he pointed out.

"That's not exactly going to catch Caleb off guard," Rhosyn chimed in. "He'll expect you to pull a knife on him as soon as the rascals are safe."

"That doesn't mean I'm not going to do it," Nate pointed out. "We're both expecting a betrayal. There's no way around that in a hostage situation."

"You have a point," Kristoff conceded, "but I'm coming too."

"I know," Nate leaned his head against the back of his chair with a thump. "We need to take Caleb out. I've been trying to avoid an all—out war with him, but if he's going to resort to using actual children as pawns, then he needs to be stopped. Honestly, we can probably fight our way out of there even if they are expecting it."

Contessa slapped the note she was still holding down on the table in front of her, causing everybody in the room to jump.

"Probably isn't good enough," she snapped. "You think I win every game of chess I play by making moves that will *probably* work?"

"Connie," Nate's voice softened, "we don't really have a choice.

Caleb is going to expect a fight no matter what, and what are our other options? We can't do nothing, and we can't give up."

"In chess, the best way to lure somebody's tile into a trap is by making them think they're escaping a different trap. Caleb won't suspect a betrayal if he thinks he's already succeeded in thwarting your plans for fighting back."

Kristoff let out a low whistle. "Where have you been while we've been planning strategies all these years? Your deception has *layers*."

"Do you really think we could trick Caleb like that?" Rhosyn asked.

"If anybody can sense that we've tricked him, it'll be Nate," Contessa pointed out.

Nate was beginning to nod along, leaning forward in his chair.

"We can lull him into a false sense of victory," Nate agreed. "Really make him think we've been beaten. And we have one thing up his sleeve that he will never see coming."

Chapter Twenty-One

Contessa looked between the spikes clutched in her sweaty hands and the tree before her with trepidation. She'd been so confident in this plan, keeping her out of any fighting as much as possible, playing to her strengths. Now, though, standing face to face with her tasks, Contessa mused that she perhaps had underestimated the difficulty of what she needed to do.

Forcing her uncharacteristically dry throat to swallow, Contessa hefted the spikes in her hands, feeling their solid weight and finding it comforting as she stepped up to the tree trunk in front of her. It was lucky that there was such a tree just outside of the fence surrounding Caleb's house in the middle city. Maybe it was hubris that led Caleb to not trim the branches that brushed up against a second story window, springy but still sturdy enough to hold the weight of someone as slight as Contessa. Or maybe he was expecting her.

Brushing those thoughts away, Contessa reached up to dig the spikes into the tree above her head before using her toes to scrabble for purchase along the rough bark. She would only need to pull herself up a few feet using the spikes before she could reach the lower branches. A better climber wouldn't have needed spikes at all, but Contessa wasn't about to turn down any possible advantage. It wasn't long before Contessa was able to loop her arm around the lowest branch and haul herself up, although she was already panting from the short exertion. She cursed the balmy night as she swung her foot onto the lowest branch and stood on it, balancing herself with a hand on the tree trunk and mapping out her path towards the second-story window of the house that Caleb used as a front for higher society Rattlesnake business. Contessa's heart pounded against her sternum as she edged herself along the branch, and she tried to tell herself this wasn't any different than when she would climb trees by the seaside cottage as a child, while her mother kept watch from below. That felt impossibly long ago.

Now, Contessa was straddling a higher branch and edging closer to her anticipated point of entry. As slow as she tried to move, the rustling of leaves she caused seemed deafening. Still, a sudden noise from the front of the house told her Caleb's men would be distracted right now.

Unable to resist, Contessa peeked over the fence towards the street, catching the barest glimpse of Nate's figure approaching the house, trailed by two smaller figures she knew to be Rhosyn and Gregor. She wished just for a moment that he would look up at the tree he would know she was climbing, but he knew better than that. Contessa watched him disappear around the corner to where the front door was, hearing voices she couldn't make out. She knew they would search him for weapons, surely be gloating and taunting him, but she tried not to think about it. Instead, she thought about the nervous kiss she'd pressed to his lips, hurried with an uncoordinated bump of their noses as she wished him luck and asked for some of her own in return. She owed him a better kiss, and they both had to succeed in their parts of the plan if she was going to deliver it.

Contessa remained perched in her tree, crouched low among the leaves, as the noises at the front door faded. Her legs trembled as she held herself tightly to the branch below her, but she knew her timing had to be perfect. Contessa lost her sense of time as she tried to remain still and inconspicuous, but eventually, the sound of more activity from the front of the house drifted through the warm evening air. The indistinguishable chattering of children's voices made a knot release in Contessa's chest, and she spotted a small herd of figures, shepherded along by Rhosyn and Gregor, set off down the street. Even though Kristoff and Nate had assured her over and over that Caleb would have no use for a herd of children and he only wanted Nate, Contessa had worried he wouldn't let them go and that the poor little ones would be harmed, and coordinating this ridiculous operation would be for nothing.

Rhosyn's bright red hair disappeared at the end of the street, and Contessa breathed a sigh of relief, even as she wished Rhosyn were with her. Nate had been right that Rhosyn was too recognizable, and the Rattlesnakes would be suspicious if she weren't accounted for, but Contessa craved the comfort of somebody more experienced at her side.

However, the other more experienced member of their team was currently slinking through the back gardens. Kristoff darted from bush to bush, hiding himself in the shadows, although perhaps not as thoroughly as he could. Reaching the house, Contessa couldn't help but sigh with envy at the effortless way he grappled up the side of the house, clinging to the stones by the tips of his fingers. Kristoff reached a window on the second floor, down the side of the house from her own post. Holding himself precariously on the slim sill, Contessa assumed he was working the lock until the window sprang open and he levered himself inside.

She held her breath for a few moments in the silence she knew wouldn't last. The sound of several shots in quick succession split the air even sooner than Contessa expected, almost startling her out of the tree even though she'd known they were coming. She was too far away to be sure, but she thought she heard the thud of several bodies falling. Contessa tried to picture the chaos in the upstairs hallway in her head as pounding footsteps and yelling were punctuated by the pop of more gunfire. Kristoff had assured her that he had a flair for chaos, and he seemed to be delivering on his promise as the racket continued. Still, after several minutes, the sound of Kristoff's twin pistols was notably absent, and silence returned not long after. It seemed that Kristoff had been subdued, but if he had landed most of the shots Contessa had heard, he had gone a long way to making her job easier. Steadying her breathing, Contessa counted to one hundred as planned. Then, she picked up her inching towards the window where she'd left off. The bough bounced precariously with every shift of weight as she reached the end. Just as it dipped so dangerously that Contessa worried it would give out altogether, Contessa's fingers reached the windowsill. She clambered onto it, crouching awkwardly as she tried to find a way to balance without using her hands. She ended up halfway crouched and halfway kneeling with one shoulder braced painfully against the brick of the window casing. Still, she could reach the lock and her boot this way. Fishing out the lockpicks that had been stashed in her boot, she made quick work of the window latch, grateful to be using legitimate picks for once. When the window swung inward, Contessa immediately tumbled through, landing on her backside with a thump. She could only pray it hadn't been heard downstairs.

Looking up and down the hallway, it seemed Kristoff had done his work well. There was nobody in sight, and a series of dark splatters on the wall suggested exactly what had happened to the thugs who had been keeping watch upstairs. With Kristoff and Nate captured, all the main targets were accounted for, and replacing these guards wouldn't seem like an immediate priority. Contessa could have taught Caleb better, though. It's always the pieces you don't count as a threat that come back to steal your win from you.

Despite the apparent lack of life on the upper floor, Contessa pressed herself to the wall, peeking in every doorway and stepping as lightly as she could as she made her way down the hall. She wouldn't be able to fight anybody off if they surprised her from behind. Reaching the end of the corridor, she could just make out voices from the lower level. Knowing she'd reached the landing at the top of the stairs, Contessa crouched down, bracing her back against the wall. Reaching into the other boot this time, she fished out their secret weapon. In one hand, she held an object that looked like a pistol but with a gap behind the barrel where the chamber would be. She set it on the ground to work on the other object. As carefully as possible, she began to screw the cap off the syringe she held, not wanting to think of what would happen if she spilled any of the contents on her fingers. Contessa loaded the uncapped syringe into the chamber of the gun, cursing at how ridiculous this felt, although Kristoff had insisted this was something they had used before, if not quite in this capacity.

With her weapon ready, Contessa inched her head around the corner to peak onto the empty landing. Straining, she could just hear the low rumble of an angry voice that sounded like Nate's, giving her the impetus to creep out onto the landing. She crouched awkwardly as she inched forward, wanting to stay low while afraid of the noise her knees would make on the floor if she crawled. Contessa moved haltingly, stopping every time the floor squeaked beneath her, a hysterical giggle threatening to escape as she wondered how Nate managed to sneak so effortlessly when he must weigh twice as much as her. Pushing down her rising hysteria, Contessa reached the railing and hazarded a peek through the balusters down into the room below.

As Nate had predicted, he and Kristoff were being held in the large room. Nate was on his knees, flanked by uneasy looking thugs. Meanwhile, Kristoff seemed to have abandoned the discomfort of kneeling for reclining on one elbow, seeming for all the world as though he were sprawled on a chaise lounge in an elegant parlor and not in enemy territory. If the thugs on either side of Nate had looked ill at ease with their charge, the ones next to Kristoff appeared utterly disconcerted by his behavior.

Contessa's eyes roved away from her friends to the figure walking back and forth in the center of the room. Although she could only see the back of his head from this angle, his incessant pacing and expansive gesturing gave him the air of a mad king holding court. Kristoff had mentioned Caleb had a flair for the dramatic, always conducting his business in the grandest room of his house, as though he were an enigmatic nobleman and not an underworld gangster. However, it served their purposes well, Contessa mused, as she let her eyes drift up from his pacing figure to the gaudy chandelier dominating the space, hanging by a thick chain from the vaulted ceiling beams.

Taking a quiet breath to steady her hands, Contessa raised the gun contraption and aimed it at the top of the chain supporting the chandelier, barely two meters from where she crouched. She squeezed one eye shut as she tried to get a line through the makeshift sight, suppressing the voice in her head that sounded like her father saying that every good shot aimed with both eyes open. It felt strange to be lining up to essentially fire a squirt gun, but Kristoff had explained they had devised it to shoot the acid they used to melt through safe doors at a long enough distance that the user wouldn't risk being splashed. Contessa sent a brief prayer to any Gods that might be listening that it was as accurate as Kristoff had claimed. Then she pulled the trigger.

There was a click, then a grinding feeling in the trigger, which caught before Contessa could compress it all the way. Pulling back to inspect it, Contessa assumed it must be jammed. She turned it this way and that, trying to find the source of the stuck mechanism, but Contessa knew little about firearms and even less about retrofitted ones like this. She tried finessing the trigger back and forth slightly, but it wouldn't budge, and she stopped quickly, afraid of what would happen if she squirted the acid onto her pants.

Contessa snuck another desperate glance at the scene in the room below her, wracking her brains for what she could do before Caleb finished gloating over his victory. Her fingers ran over the catch to her knives at her wrist as Caleb paced near the edge of the landing where she perched. A skilled assassin might be able to jump down onto Caleb and take him out before he could throw them off, but Contessa dismissed that idea as quickly as it came. She was as likely to hurt herself in that endeavor as Caleb, and something about driving her knife into his throat made her shiver. As much as she burned to see him pay for the things he had done, the wet sound of blood splattering when Nate slit Thomas's throat haunted Contessa in quiet moments. A more hands-off approach was preferable, which is why they had made this plan in the first place.

Looking back down at the contraption in her hands, Contessa twisted the syringe free, pulling the cap from her pocket and screwing it back on. Contessa patted her thighs for a moment, forgetting these pants didn't have pockets, and cursed. Reluctantly, she placed the vial between her teeth after double checking she'd screwed the cap on tightly. She would need both hands free. Edging back towards the corner of the landing, Contessa straightened until she could reach the ceiling beam where it emerged from the wall. Before she could second guess herself, she hoisted herself up until she managed to swing one leg over the beam, trying not to bite down too hard on the metal cylinder in her mouth as she struggled awkwardly for a few moments.

This close to the wall with the ceiling dramatically pitched, Contessa had to press her stomach flat against the beam as she straddled it, and she remained wedged there as she caught her breath, the taste of metal strong on her tongue. As she began to edge forward, sliding on her belly, the ceiling pulled away from her back and she managed to gain more leverage. She looked down as she started to get the hang of the awkward sliding wiggle, only to immediately press herself flat against the beam again as she found she had passed the edge of the landing and was now in the open space above the hall. From this angle, Nate and Kristoff, as well as a few thugs, might be able to see her if they happened to look up, but Contessa kept herself from looking down in favor of focusing on the chandelier chain a meter or so in front of her. She wriggled forward. The rough wood of the beam scratched against Contessa's ribs through her shirt, but it wasn't long until she reached her goal.

Prying one hand away from its death grip on the wood supporting her, she plucked the syringe from between her teeth. Needing both hands to unscrew it, she awkwardly hugged the beam so as to not slide off as she worked. With the cap off, she aimed the syringe at the narrowest point of the chain, right where it screwed into the beam, her thumb braced on the plunger. She chanced a glance down. Caleb was directly below her. Just as she pushed the mechanism, Nate looked up as if he could sense Contessa and jerked in surprise.

Several things happened in quick succession, Contessa's mind seeming to slow time to absorb the mayhem, futilely trying to find a way to prevent catastrophe. Caleb, alerted by Nate's surprise, followed his gaze to find Contessa perched in his ceiling like some sort of overgrown squirrel. The chain holding the chandelier groaned as the acid immediately went to work, creating a fizzling, foul smoke, and a second later, an ear-splitting cracking rung through the hall. Looking up from the people below, Contessa's heart dropped when she saw the acid had splattered off the chain and was eating through the beam. There was a heart wrenching moment when the beam started to buckle and then stopped, as if it might hold. Then Contessa's stomach flew into her throat as the wood gave way completely and she hurtled towards the floor below.

A sickening crunch filled Contessa's head as she hit the ground, rolling to one side, multicolored lights dancing behind her eyelids. For a few stunned seconds, Contessa struggled to draw in the breath that had been knocked from her, her panicked brain trying to find which bone she had heard breaking. After a few seconds, pain set in, but it appeared to be nothing more than the dull ache of bruises.

She pushed herself to sitting among the ruins of crushed furniture and the shattered remains of the chandelier, looking around. Nate was on his feet, shaking out his hand and standing over the moaning forms of the men that had surrounded him and Kristoff. A sharper groan caught Contessa's attention, and she found she'd partially missed her target. Caleb was several feet away, apparently having to tried to jump out of the way, but not quite making it.

Instead, his legs were caught under the heavy wooden beam, one of them sticking out at an odd angle from his knee. Seeing the back of his head had been one thing, but looking at the pointed face of the man who had killed her mother and framed her husband for it ignited something inside Contessa that had been quelled in the past weeks.

"Well, I suppose that is one way of cutting the chandelier and riding the rope down, but we need to work on your form," Contessa heard Kristoff comment, light as ever, but she was already scrambling to her feet. The hilt of her knife was cold against her palm, even though she didn't recall unsheathing it.

She'd clambered through the wreckage of the chandelier in the blink of an eye, her knife coming up to point at the hollow in Caleb's throat. He froze, ceasing his struggles to free his legs. Contessa's grip on her knife may not have been as sure as it could have been, and the tip may have involuntarily scratched along the lump of his throat, but her intent was clear.

Caleb was still, but despite his crushed legs and the knife at his throat, he only looked faintly amused. His eyebrows raised a millimeter, his face otherwise barely even betraying surprise.

"Why, if it isn't Mrs. Woodrow. What a pleasant surprise," Caleb commented.

"Be quiet," Contessa spat, pushing closer to her captive, the tip of the knife scratching a bit deeper into his neck. His eyebrows raised a tick higher, but instead of feeling pleased at getting a reaction, Contessa just felt like he was mocking her.

The silence stretched thickly through the room, and Contessa knew everybody was waiting for her to speak. Now that her mother's killer was at her mercy, though, nothing felt like the right thing to say.

"I don't know what you want with my husband, but you're not going to get it," she settled on, buying herself time.

"Ha!" Caleb's short exclamation of amusement was jarring, like an off-key note in the middle of a song. "I wanted him out of the way. For him to stop ruling the slums of the town quietly and make some noise. If I was running this town, nobody would have to slink around in the shadows anymore."

Caleb's thoughts seemed to come chaotically, his words spilling from his mouth in fits and starts, disorienting Contessa even further.

"Well, you're not killing him. Not today," Contessa announced as firmly as she could, trying to regain her footing.

"Perhaps not," Caleb raised one shoulder carelessly. "But maybe I got something better. The daughter of the police chief crashing down from my ceiling with a knife in her hand to participate in gang dealings is certainly a degree of chaos beyond what I'm usually able to achieve."

"Chaos? Is that all you want?"

"Chaos is the catalyst for change, my dear Mrs. Woodrow," Caleb explained grandly. "For new things to grow, everything old must come crashing down. And this city is ready for something new, wouldn't you say?"

"If you're so invested in causing chaos, then why did you agree to work with the Royal Police? Do you hate Nate that much?" Contessa hissed.

Caleb chuckled, and it sounded like the rasp of a match striking tinder. There was a rustle behind her, as if Nate were shifting his weight between his feet.

"Oh, I didn't agree to work with the Royal Police. *They* agreed to work with *me*." Caleb sounded giddy. "Your father may have tried to play it off as his idea to the rest of the police force, but he had to agree to help me when I threatened to reveal his little secret."

"You don't make any sense," Contessa hissed, "and I have no reason to trust a murderer like you. It's a shame that chandelier didn't finish you off so I wouldn't have to listen to your nonsense."

The venom in Contessa's statement was diluted by the fact that she hadn't moved to kill Caleb yet.

"It's hard to say who is a murderer and who is doling out proper justice sometimes," Caleb commented, as slippery as ever.

"You're the murderer!" Contessa finally snapped. "You murdered my mother, and there is no way you can call what you did justice! There was nothing *just* about me helplessly trying to stop the bleeding with my bare hands after you slit her throat and blamed it on somebody else! Was that just to cause chaos too?"

Contessa's chest was nearly heaving from the force of her outburst, but Caleb looked delighted.

"Oh my. You think I was the one who murdered your mother. What a delightful twist indeed!" Caleb let out a giggle that was borderline hysterical. "It was obvious you had figured out it wasn't your dear husband, but I thought you would have put the pieces together by now. Oh—and even better! This means you turned against your father without even knowing...chaos indeed!"

"Speak plainly or shut up!" Contessa shouted, feeling wobbly, as if she were tumbling down from the ceiling all over again.

"Oh, I'll speak plainly," Caleb's face spread into a gleeful grin. "I wasn't the one who slit your poor mother's throat. That was all your father's doing."

"Liar!"

Contessa barely heard herself shout over Caleb's words echoing in her head. Her father wouldn't. Couldn't.

"You're a liar, and I don't know why anybody has let you live so long." Contessa pushed the knife against Caleb's throat hard enough a drop of blood ran down to pool in the hollow of his collarbone.

"Contessa." Nate's soft voice behind her managed to cut through the clamoring in her head. "He's telling the truth. I don't know how but...he's not lying."

"Oh, I'll tell you," Caleb said with all the joy of a child being presented with a sweet. "When I heard that Nate here had killed the wife of the police chief, I knew it had to be a lie. It's the type of bold move I would have wanted him to make, but he was never daring enough for it. He should be called the Mouse, not the Beast." Caleb paused to chuckle at his own joke. "I was the only person I knew of who tried to pass murders off as Nate's at the time. Trying to sow fear and all of that. So, I decided to do some snooping of my own, steal some police records to see what new face on the scene would make a move like this. And as I went searching through the report on the murder, I found a lot of missing information and sloppy investigating. A report that Chief Cook never would have signed off on if he himself weren't trying to cover something up."

"That's shoddy evidence at best," Contessa argued, but her voice wavered on the last syllable. "Why would he murder his own wife? He loved her!"

"And what might make a man, who has made it his life's purpose to rid the city of the Talented, feel so betrayed that he would resort to murder? Maybe finding out that his dear wife was Talented herself?"

"My mother wasn't..." Contessa trailed off.

"Oh please. I guessed that one with barely any investigation."

"Oh, is that all this is? Guesses?"

"It may have started that way, but I was proven right by your father himself when I threatened to expose him." Caleb's grin was positively feral. "I just had to pretend to have evidence, and he rolled right over to show me his belly. Why would such a powerful man be afraid of being accused of murder by a criminal, unless he was guilty?"

Maybe Caleb was just cooking up this lie to cause more chaos. Maybe this was all just part of the massive, twisted game he played. Still, the icy shard of rage that had been driving Contessa forward had evaporated, and now she was left feeling an entirely new brand of rage, hot and trembling and directionless.

"Nate?" Contessa whispered, not entirely sure what she was asking him for, even though Nate seemed to be able to interpret her intentions just fine.

"It's true, Contessa. I'm so sorry but...he's not lying."

The hand holding the knife to Caleb's throat dropped to Contessa's side, as though she were a marionette that had a string cut. She took one step backwards, then another. She could sense the warmth of Nate standing just behind her now.

"You're not even worth the time it would take to clean your blood off my knife," Contessa stated before turning towards Nate. She couldn't stand to look at Caleb's pleased expression any longer.

Nate was there immediately, and she stepped into his already open arms to press her face to his chest. It was the type of comfort she might have ridiculed herself for wanting just weeks ago, thinking it made her weak, but she would have been wrong. She'd been wrong about so many things.

The sharp smell of the sweat on Nate's shirt had just started to clear Contessa's mind when it was filled with the shrieking of alarm bells. Nate felt it, too, his arms instantly tensing around her as there was a loud movement behind her. Before they could react further, the air was split by the loud crack of gunfire and the thud of a body falling to the floor.

Whirling around, Contessa was greeting by the sight of Kristoff holding the world's smallest pistol in the air, a satisfied look on his face and, for some reason, his pants entirely unbuttoned. The oddness of the sight alone was enough to drive some of the fog from Contessa's mind.

"Kristoff, why were you taking your pants off?" Nate asked exactly what Contessa had been wondering.

"Well, I had to get my gun out of course!" Kristoff waved his ridiculous weapon in the air as if this should have been obvious. "And for the first time in my life, I don't mean that as a euphemism."

"How on earth did you get that gun in here? Weren't you searched when you were caught?" Contessa asked. Her mind seemed to be rejecting the shock of the past minutes' revelation by grasping onto a more easily understood issue.

"Ah, thus why I was unbuttoning my pants," Kristoff explained conspiratorially. "You see, very few goons pat down the front of my trousers as thoroughly as they should, especially given my widespread reputation with men. It's as if they think it will catch or some such thing! Or maybe they just don't want to seem too eager."

"You snuck in a pistol in your underclothes," Nate commented as if he were disappointed in himself for not expecting this. "And why did you not mention to me that we had a contingency plan?"

Kristoff shrugged. "I know you expect me to say it would ruin the surprise or some nonsense, but it seems like one is much more likely to fall back on a contingency plan when you know it's there. I had hoped we would be able to avoid a standoff and it would never come up."

Kristoff's words had a sobering effect on Contessa, and she glanced over to Caleb's body where it was crumpled on the floor, limp finger still resting on the trigger of a pistol. She instantly regretted it. Nate stepped between her and the sight of Caleb's mangled head reflexively, and Contessa edged away from the spreading pool of blood that inched dangerously close to her boots.

"We should get out of here," Nate suggested. "No need to wait around for more trouble to find us." He quickly gathered his knives from the unconscious guards on the floor, sliding them each into their place with practiced efficiency.

Contessa nodded, grateful for the warm, rough fingers that wove between her own to lead her out of the ruined house. She'd thought when this mission was finished, she would have felt some sort of completion. A wholeness that made her feel as if she could move forward. Instead, as Nate led her out into the fresh air, her mind felt as splintered as the chandelier destroyed on the floor behind her.

Kristoff turned up the street, leading the way to the upper city and the house with the blue door. He was uncharacteristically silent, as if sensing it wouldn't be much use to distract Contessa from the whirling thoughts in her head. Her feelings were oscillating so wildly that she wasn't even sure what emotion was dominant, be it rage, sadness, or confusion. She had no idea how it must feel to be Nate. If he could sense each separate emotion tangling together like hopelessly knotted embroidery threads, or if it simply felt like an incomprehensible storm. Either way, he didn't comment, nor did he let go of her hand.

Contessa had been walking so blindly that if Kristoff had led her off a cliff, she might have followed over the edge without noticing, but she stopped suddenly as they passed a familiar street. Nate pulled to a stop beside her, Kristoff pausing when their footsteps went quiet.

"Connie," Nate said. She wasn't sure if it was a question or simply a statement.

"I have to know," Contessa answered.

Nate was silent for a beat, following her gaze down the dimly lit street.

"Alright," he said simply.

"Kristoff, go update Rhosyn and Gregor before they worry too much. We have some business to take care of."

Kristoff nodded and stepped forward hesitantly as if to say something to Contessa but settled for a comforting squeeze to her shoulder before turning and jogging towards home.

As his footsteps retreated, Nate took an audible breath beside Contessa before asking, "So, do we have a plan, or do you just want me to kick down your father's front door and stab anybody that has a problem with it?"

Chapter Twenty-Two

Contessa wondered why she hadn't thought to wear trousers when she snuck out of the house as a child. Crawling under the gap in the back hedge was easier without worrying about tearing cumbersome skirts. She emerged from the thicket, crouching behind a strategically placed bush of rhododendron as Nate wriggled through behind her with considerably more difficulty. The heavy smell of the flowers in full bloom was thick on Contessa's tongue, and while it once would have reminded her of her youth, now it just tasted bitter.

Nate came to crouch beside her and survey the side of the house, his eyes narrow and a few leaves from the hedge caught in his untamed hair. For a moment, she was reminded of the fearsome way he looked when they had first gotten married, and she was grateful to be beside him instead of against him.

"If we break into the cellar there, we can enter through a secret panel in my father's study," Contessa whispered. The shadow of the gray stone house before them weighed on her like a physical presence, and as she looked up at it, the architecture she'd once thought stately now seemed hostile.

They picked through the shadows of the garden, Contessa alert for any sign of her mental alarm bells even though she knew her father never had police patrolling inside the limits of his own property. He was adamant that having the force he commanded protect him too closely would project weakness. The lack of security had seemed overly proud to Contessa, especially after her mother's death, but it made sense now. No need to keep the criminals out of the house when they already lived inside.

Reaching the cellar door, Contessa slipped her lockpicks out of her boot and set to work. In the darkness, she had to go by feel alone, tumblers clicking into place slowly as the puzzle came undone in her hands. It took her longer than usual to work the lock, this one being a more sophisticated design. It would have proved a challenge for somebody less trained than Contessa, and the irony of that wasn't lost on her.

When the door was open, Contessa waved Nate inside and eased the hatch closed behind her as they descended into the cellar. She left it open just a crack so a sliver of moonlight lit their path. The cool air was refreshing after the humidity of the early dawn.

Contessa led the way through the cellar, letting her eyes adjust to the near blackness. It wasn't far to the secret door leading into her father's study, and they hadn't brought a lantern. Besides, a sliver of light coming from under the bookcase in her father's study might alert him of their presence, and she wasn't sure they would be able to corner him without drawing attention if they lost the element of surprise.

"Why isn't this passage protected if it goes straight to your father's study?" Nate breathed right behind Contessa's ear.

She paused to ease around a stack of crates, whispering over her shoulder. "It's an escape route for my father. He's paranoid, and so the only people who know of its existence are me and him. A secret passage stops being secret when you post guards outside of it."

Contessa put her hand on Nate's arm for silence as they took a few steps up to a panel set into the wall. She approached it, gingerly pressing her ear to the door to see if her father was inside. If she strained, she thought she heard the shuffle of papers, but it could have been her imagination. Her Talent wasn't alerting her to any danger, but she didn't think it would unless she'd been discovered.

She motioned Nate forward, and he slunk up next to her, a soft *shink* indicating his knives had slid into his hands. The noise made her shiver. Accosting her father in his own home didn't come without the risk of bloodshed, and she wasn't even sure she was trying to avoid it. She wasn't the one who had drawn first blood in this war after all.

Contessa braced her hands on the door, ready to swing it open into the room, mentally preparing herself. Nate nodded to her, indicating he was ready when she was.

The moment Contessa pushed the hinged bookshelf open, Nate was moving, faster than one of the bullets from Kristoff's guns. Contessa pushed into the room after him, finding her father sitting at the desk. His hand was already moving to grab the loaded gun in the drawer, and a sense of danger was screeching at the base of Contessa's skull. Nate was one step ahead, though, and already he was hurling one of his knives. The pommel hit her father squarely in the wrist, the pistol falling to the carpeted floor with a dull thud.

Her father wasn't stunned for long, grabbing the letter opener on his desk, but Nate was quicker. He leaped over the top with the power of a lion hunting down its prey and grabbed her father's wrist, digging his fingers in until he dropped the letter opener. Nate ducked under his arm, still holding his wrist so it was twisted up behind him.

A matter of seconds after entering the room, Nate had her father immobilized, a knife pressed to his throat.

After such a rapid series of events, the room fell unnaturally still as two sets of eyes fell expectantly on Contessa, one trusting, one cold.

Contessa took a shaky breath, clenching and unclenching her fists a few times, suddenly wishing she had skirts to hide the action in. The odd, hot anger was washing over her again, making her tremble and her face flush.

"Well, I knew you'd been poisoned against me, but this is an unexpected gambit for you," her father said casually. Contessa knew he wanted to make her doubt herself, get her on uncertain footing—but she was here for a reason.

"Why did you kill mother?"

To his credit, Chief Cook barely blinked, but Contessa knew him well enough to know he was surprised.

"I'm impressed you figured it out. I knew I had given you the necessary skills, but it seems your investigative abilities surpassed even what I expected," he said smoothly.

"So, you admit it," Contessa said coldly. "Why?"

Chief Cook laughed humorlessly, and Nate tightened his grip, causing the chuckle to be cut off by a grimace.

"Considering you have your once sworn enemy holding a knife to your father's throat, I would think you would understand that sometimes the only way to respond to betrayal is with betrayal."

"You murdered your wife," Contessa's hands were shaking, but her voice came out hard. "There's no betrayal that could possibly be as great as that."

"She wasn't my wife when I killed her, not really. She had lied to me, tricked me. She wasn't the woman I thought I had fallen in love with," Chief Cook said emphatically, with all the conviction of a preacher at the pulpit.

"She loved you!" Contessa nearly shouted.

"She was a monster! She manipulated people with that Curse of hers, that singing voice. I don't know how I didn't see it at first, but for all I know, she could have used it to trick me into thinking I loved her, so she could take me down. Finish what the Talented had started when they assassinated King Royce and fully disgraced me. But I knew when I saw the way she could calm you with her singing, and I had to do something before she poisoned you too. Before the world found out I had been sleeping with the enemy."

Contessa had always thought her father to be the epitome of reason and cold logic, but that façade unraveled before her eyes.

"Is that what this has all been about? Have you been murdering innocent people because your pride was hurt when a Talented assassin got past you?" Contessa demanded.

"I had everything!" Chief Cook's gray eyes were unyielding, and for a moment, Contessa wondered if that's what her eyes had looked like when she first looked at Nate. "I hadn't been handed success and status; I had earned it by being the best at what I did. I was a good bodyguard, and the King trusted me, giving me status, power. Then one day, it was all taken from me by a perversion of nature. The world had to be rid of those who could gain an advantage through abominations, and I had the skills to do it."

"Mother was not an abomination," Contessa said, her voice hard.

"You were blinded to it," Chief Cook scoffed. "But you're lucky I dealt with her before you became like her and used tricks to get ahead. No, you're like me, and you get what you want by using the brains in your own head."

"I'm more like Mother than you might think," Contessa squared her shoulders and stared her father down with all the rage she could muster. "And I am nothing like you."

Chief Cook was unphased.

"You say you're nothing like me, but here you are, willing to slit your own father's throat in the name of justice. Go ahead, have the Beast kill me, then look in the mirror and tell yourself you aren't your father's daughter. At least I have a warrant when I have people killed."

Contessa looked over her father's shoulder at Nate, who had been notably silent the whole time. He met her eyes steadily, his eyes holding no judgement—just trust.

"You just admitted to murder," Contessa said. "I could have you hanged for that as well."

"I'm the Chief of the Royal Police, and you're holding me at knife point. I don't see this going in your favor," he commented.

Silence fell in the room, and Contessa's balled fists trembled. He was right. Nobody would believe her and Nate.

"Maybe not, but she has a witness."

Everybody jerked collectively as Joseph rounded the corner, holding a pistol aimed squarely at the men behind the desk. Contessa couldn't say whether he was aiming for her father or the Beast. From the wide-eyed expression on Joseph's face, she thought he might not be sure, either.

"Joseph," Contessa murmured, not sure what to say to the man who had once been her closest friend, now holding the justice for her mother's murder in the palm of his hand.

"Not now, Contessa," he snapped. "You're not innocent here, either."

"Joseph, seize her," Chief Cook commanded smugly. "She assaulted me in my own—"

"Not a word from you, either!" Joseph practically yelled before

Chief Cook could finish giving orders, leaving him sputtering in disbelief. "I dedicated my life to upholding the law because of your mentorship, and now I find you've spit in its face?"

"I was doing what was right—what the law couldn't do. Sometimes you must go beyond what's legal and get your hands dirty to get the job done," Chief Cook explained, fanatical in his fervor. His eyes took on the unholy glint that Contessa had long thought was determination, but she saw now as being lust for power and vengeance.

"I have always followed the law to the letter." Some of the anger seeped from Joseph's voice, but still he held his gun steady. "I thought that would make me the only innocent one here. But I see now that following the law does not save me from guilt. Not after I heard you admit we've been killing Cursed—Talented—because you couldn't stand losing power. I've had people put to death because of the law, and now I'm finding out I might be just as guilty as everybody in this room."

"She's poisoned your mind too," Chief Cook insisted, a vein throbbing in his temple.

Joseph finally looked at Contessa after pointedly avoiding her gaze for the whole conversation. The expression on his face sent a crack rattling through her heart. It was the expression of somebody who was having the truths they held dear crumble around them and being forced to reassess everything in their reality. It was what Contessa had gone through, too, although over several months, with Nate at her side. Now Joseph was watching it happen over a matter of seconds, and Contessa wouldn't let her friend go through it alone.

"Only you can decide for yourself what is right," was all she offered.

Joseph blinked and took a shuddering breath before turning back to the men.

"Chief Cook, you are under arrest for murder," Joseph said, his gaze flicking to Contessa and then back to her father's purpling face.

"How— They're...they're criminals! How could you betray me like this?" Her father's cool demeanor had evaporated, leaving no traces of the man Contessa had thought him to be.

"How could *I* betray *you*?" Joseph asked. "I looked up to you, and you just admitted I have been following the command of a murderer. At the end of the day, I trust Contessa because she is the one who told me to think for myself, while you always told me to follow you blindly."

Joseph pulled a set of cuffs from his belt and approached Chief Cook, Nate still pressing a knife to his throat. Nate shook the Chief, prompting him to hold out his wrists for Joseph to bind.

"I thought at least you might be smarter than Contessa," he spat as his wrists were fastened into the cuffs, "but it turns out you're no smarter than a girl who's had her head turned by a criminal."

"No," Joseph replied, finishing his work and yanking Chief Cook forward by his cuffs. "She's the smartest of us, seeing through your manipulations first. And me? I wasn't smart enough to listen to her the first time she told me to think twice."

Contessa let out a noise somewhere between a sigh and a sob, clapping her hand to her mouth. Nate, now no longer holding Chief Cook, strode over to her, pulling her to him as she shook with relief. Joseph glanced at her, an apology and regret mixed in his gaze.

"Now, Chief Cook, you will stand trial for what you've done."

♟♟♜♟♟♟

Contessa gripped the bench she sat on so hard the wooden edge bit painfully into her palm. Nate reached down and pried her fingers from their death grip, instead clasping her hand in his and stroking it gently with his thumb. Still, Contessa felt so tense that she might snap as the new King Byron stepped up to the stand to pass down her father's sentence.

"I find the former Chief of the Royal Police, Emil Cook, guilty of murder. However, given his years of service to both London and my grandfather during his time as his bodyguard, I have chosen to be lenient. He is sentenced to life in prison."

Contessa trembled even as the knot in her chest released. Justice was served, but she wouldn't have to watch her father hang. Caleb had been right, and the records and police reports regarding her mother's murder had been sloppy, missing information. After that, Joseph's testimony alongside hers had been enough to convince the court of her father's guilt.

Contessa didn't even remember standing up and leaving the courtroom. She felt as if she were floating as Nate led her through the halls. She barely paid attention to where they were going, instead focusing on her intense relief. She was startled, almost colliding with the figure who stepped in front of them, forcing them to make an abrupt halt.

Contessa looked up to apologize to the man for almost running into him, only to choke on her words. Standing in front of them was King Byron himself. He had taken the throne several weeks ago, after his older brother, Prince Albert, had abdicated after only two days as king.

Contessa shook herself, curtsying awkwardly. She hadn't been prepared to greet royalty today. Nate was even worse, bowing so stiffly she thought he might topple over.

The King waved away his retinue, and they stepped back, giving them some space.

"I must thank you," he started.

Of all the things Contessa expected him to say, that hadn't been one of them.

"It's hard enough learning how to be a ruler, having the head of the Royal Police be corrupt would have only made things worse. I need people I can trust in positions of power."

Nate was opening and closing his mouth soundlessly, so Contessa jumped in.

"We are glad we could be of service, and I am thankful for your mercy towards my father."

King Byron nodded, making the golden crown on his head flash in the sunlight. He wore it well.

"I think London has seen enough executions in the past years. A lot of people would be happy to see them end." He shot a pointed look at Nate, who coughed.

"You know," Byron continued casually, as if it had just occurred to him, "I need people who care about this city—and all its people—to help me rule. I have some changes I would like to make, some policies I think are outdated, especially when it comes to the Talented. It would be great to have people who understand other sides of the issues to council me."

Byron looked between the two of them pointedly, and Nate finally found his voice.

"Connie here—Mrs. Woodrow, that is—has a good handle on many issues, given her history."

Contessa flushed but held King Byron's gaze as he nodded thoughtfully. "Then we shall have to meet sometime. See if we can come up with an arrangement." He turned his attention to Nate. "I also was thinking how I myself will need a personal bodyguard. Somebody skilled, who understands the concerns and moods of the public. Maybe somebody who would consider working inside the law to help the people, instead of outside of it."

Nate blanched and offered a stilted bow. Contessa took pity on him.

"Thank you for your kind considerations, King Byron. We will have to meet to iron out more arrangements some other time. For now, it has been a long trial, and we have some affairs to see to."

The King nodded understandingly as his retinue stepped up behind him once more.

"I will be in touch," he said as he began to walk away. "And do try to stay out of trouble until then."

Contessa could have sworn she saw a devious twinkle in his eye before he turned away.

As Contessa and Nate walked out of the palace to the carriage that Gregor had waiting to take them back to the upper city, Nate eventually spoke.

"Were we just offered jobs by the King?"

Contessa couldn't help but smile at the stricken look on Nate's face.

"Now everybody is going to know how great of a man you are, and there is nothing you are going to be able to do about it."

Nate helped her up into the carriage, offering her a smirk.

"Well then, I guess, when we get home, I am going to have to remind you just how bad I can be."

♟♖♞♗♛♝

Standing in the dazzling sunlight next to the trickling fountain in the back garden, Contessa couldn't help but think how this was a much better wedding than her first one, despite the non-traditional setting and small number of guests. She smiled up at Nate instead of staring at his buttons, and now she wore her mother's veil out of pride instead of as a symbol of vengeance.

"I now pronounce you husband and wife...again," Kristoff declared grandly.

His statement was greeted by small applause and whoops from Gregor, Rhosyn, and Julia. Even Joseph offered a shy cheer, despite still seeming surprised that he was now friends with a haphazard crew of gangsters. He and Contessa had begun mending their friendship, working together through the confusion of feelings caused by her father's conviction. Having him here, among all the people who mattered the most to her, was one of the nicest wedding presents she could have asked for.

Contessa's heart swelled at the feeling of having friends here to witness this second wedding. The wedding they had planned to have to show they were choosing to love each other—that they weren't married for schemes or politics, but because they never wanted to be apart again.

"You may now kiss the bride!" Kristoff exclaimed.

Nate wasted no time in grabbing Contessa by the waist and kissing her so thoroughly that she bent backwards, supported completely by Nate's arms around her. The small group cheered again, this time accompanied by some whistles from Kristoff. Contessa laughed into Nate's lips with the sheer joy of it, and she felt him smile in return. This may not have been the official start of their marriage, but it was the start of a new life together, and Contessa couldn't wait.

Acknowledgments

One might think that as you write more books, you get more experience and therefore need less help. One would be wrong. My writing and publishing support system continues to grow, and I couldn't be more grateful. Still, it becomes increasingly hard to thank everybody who deserves my appreciation in these few short pages, but I will do my best.

Getting to this point with this book has been a tumultuous journey with many twists and turns. I can't thank all the readers and fellow authors who stood by me through those plot twists enough. Charissa, Lisa, Lily, Emily, Erin, and Alexis all have my eternal gratitude for having my back as I navigated my way towards publication.

My family, as always, continues to be the safe space from which I can explore my creativity and write my stories. A big thank you to my sister, for being one of the first people to nurture my love of fantasy and fairytales. My parents continue to move through this adventure with me with no loss of enthusiasm, a feat worthy of endless recognition and appreciation. And Rhys, thank you for encasing me in a bubble of love and support that allows me to ask myself "*What would I do if I could not fail?*" and then go do exactly that.

And lastly, and most importantly, thanks to those of you who are reading this book. Stories can't exist in a vacuum but need to live and grow in the minds of those who read and love them. I continue to appreciate you giving my stories a home in your brain. I hope you have room for a few more.

About the Author

S.C. Grayson has been reading fantasy novels since she was a little girl stealing books from her older sister's shelves, and that has developed into a love of writing and storytelling. Her writing is currently focused on fantasy romance and fairytale retellings. When she is not sitting in a local coffee shop writing and consuming an iced americano, Grayson is a nurse working towards a PhD in nursing with a focus on breast cancer genetics. She lives in Pittsburgh with her loving husband and their two cats, who enjoy contributing to her work by walking across her keyboard at inopportune moments (the cats, not the husband).